PRAIRIEVILLE

MATT BANNISTER WESTERN 6

KEN PRATT

Published in the United States by Wolfpack Publishing, Las Vegas

CKN Christian Publishing
An Imprint of Wolfpack Publishing
6032 Wheat Penny Avenue
Las Vegas, NV 89122

christiankindlenews.com

Paperback ISBN: 978-1-64734-151-0
eBook ISBN: 978-1-64734-152-7
Library of Congress Control Number: 2019956857

PRAIRIEVILLE

This book is dedicated to my friend,
Glenna Brown.
Thank you.

ACKNOWLEDGMENTS

I find it amazing how much support I receive from my family. My wife, Cathy is always the cheerleader captain of the Pratt team. Our three daughters, Jessica, Chevelle and Katie are always right there to cheer the next story on and their amazing husbands are too. Our son, Keith is the first person to read whatever I write, and although he's a great encouragement as well, he is brutally honest and holds nothing back. I appreciate that though, because he makes some great points that send me back to the computer and the dungeon, I write in. I am blessed to have you all in my life. I love you all.

I must also thank my publisher, CKN Christian Publishing and those folks who work so hard to make this book possible. My sincere appreciation to Mike Bray, Lauren Bridges and Rachel Del Grosso.

Prologue

"Right on time," John Mattick said as the black privately owned Concord, custom made stage coach came up the rough mountain road that crossed over the mountains. It stopped at the agreed-upon location marked on the road by a large chunk of black obsidian set there the evening before by John and the stagecoach driver, Herb Johnson. Herb was a local freight hauler for the local lumber company who had been approached to use his team and knowledge to drive a wealthy couple from Prairieville to Galt, where another team and local driver would take over to get them to Branson. He was being paid thirty dollars for a long day's trip, but one he agreed to. Herb was hired on a confidentiality basis, meaning he wasn't supposed to let anyone know what he was doing or the route they were taking. Whoever he was hauling sounded important and had a great deal of money. Herb told his friends about the deal, and together, they planned to rob the luxury concord. As planned,

Herb stopped the coach unexpectedly, stepped down and urgently went into the thick woods to relieve himself. "Devin, when Herb reaches those trees, blow that guard out of his seat, and we'll ride down and surround the coach. If they fire a single shot at us, fill the whole thing up with lead. Let's make this fast and clean and get out of here. Okay, there goes Herb. Let's go!" John said as Devin aimed his rifle over a tree limb and squeezed the trigger.

The guard riding beside the driver fell off the bench seat to the ground with a bullet penetrating through his heart. John and three others surrounded the coach quickly with their weapons drawn. "Get out of there, or we'll start shooting!" he shouted to the occupants inside. John wore a gray cloth bag over his face with holes cut out of it for his eyes like the others in the gang. He held his revolver pointed at the coach. "Hurry up! Give us your money and goods, and you can move on!" he demanded.

A short and thin man with a weasel-like face wearing round silver-rimmed spectacles and dressed in a suit stepped out of the coach first. He turned to help an attractive older lady in her late forties or early fifties step down to the ground. She was dressed in a beautiful dress and was quite well-to-do. The diamond ring of her wedding finger was bigger than any diamond John had ever seen. The skinny weasel of a man kept his head downward and whispered for her to do the same. He didn't need to, though; she was too afraid to look John in the eyes. A tall, dark-haired man with a mustache and a suit stepped out of the stage and glared at

John. "The money's for my daughter, and you're not taking it!"

John pointed his revolver at him. "Stop me." He looked at one of his friends. "See what they got."

The robber stepped out of the saddle and walked to the coach. He began to step up inside when the taller man turned around and grabbed him by the back of his coat and jerked him out of the coach, forcing him to the ground. He then kicked the robber's covered face when he landed and then shouted at John, "You're not taking it!"

"Louis, knock it off and let them have it!" the weasel looking man said anxiously.

"No! I'm not losing my daughter again because of some cockroach highwaymen don't want to work for their money!" the man called Louis shouted at his friend.

"Cockroach?" John asked.

Louis glared at him. "Yeah, you are a cockroach! A damn worthless cockroach that needs to be stomped upon before your nit headed children grow up to be the same kind of pestilence on humankind. Do you know who I am? I'm Louis Eckman! If you rob me, every law enforcement officer from the Mexican border to Canada will be looking for you! Including Matt Bannister, who happens to be my friend. So, take your cockroach friends and get out of here!" he shouted.

"Louis, shut up!" The weasel looking man hissed under his breath.

"Louis Eckman...of the railroad?" John asked.

Louis sighed with a sense of relief of his importance being recognized. "Yes! I am. Now please leave us to our travels. I'm nothing but trouble for you."

John pointed his revolver at him. "My father was killed digging a tunnel through a mountain for your railroad. They blew some dynamite in the tunnel, and a rock from the blast hit him in the head. He died working for you, and you got rich off his labor. Let me ask you, do you have a list of the men who died so you could get rich?"

The short and skinny man whose name was Carnell Tallon, spoke quickly, "Sir, the railroad does. I'm the company bookkeeper, and I could send you that list. I am confident your father's name would be on it. The railroad kept careful records of the lives lost tragically while building the greatest accomplishment in humankind. You should be quite proud of your father for his labors. What he helped build will last forever."

John took a deep breath. "Shut up!" he warned. "The railroad couldn't care less now, nor did it then! Do they Mister Eckman?"

Louis smirked. "Your father should've ducked. I weep every day for the men who never went home to teach their nits how to work," he said pointedly.

Carnell yelled. "Damn it, Louis, shut the hell up and give him the money!"

John interrupted sharply, "You weep every day, you say." He nodded slowly, "Well, I did too for a long time. But what the hell, I got over it. Your daughter will, too," he said and pulled the trigger, shooting Louis in the stomach. He backed up against the

Concord with an expression of shock, while the woman screamed. Louis looked up at John just as he fired his weapon again, hitting Louis in the forehead. He crumbled onto the ground, dead.

The woman fell to his side, screaming over his dead body. Carnell Tallon cursed and looked at John. "Please, just take whatever you want and go! You didn't have to kill him."

John looked at him and shrugged. "He should've ducked," he said. He spoke to his men, "Take what they have and let's go. Check the late Louis Eckman's pockets and their bags too. He's a rich man so he must have money don't hesitate to take it all. And take her wedding ring and jewelry. That might shut her up!"

One of the robbers threw Carnell up against the coach to search him. "Here!" he yelled and pulled a leather billfold out of his jacket pocket, opened it and pulled out over two hundred dollars of cash money, and handed it over. "Take all I have, just please don't hurt us." The robber began counting the money. "Mister Eckman's billfold is in the coach. There's more money in it. Please, take whatever you want, but don't hurt Misses Eckman or me, please!" he bent down near the woman like a coward and put his billfold back in his coat.

The robber laughed with excitement. There's over two hundred dollars here!"

John's friend Charles Hammond stepped into the coach, and momentarily his excited voice boomed out, "Oh my! Dang! There's like two thousand dollars in his billfold!"

John ordered the other robber to take the woman's ring and jewelry. Adrian did so without any mercy while the lady screamed. The cowardly man beside her remained down on the ground, afraid for his life.

The driver, Herb Johnson, came walking out of the woods horrified to see the woman screaming beside a dead body while Adrian Crowe yanked the ring off her finger mercilessly. His brother Bo Crowe sat on his horse with a rifle watching the road for any witnesses. "Why'd you shoot him? You were just supposed to rob them!" Herb questioned loudly.

John turned his horse towards Herb and without saying a word, shot him in the chest and watched the man fall. He turned his horse back towards the Concord coach while yelling, "Let's go!"

They rode quickly to where Devin stood by a tree with his rifle in his hand. "John, that skinny guy is talking to Herb. Do you want me to shoot him?"

John looked back and seen Carnell stand up and walk back towards the coach, shaking his head. "No, Herb's dead. I shot him in the heart. Let's get away from here as fast as possible. I killed Louis Eckman, and that's no small thing," he sounded a bit anxious about it.

"Who?" Devin asked.

Charles Hammond answered bitterly, "The California railroad tycoon, Louis Eckman! John killed him for no reason!"

Devin grinned at John. "There had to be a reason, right? I mean, I killed a man so we could rob the stagecoach." He chuckled. "How'd we do?"

John nodded. "Very good, I think. There's probably more we could take, but I don't want to stick around too long."

Charles pulled the hood off his face and looked at John. "He was unarmed!"

"Herb would've given us up, and you know that. It was part of the plan."

"No, I'm talking about Eckman!"

John looked down for a moment and answered. "He was rude and disrespectful. You don't call my kids nits and you sure as hell don't tell me my father should've ducked! My father was killed digging a tunnel in the Sierra's. And that man got rich off the blood of many men, including my father!"

"You're blaming him for an accident?" Charles asked bewildered.

"No. I was asking if the railroad kept the names of those who died to build it. He should've said yes or no, instead of calling me a cockroach and my kids nits! He should've kept his mouth shut like his cowardly friend!"

"What's done is done," Adrian Crowe said to end it. "Let's not argue about it. I wanted to shoot him too, by the way. We need to get rid of these horses and get back home." They had stolen the horses from three small farms along the way to the mountains the night before. Their horses were tethered two miles away under the care of Devin's youngest brother Dane. They would let the stolen horses run free and return home on different routes.

John nodded. "Let's go," he said and began to ride forward.

Charles spoke as they rode, "You do know the marshal's going to be coming for us. Probably the Pinkertons and everyone else too."

John smiled slightly. "Yeah, I know. Did I ever tell you about the time I whipped Matt Bannister in a fight? I whipped him good. Did I ever tell you about that?"

"A few times, yes," Charles said.

"He was a friend of mine, you know. I liked him until he accused me of being a thief. Funny how time has led us down different roads, huh?"

Adrian Crowe smirked as he took off his white hood. "You are a thief."

John chuckled. "Yeah, I suppose so. I probably shouldn't have taken his money, but none the less, I won the fight. I left him bloody and bleeding on the ground. He ran away after that like a scared jack-rabbit. You boys can be afraid of him if you want, but I've seen the other side of him, and I think he'll be more afraid of me than I will be of him. Too bad, he accused me of that, though; he was a good guy. We could've been great friends. It'll be good to see him again if he shows up."

Devin chuckled. "Only you can kill someone important and then say it'll be good to see the most dangerous U.S. Marshal in the United States. You're crazy, John."

"Not crazy at all. Heck, Devin, I'm at work right now, don't you know that? So are you. We're going to get away with this just like always. We have nothing to worry about as long as we don't blow it ourselves. Those folks have nothing to tell the sheriff that will matter; nothing at all. This robbery will be blamed on the Sperry-Helms Gang or those heathen cousins of theirs the Crowe Brothers."

Adrian Crowe smirked. "If it were my brothers and me, there would be no survivors to tell a story. Would there, Bo?"

Bo Crowe shook his head.

Devin spoke quickly, "I know! That's why John was put in charge of this deal. And he screwed it up! There were only supposed to be two deaths, the gunner and Herb. I don't think anyone was expecting Louis Eckman to be in the coach, let alone to be killed! And John, I don't know you'd be so offended, you don't even have any kids!"

John shrugged. "I might somewhere. But my father's death is now justified. I feel better."

1

Matt Bannister opened his eyes tiredly as the loud knocking on his door woke him up. It had been a stressful weekend that had left him physically and emotionally exhausted. He had taken the day off to catch up on his sleep after being woken up early to investigate the hanging of Pick Lawson. Matt had made a deal with Pick to get him out of the Branson jail for the kidnapping of Christine Knapp. He would have had to arrest Pick himself for the murder of a young man named Brent Boyle and for the bank robbery of the Loveland Bank anyway. It was the Sperry-Helms Gang that had taken Pick from the jail and hung him. Matt had gotten the truth out of Tim Wright, the Branson City Sheriff. However, Tim refused to acknowledge it officially and fabricated his report to say he had forgotten the keys in the jail cell door. Pick chose to escape and was hung by unknown persons who had left a note written in Chinese nailed into Pick's chest. Matt was infuriated and could not legally go after the Sperry-Helms Gang for hanging Pick with the Sherriff's refusal to admit the truth. It had been a stressful weekend and one that left Matt broken-hearted. He had fallen in love with Felisha Conway, who he had met in Sweethome. Unfortunately, this one weekend had ended their young relationship. It was easy for Matt to communicate through writing long letters, but it was a bit harder to communicate in person. Especially when unknown assailants had taken his friend Christine, and at the same time, he was under investigation by the Pinkerton Detective Agency for a crime in which he was guilty. It had worked out for the best, but not before he had to kill two men and lost Felisha in the process. Matt was exhausted and wanted to sleep for a few hours. The knocking became loud, pounding on his door.

"Oh, for crying out loud!" he said bitterly and got out of his bed. "Oh Lord, I would sure like to get some sleep." He grabbed his revolver and went to the family room. "Who is it?" he asked firmly. If there was one thing, Matt knew it was jerking the door open in frustration could lead to a shotgun blast to his chest. Caution had become a normal way of life.

"William, open up!" his cousin said loudly.

Matt frowned and opened the door. "What do you want..." he paused when he saw the Pinkerton Detective, Sabastian Worthington standing beside William.

William stepped inside out of the cold. "I brought the detective over to see you because he couldn't find your house. Doesn't that make you want to become an outlaw? We'd get away with murder with him chasing us."

Sabastian stepped inside and closed the door behind him. He was a heavy-set man with a round face and a derby hat. "Matt, I apologize for the unexpected visit. I assure you I could find your home just fine, but William offered to bring me over. I want to talk to you if I could, about something." He held up his hands, showing his palms. "It has nothing to do with why I was investigating you before. I'm afraid it became quite obvious that Catherine Eckman was never kidnapped and she certainly didn't hesitate to speak her mind. I'm glad she's alive, though. Maybe there's hope she and her mother can make amends down the road."

Matt waved towards the davenport with a yawn. "Sit down. What can I help you with today?" Matt sat down on a smaller davenport heavily. "William, are you going to sit down?" Matt asked.

William moved towards the door. "No, he wanted to talk to you alone. I'm going back to the hotel. I'll talk to you later."

Sabastian frowned as William closed the door behind him. "Your cousin's an interesting man. He kept me entertained for the past few days," he said with a quick smile.

Matt nodded. "So, how can I help you?" he was in no mood for idle chit chat.

"Well, it seems I have been promoted to head of security detail for Divinity Eckman now that her husband and Carnell Tallon are both dead. Carnell was my boss for a few years now, and I can't say I necessarily agreed with the way he and Louis ran their business. I'm not sure how I'll like working under Divinity now that she'll be taking over the Eckman dynasty either. I don't know who is more brutal she or her husband. Carnell was an evil man under his meek exterior. If Louis wanted someone beat up, Carnell would have them beaten almost to death. Sometimes they didn't survive. He had a way of multiplying the violence for the pure pleasure of it."

"Should I congratulate you or no?" Matt asked, not knowing what Sabastian was getting at.

Sabastian chuckled. "Maybe, maybe not, I don't know yet. I prefer to be straight up and honest. I never took part in the brutality; I was primarily an investigator that dug up dirt and ways to blackmail Louis' enemies. Carnell and the others did the dirty work."

"Why are you telling me this?" Matt asked, curiously.

"Because it's your fault, Matt. You killed Carnell. Now I'm stuck riding back to California with Divinity. I enjoyed my job traveling around and working alone, but now that's gone," he chuckled.

Matt shrugged. "Not much I could do about that. I warned him."

Sabastian nodded. "I know. Matt, I'm here to ask a favor of you. You know Louis was killed in a stage robbery. Carnell didn't get much information other than the descriptions of clothing and horses, but he did get one name or maybe a part of a name, 'Dall.' Apparently, Dall's father worked for the railroad as a laborer and was accidentally killed in an explosion at some point. I know that isn't a whole lot to go on, but in small rural areas, you may not need much more than that. We would like for you to go after him and his gang. Before you say no, I'll remind you it is your duty as a lawman to go after murderers, and certainly, the killing of Louis Eckman is an important one to solve. These men killed two of my friends with no warning. And to top it off, Miss Divinity has offered you quite a sum of money to bring them in dead or alive. Your preference is fine either way."

Matt shook his head slowly. "I once had a friend whose father was killed on the railroad like that, but that was years ago over in Boise City. You know, Sabastian, I'm not particularly interested in bringing them in either way. The county sheriff down there can solve that crime better than I can anyway. He would know folks; I don't know anyone down there."

"The county sheriff has lost their trail. It seems the horses they used in the robbery were stolen from three different farms from varying areas of the valley and released in the mountains. The only real clue we have is their clothes and the name Dall. The sheriff down there is named Chuck Dielschnieder, and he is a weak link. We need you, to assist, we have two of our best detectives coming over from California as we speak. They should be arriving in Prairieville in a week. I notified them today to prepare to leave. They will meet you in Prairieville."

Matt yawned. "If you have two detectives going

there, then why do you need me? Two detectives ought to be able to figure out who they are as well as I could, if not better. Not many people go by Dall. It's not a common name like John, Jim or Jake. It should be easy even for a weak link of a sheriff to find someone named Dall."

Sabastian smirked with a hint of shame. "I'm afraid the way Carnell ran things was a bit different than I hope to. Those two men I am sending are not trained detectives, nor were they ever detectives. They are for lack of a better word, gunmen. They are being sent there to take orders from you and to be your back up since you are going against a gang of killers. The two I'm sending could barely figure out how to untie a grain bag, let alone solve a crime. But they are good with a gun and their fists. They are simple thugs used for their muscles to intimidate Mister Eckman's competitors. However, for your purposes, they will be quite useful. Can I tell them when they can expect you?"

"I prefer to work alone."

"Not this time, you won't. Matt, I don't know who these men are, but I can tell you they are a bad bunch. You will need help, and we are supplying two of the best, maybe three of the best we have. And I assure you, Carnell always wanted the best for whatever purpose he needed them for. If you get into a shootout with this gang of killers, you will appreciate having these men with you. They may not be the brightest candles in the chapel, but they are tough, experienced, and brave. They will not run from trouble. These men will stand behind you and work with you to bring this gang to justice. And if I can add, the world's going to be watching because the death of Louis is front-page news across this nation. Bringing them to justice will be too. And that is why we need you. You are the best at what you do."

"Used to do. Now I sit in my office a good portion of the time."

"Bull. The two men I am sending are named Ivan Petoskey and Pete Logan. They'll be waiting in the Grand Lincoln Hotel in Prairieville for you. Your room and board will be paid for by us, and other expenses as you require them as well. I already reserved your room. Today is Wednesday, shall we say you'll be there next Wednesday? That way, you have a few days to get things situated here before you leave. And just in case I forgot to mention it, Divinity Eckman is offering you a sizable reward for bringing them to justice."

"So, you said. I don't know if I can accept that, but I'll do what I can. I'll be there on Wednesday. However, I will let you know I don't want your men getting in my way. So, if they get out of line, I'll send them back to you and use local law enforcement or my men for help if I need it."

Sabastian smirked. "Matt, we both know your deputies are green. You'll need experienced men, and I have them for you. Rest assured, when this is all over; you might even want to hire them for your own office."

Matt chuckled. "I don't put badges on thugs, Detective Worthington. Life's too valuable to take a chance on that. The authority behind a badge is corruptive to the wrong sort. I've seen it before, and I won't have it in my office. You can keep your street thugs."

Sabastian raised his eyebrows and shrugged. "I think they'll impress you when it's all said and done."

"Maybe. I hope your right."

"Well, Misses Eckman is waiting, and we have a long trip back to California. I wish you well, and good luck. I look forward to reading about your success."

Matt nodded. "I'm sure it'll be incorrect and spiced up a lot. Lying writers always try to make it sound grander than it really is to sell papers. I can't stand most of them."

2

Christine Knapp was dressed warmly in a long wool coat as she walked towards Matt's house on Sunday afternoon. It was a cold misty day with heavy gray clouds filling the sky. She carried her umbrella to keep the drizzling rain off her. She knocked on Matt's door knocked again with no sound coming from inside. She frowned with disappointment but decided to walk the three blocks to the marshal's office to see if Matt was there by chance. She had her doubts since it was Sunday, and he normally took Sundays off. As she approached Main Street, she could see the faint blue smoke rising from the stovepipe of the marshal's office. With renewed excitement, she tried opening the door, but it was locked. She knocked as she peered through the door's window. She smiled when she saw Matt step out of his office and come towards her with a slight smile on his lips.

He unlocked the door and opened it for her step

inside. "Christine, what are you doing out and about on this cold, wet day? You're going to get yourself sick, young lady. Come on in and warm up. Do you want some coffee? I don't have any tea or anything fancy like that."

She giggled lightly. "Coffee will be fine today. But I will have to convert you to tea one of these days." Her expression grew serious. "So why are you here on Sunday? You usually don't work on Sundays, do you?"

"No," he answered as he held open the three-foot-tall partition gate for her walk through so she could walk back to his private office. "I'm leaving tomorrow to go to Prairieville and track down the men who killed Louis Eckman. I wanted to leave some instructions for my deputies, and I'm looking over the census from three years ago for any names with 'Dall' in it. I'm not finding very many. Dallas is the only name I can think of that starts with Dall. There's a couple of Daltons, but that sounds like doll, not dall. So, I'm not finding very much to go on." He walked to the woodstove and took a clean cup down from the wall. He filled it with coffee for Christine.

"How long are you going to be gone?" she asked.

"Let's go sit down in the office," he said as he led her to his office door.

She entered, noticing the papers spread out on his desk. She sat down and looked up at him, waiting for his answer.

He set the cup of coffee in front of her and then sat down. "I have no idea how long I'll be gone. It could be a week or two, three, maybe. It depends on what or who we find. I'm meeting two of the Eckman detectives there. They're going to help bring these guys to justice. But we haven't got too many clues. I'm hoping things open up a bit when we get down there. I do know it all starts with the man who was driving the stagecoach. And that's where I am going to start the investigation. So, what are you doing walking around today anyway?"

"Looking for you. I haven't seen you since Tuesday. I was just wondering if you were avoiding me or something. I thought you'd come by the dance hall sometime, but you haven't. If you're mad at me because of what happened between Felisha and you, I never meant to cause any trouble. I'm sorry if I did."

Matt smiled, sadly. "I'm not mad at you at all. I have been exhausted since last weekend and just trying to keep up with my work here. Friday and Saturday, I was over in Willow Falls, visiting my aunt and uncle. I got home last night, and today I'm here. I don't want it to sound like an excuse, but I've been busy. By the way, what do you have planned for Thanksgiving?"

"So, you're not mad? We're still friends?" she asked, sincerely.

He chuckled lightly. "Yes, we're still friends. What are you doing for Thanksgiving?"

"Nothing. Do you want to come over to the dance hall for our thanksgiving feast? There's always lots of food."

Matt shook his head. "No. I thought you might

want to join me and meet my family out at the Big Z."

"Oh…" she said hesitantly. "I don't think your family likes me."

"My family doesn't know you. Have Thanksgiving with me, and let them get to know you. I think even Regina will apologize for her misjudging you once she gets to know you."

"How do you know you'll be home from Prairieville by then?"

Matt shrugged. "It's almost three weeks away. If I'm not back, then we're not going to be at the Big Z for Thanksgiving. But if I am back, then come to Willow Falls with me. I would like for you to meet my family and for them to get a chance to get to know you."

She took a deep breath. "What if Regina makes a scene again? I would be horrified."

"She won't, because I won't let her. No one's going to…"

The cowbell rang as the front office door opened, followed by William Fasana yelling, "Matt! Are you in here?"

Matt frowned and stood up to open his office door. "I am."

William had already stepped through the partition gate and stepped towards Matt. "I have to talk to you, bud. Do you know Carol, the housekeeper at the hotel?"

Matt shook his head. "I don't think so."

"Doesn't matter, she's too old for you anyway." He laughed. "What are you doing here, anyway? I went to your house, and no one was home. Where's Truet? I like him and all, but he's never home. Does that ever seem strange to you? He's always going somewhere," William said suspiciously, wondering if Matt would ever catch on to Truet courting his sister Annie. "Whoa!" he shouted as he stepped into Matt's office and seen Christine sitting in there. He looked back at Matt with a smile. "You were going to tell me you were working, weren't you?"

"I am. I'm working on trying to convince Christine to come out to the Big Z for Thanksgiving with me."

"Oh?" He turned back to Christine. "Well, yeah, you want to do that! That's not even a question. Yeah, you'll be coming. We'll be glad to have you there. Just remember to make a loaf of your best bread, okay?"

"Okay," she answered through a chuckle.

"Promise? And you'll bring a loaf of your best bread, yeah?" he asked.

"I promise."

"Okay. It's settled, she's coming to the Big Z for Thanksgiving. Awesome! Now," he added seriously, "I need to ask you to leave Matt and I alone for a bit if you would. I have to talk to him and normally wouldn't want to interrupt, but it's important."

"Oh, sure." She stood up and moved towards the door and looked at Matt, who waited outside of the small private office. "I guess I'll see you later?"

Matt nodded. "I'll come to the dance hall later. I won't leave without saying goodbye."

Matt walked her to the front door and watched

her leave. He went back to his private office and sat down behind his desk. William sat in the chair with his feet up on the desk and drinking the cup of coffee Matt had poured for Christine. "Get your feet off the desk. What's this all about, William?"

William moved his feet to the floor. "So, you don't know, Carol, the housekeeper?"

Matt took a deep breath. "No, but I heard she was too old for me anyway."

William laughed. "That she is. But when she heard you were going after the men who killed Louis Eckman and meeting up with a couple of Eckman's men, she wanted me to tell you to be careful because Carnell, the man you killed, had a thing going with Misses Eckman. Oh yeah, they were close. Like romantically close, you know sporting their own show behind the curtains where no one knows. Except for the cleaning lady, but isn't that the way it always goes?"

Matt was looking at him awkwardly. "Um... and?" he asked with a slight shake of his head.

"In short, I'm going with you tomorrow."

"No. You're not..."

"Yeah, I am. You can't stop me, so you might as well agree to it."

"Why do you want to go, William? There's no gambling halls or money to be made over there." Matt stated sharply.

William took a deep breath and answered sincerely, "I need some excitement. An excursion across the Blues into new territory and a new adventure might just be what I'm looking for. Besides, that's the territory the Crowe Brothers run in, and if you have a scuffle with them, I want in on it. I already got it okayed with Lee, and I'm free to leave for a while."

Matt sighed. "William, I don't need any needless trouble."

William gasped. "You must be joking. I cause trouble? Never." He chuckled. "I won't cause any trouble."

"You better not. Well, if you're coming, don't wear a suit and don't wear your silver ivory-handled revolvers either. We don't need the attention, okay? One more thing, I'm leaving early, and I'm not waiting. So, go to bed early. We have a long and cold few days of traveling ahead. Dress to be warm, not pretty."

"I'll be ready to leave in the morning bright and early. I'm not inexperienced when it comes to winter traveling, Matt. I've done my share of it too. Hey, we're going to have some fun, huh?"

Matt smiled as he shook his head. "We'll see. But again, I don't want any needless trouble."

William scoffed as he sipped the coffee. "You know me better than that."

"I know. That's why I'm worried."

William laughed. "I'll be good. I promise."

3

After two and a half days of long hours in the saddle in the cold low thirties of the Blue Mountains, Matt Bannister and William Fasana arrived in the town of Prairieville in the late afternoon of Wednesday. They were both dressed in buckskins, and both wore moccasins on their feet as they crossed the mountains. Matt wore his long buffalo hide coat, and William wore his bearskin coat. Both men were hungry, cold, and tired. William went to the Grand Lincoln Hotel to check-in and find a place for them to eat dinner. Matt went to check in with the Aurora County Sheriff. Prairieville was a medium-sized city of two thousand people located at the east end of Aurora County in the Wabeno River Valley. The base of Prairieville's economy was farming, ranching, and the lumber industry, but it was the gold rush that had brought more men to the region than gold, or the labor industry could support. Those who had good jobs did well enough, but the wages were low for the laborers, and the owners, investors, and bankers collected like kings. Unlike Branson, which was the main stop for the Oregon Trail and anyone traveling east or west, Prairieville was a hidden town set apart to soak in its own corner of the world. It did not have a city marshal or police force; the county sheriff's office was the only law around Prairieville and the whole Wabeno River Valley.

Matt hitched his horse in front of the sheriff's office and stepped inside. He pulled the hood back off his head and looked at three men who were standing around the woodstove drinking coffee, staring at him.

"Can I help you?" one of the men asked, sounding annoyed by the intrusion of their conversation.

"Is the sheriff in?" Matt asked as he unbuttoned his buffalo skin coat.

A big man stepped forward. He had light red hair that was thinning on top and cut short and a groomed red goatee on his round face. "I'm the sheriff. How can I help you?"

"Can we talk in private?"

He raised his eyebrows. "Well, we don't have much for privacy, as you can see. Beyond that door is the jail, and there's no privacy in there. Who am I talking in private with anyway?" he asked sarcastically while he waved his hand to show the open office building. It was a square room with four desks, one long table surrounded by chairs, a gun cabinet, and other cabinets and shelving, and a wood stove where the men stood around a pot of coffee. His two deputies chuckled smugly while looking at Matt.

"I'm Matt Bannister, United States Marshal."

The sheriff's sarcastic smile faded, and a serious look of concern took over. "Well, what brings you into our neighborhood?"

"Do you think we could excuse your men and talk in private?" Matt asked while casting his eyes over towards the two deputies who were now looking at him with a touch of nervousness to their faces.

"Well, we all work on the same side of the law. And these are two of my deputies, my brother, Troy. And my number one deputy, Charlie Hammond. I have four more out there running around somewhere. I don't keep anything from my guys, so if it's okay with you, how about we talk here?"

Matt looked at the other two men and nodded. "Fair enough. I'm here to discuss the murder of Louis Eckman and two other men during a stage robbery outside of town here a couple of weeks ago. I know you investigated it, and I'm here to see what you found out and take over from there."

"Oh!" Chuck exclaimed and looked at his two deputies. "Well, I can tell you we were shocked to hear that happened around here. We did try to track the thieves, but all we found was their stolen horses. They must've had other horses stashed up there somewhere and split up to confuse us. There was no way to track all the horse tracks we came across. There were horse tracks spread out everywhere between the stolen horses wandering around and the other horses they rode out of the mountain on. We are not bad trackers, Marshal, I believe the bandits split up and rode down five different stream beds to leave no tracks. We couldn't find anything. But sit down, let's talk." He walked over to the table and sat down.

Matt removed his coat and hung it up on a rack inside the door. "You don't have any suspects?" he asked as he stepped to the table and sat at the opposite end of Chuck.

Chuck took a deep breath and raised his eyebrows. "Believe it or not, no." He waved his deputies over to join them at the table. "Come sit down, boys, let's talk to the Marshal."

A tall man about six-foot with solid broad shoulders stepped towards the table. He had red hair like the sheriff's, but this man's wavy red hair fell to his shoulders. He had a strong face with high cheekbones and a mustache and a goatee. Both sides of the mustache fell below his chin about three inches long. His goatee was three inches long as well but braided with turquoise beads. He reached out a muscular hand. "I'm Troy Dielschneider. I'm Chuck's younger brother." He was in his late thirties, and unlike his brother, Troy came across as a hard man. Though the braided hair on his chin was noticeable, what Matt noticed most was the coldness of his light blue eyes.

Matt stood and shook his hand firmly. "Nice to meet you."

The other deputy reached his hand across the table to shake Matt's as well. He was a rough-looking man in his mid-forties with short brown hair and a mustache that grew down below his chin a good four inches long as well. "I'm Charlie Hammond. I run the office when the sheriff's out of town. I was one of the first ones up there when we heard about that robbery, and it was a nasty scene. Of course, travelers had found the Eckman party and sent someone to our office. When I arrived, a short skinny guy, whose name I forget, said a gang of highwaymen robbed them, and he would take care of it. He was anxious to keep moving over the mountain. He didn't give many details, but we tried to track four or five deviants in those woods but found nothing except tracks going in circles and stolen horses."

"And the driver?" Matt asked.

Charlie replied to the obvious, "He was killed."

"I know. Carnell Tallon, that short skinny guy, said the driver was in on it. He knew the gang, and he was shot without any explanation when he asked the leader why they killed Louis Eckman. Carnell went to him as he was dying and got one name or a part of a name. The driver said, 'Dall' before he died. So, does that ring any bells?" He noticed the surprised expressions cross all three of the men's faces.

"No one mentioned any of that to me up there," Charlie said, sounding surprised.

"Does it help?" Matt asked.

"It might," Sheriff Chuck Dielschneider said slowly. "Let me do some investigating before you spend your time on it."

"So, you gentlemen don't have any suspects at all? In my county, I automatically think of the Sperry-Helms Gang. You fellas can't think of anyone around here? Even I have heard of the Crowe Brothers, is there any chance they may have been involved?"

Troy Dielschneider shook his head. "No, we had two of them in jail for fighting the night before, and the others were in town trying to get them out. It wasn't them, or we might've suspected them right away. We did think it might've been the Sperry-Helms Gang, though."

Chuck added, "We have a wide territory to protect, and there are so many people without jobs; it's not even funny. Most folks who don't have a job, and there are few jobs around right now, have a claim they work, but winter's closing in and some might be getting desperate. It could've been anyone."

"And the name Dall, how does that ring a bell?" Matt asked.

The table was silent for a minute. Chuck spoke softly, "Troy's and my brother-in-law is named Dallen. I can't imagine him getting mixed up in something like this, though. Can you, Troy?"

Troy shook his head.

Chuck continued, "That's why I want to confront him tonight instead of you, Matt. You do understand; it's family. Yeah?"

Matt nodded. "I get it. But no matter what you find out, I'll want to talk to him tomorrow — also any relatives or friends of Herb Johnson. I want to find out as much as I can and bring these men to justice. The Eckman's are sending two men to help me; they are at the hotel now, I imagine. I will introduce you to them tomorrow. They are Pinkerton's, but more on the violent side, I understand. Anyway, talk with your brother-in-law and arrest him if he was involved. I'll talk to him tomorrow." He paused and added, "I've been riding a long way, and I am done for the day. I'm going to the hotel, and I'll see you gentlemen tomorrow."

The Sheriff stood up and offered, "Herb was a lifelong bachelor, Matt. He didn't have any family that we know of."

Matt reached for his coat. "Someone knows something. It's my job and yours to get it out of them and bring those men to justice. I'm not leaving here until we do. Nice to meet you, gentlemen."

"Enjoy our town, Matt."

Troy smirked as he stood up and asked, "How are you at throwing hands, Matt? You know fighting?"

Matt looked at him evenly. "Not too bad."

Troy snickered under his breath. "I'm the local champion around here."

"It's a good thing we're on the same side then. Huh?" Matt answered simply.

"Indeed. Hey, why don't you come out to the Blazing Bull Saloon with us tonight? We'd love to discuss the robbery and hear some of your stories."

Matt shook his head slightly. "I don't drink, Troy. There are too many people who'd like to shoot me or want to fight. Either way, staying sober keeps me ready for either one. I'll meet up with you gentlemen tomorrow."

When Matt left the office, Chuck sighed. "Damn. Well...I guess I better go talk with Danetta. You boys stick around here, we might have to go arrest Dallen."

Troy took a deep breath. "I have a feeling this is going to get dirty."

Charlie chuckled lightly. "We haven't got much of a choice now, do we boss?" he asked Chuck Dielschneider.

Chuck shook his head. "No, we don't. I'll be back."

4

Tiffany Foster stood in front of the cookstove, stirring a pot of cabbage stew with some chopped venison mixed in with it. She added what little pepper they had left into it and stirred some more as the stew began to boil.

"When the coals burn out, I need you to clean out that firebox tonight. The ashes are getting too deep, and they never should get up so deep to begin with. You'll never be a good wife if you can't clean out the firebox of the cookstove! It's the easiest job in the world, and you can't even do that right. I swear, Tiffany, your father should have left you on a corner somewhere," Danetta Foster said bitterly while she watched her fourteen-year-old step-daughter stirring the stew.

"I'll clean it after dinner," she answered without any emotion. It had only been eleven days since her father had confronted Danetta about the way she treated Tiffany. She had gone to her father's claim on a Saturday and confided to him that Danetta had been beating on her. Dallen Foster was furious and came home to confront Danetta. For a while, it seemed to have helped. Danetta had treated her well for a week or so without so much as a negative word or a raised voice. However, in the past three days, Danetta had been a bit ruder and more vocal. She had not laid a hand on Tiffany, but she was going back to her old ways little by little. Tiffany had done her best to be more respectful and not give Danetta a reason to get upset with her. It wasn't that she liked Danetta as much as she had promised her father that she would try to get along with her.

"And another thing," Danetta continued, "is that porridge the only crap you know how to make? Most of us are sick of eating cabbage! You're old enough to be out there working to bring some money home and help your father out around here. I don't know why your so content to lay around here on your butt like some special princess. I'm going to talk to your father about you getting out of the house and bringing some money in to help the family out. Lord knows we can't afford to feed you! People ask me all the time when you're expecting or who the father is, and I have to tell them, oh she's not pregnant, she's just fat and lazy! And they always say, I'm sure glad she's not looking for a husband because she'd never find one! A china man, maybe, but not a gentleman. And if you think that Author James is a gentleman, well…just know he's moved on to Janice Woodland. Yep, you've been passed over again! I suggest you quit eating and buy yourself a tighter corset until your married to the first china man that pays us two dollars for your ton. When you take that corset off, and all that fat comes bubbling out like a flash flood of flesh, your husband's eyes will pop open so wide he'll be American!"

"Why are you so rude to me?" Tiffany asked softly without looking back at Danetta. Her green eyes filled up with tears, but she refused to let her stepmother see them.

"Rude?" Danetta gasped. "I'm not rude, Princess!" she exclaimed bitterly. "I am honest. I don't know why you can't see that. I'm trying to help you become a woman. I go out of my way to shape you for the world, and all I get is dog crap! It's a losing battle that I can't win! I swear, I'm going to talk to your father about sending you away! I can't take it anymore! I mean look, there are crumbs on the table! How are we supposed to eat when there's crumbs on the table? Get a rag and wipe it down!" she yelled. "For crying out loud, Tiffany, I don't even know why you're here, you don't do anything!"

Tiffany sighed with frustration. "Nope," she agreed. She would tell her father when he got home from his claim what Danetta had said.

"Well, at least you acknowledge it! That's a start. And now that you admit it finally, I found a job for you at Chuck's place cleaning his house. I talked to him, and he'll pay you seventy-five cents a day for a job well done. You'll be bringing home fifty cents to me every day you work for putting up with you. Trust me, Princess, I'm looking forward to the day you are gone! Your father, too, for that matter. I never dreamed my life would become a burden on my brothers because my husband can't support his family, and his daughter can barely walk without starting an earthquake!"

Tiffany shook her head slightly and answered without looking back, "I weigh a lot less than you do."

Danetta stood up out of her chair and walked forward quickly and slapped the side of Tiffany's head as hard as she could. Tiffany tripped over her own planted feet and fell to the floor sideways and holding her ear; she began crying in pain.

Danetta leaned over her and pointed a finger in Tiffany's face. "Don't you ever say that to me again!" she yelled. "Who in the hell do you think you are to say something like that to me? I am the woman of this house, and you will respect me as such, or you can get out! And I can't wait until you are gone! Your father and I are both sick of you and your laziness! You're as useful as a cow without legs, eat and eat and have no purpose what-so-ever at all!" She paused to catch her breath. "Now, stop whimpering like a baby and get this table cleaned off. And tomorrow, you're going to Chuck's house to earn enough money to buy some food to cook for dinner. I'm tired of eating boiled cabbage! Everyone else in town can afford to eat filling meals; we get cabbage! You and your father have ruined my life, and I'm tired of it. Me and my girls deserve better than this. Get to work!" she yelled and kicked Tiffany while she tried to stand up.

Tiffany fell back to the floor and stood up quickly with rage glaring in her eyes as her stepmother stepped away from her. "I'm telling my father what you said! I'm telling him everything! All I do around here is work while you lay in bed or sit in your chair. My father and I were better off without you! At least we could afford to eat back then."

"How dare you?" Danetta asked as her blue eyes widened in anger. She stepped forward, and Tiffany covered her face knowing she was going to get hit. Danetta made a fist and hit her in the stomach. Tiffany fell to the floor, gasping for breath. Danetta grabbed the potholders off the counter and picked up the pot of boiling stew and held it over Tiffany. "What are you going to tell your father now? Huh? Are you going to tell him anything at all, or do I need to dump this on you accidentally? Answer me!" she yelled and poured a little of the scalding water onto the floor near her.

Tiffany scooted across the floor to get away from Danetta while fearfully staring at the steam that was coming out of the top of the pot. "I'm sorry. I won't tell him anything, I promise! Please..." she began to cry in fear. Silently, she pleaded with Jesus to protect her from Danetta and the scalding contents in the pot that was held above her.

"Look at me!" Danetta demanded. Her cold eyes glared dangerously at Tiffany. "I don't like you. I have never liked you. It wouldn't bother me at all to throw this onto you. If the burns don't kill you, then maybe the scarring will cover the ugliness of your face. If you ever...Look at me!" she demanded.

"I will kill you and say it was an accident, and it won't bother me at all." She looked around the cabin to make sure her two girls were outside before she continued. She whispered, "What do you think happened to the girls' father? What do you think happened to their first stepfather? What do you think will happen to your father and you if he ever tries to leave me? Do not cross me and do not say another word to my husband about anything! He thinks we're getting along like a loving mother and daughter right now. Well, we know that's not true, but what he doesn't know won't hurt him, unless you say something again." She put the scalding pot back on the stovetop. "I want you to start calling me 'Momma' when your father is around. I think that would make him happy. And his happiness is all I care about, not yours! You can die as far as I'm concerned. Me and the girls come first, then your father, the horse, the saddle, and then the weevils in the flour, then comes you. Know your place and obey it! Get the table cleaned off, and dinner served."

Tiffany sat on the floor against the wall and began to cry as she watched her stepmother step out of the kitchen and go into the crowded family room of their shack. It was a narrow but long cabin with a small kitchen for cooking, a dining table, and chairs, a family room with a small wood stove, and two filthy padded chairs with a small table between them. For more seating, the dining chairs were used. A hallway led past the bedroom all three girls shared and ended at Danetta and her father's bedroom. Tiffany watched Danetta sit down in her chair and pick up her knitting needles to begin knitting a wool sweater for her nine-year-old daughter Thelma. She already knitted one for her eight-year-old daughter Lynn. There wasn't much money to spend, so most of their clothing was hand made or patched up to work. Even their Sunday best were shabby and worn out by others before giving them to the Foster family. If one could call them a family, Tiffany certainly didn't call their home a family. She called it hell. She despised her stepmother and longed for the days when it was just her and her father living in the small shack.

Her mother and younger   sisters had died of a Diptheria outbreak in California where their father had a gold claim. Devastated by the loss, her father moved to another town and worked at a grist mill for a while until they moved to Portland, Oregon where he worked on a farm. After a few years in Portland, he heard of the goldfields in Aurora County and moved Tiffany to Prairieville when she was twelve years old. He filed a claim, and they lived in a tent for a few months, but her father was a decent man and knew a tent was no place for a young lady to grow up. He bought the cabin on the outskirts of town when he could afford to. It came with three acres of land and a small barn behind the cabin. He met Danetta at the local saloon a year ago and soon they were married. Danetta was a widow with two little girls, and they moved into the cabin with Tiffany and her father. The transition had been tough, but it wasn't too bad at first until Danetta began to get bitter for some reason that Tiffany never understood. She didn't know why her stepmother hated her; Tiffany certainly never gave her a reason to be so bitter. She had been courteous and respectful of her father's wife, but Danetta didn't like her from soon after the wedding. Now her contempt was not hidden in the slightest unless her father was at home. When he was home, she was kind, loving, and as fake as a harmless rattlesnake.

"I'm hungry," Danetta said as her eyes glared at Tiffany. It was a hint to get busy and get her a bowl of stew. She wanted the table cleaned off, but she never sat at the table anyway. The three girls had to, but Danetta hardly ever moved out of her chair. It was uncanny how she called Tiffany fat and made a big deal of it, but the fact was Danetta was the obese one, not Tiffany.

"I'll get you some stew," Tiffany said softly. She grabbed the ladle and scooped out some of the cabbage stew and took it to Danetta with a clean spoon. "Enjoy."

"Momma! Enjoy Momma. Remember, or do I have to whip it into you?"

Tiffany grimaced with a repulsive sneer. She had never wanted to call anyone what was rightfully deserved by her only mother. "Enjoy...Momma."

"That wasn't so hard, was it? But this food is like choking down dog vomit!" Danetta stated bitterly. She was a tall woman, nearly six-foot, and had broad shoulders on a thick body. It wasn't all bone structure like she claimed either, she was fat, and it showed most of all when she sat down, and her belly went halfway to her knees. She was simply a large woman with a lot of strength behind her fiery, ice-blue eyes and red hair. Tiffany had no idea what her father seen in Danetta, but whatever it was she couldn't imagine her father still seen it after a year of marriage to her. She had heard them arguing more in recent months over money, mostly about the lack of finances his mine claim brought in. She wanted him to hire on as one of her brother Chuck's deputies, but he always refused. It seemed to be a source of hostility to her. One of Danetta's most incessant complaints aside from the lack of finances was Tiffany herself. Tiffany had never thought too much about it until just recently that her father's claim was doing well when they met. But now it wasn't, and all Danetta did was complain.

A knock on the door startled Tiffany a bit, but as soon as the knocking ended, the door opened, and Danetta's oldest brother, the sheriff Chuck Dielschneider stepped inside. "Danetta, you're eating again, huh?" he teased.

"Shut up, Chuck. What do you want anyway?" she asked as she took a hungry bite of the stew.

He paused as he looked at Tiffany. "Tiffany, you're getting more beautiful every time I see you. It smells like you made that cabbage stuff again. Here," he pulled out his leather money bag and handed her a few dollar coins. "Go to the store before they close and buy some food, will you? And take your stepsisters too. I have to talk to my sister about some family stuff."

Danetta spat a mouthful of stew back into her bowl. "And bring me back one of those chocolate cakes Doris makes! Do you hear me?" she shouted.

Tiffany frowned irritably. "Of course, I heard you. I'm sure the whole town heard you."

"Smack her mouth, Chuck! I'm getting so sick of her!"

"No, she's right. You were loud."

"Then why don't you take her back to your place? She's old enough for you to marry if you asked me. And I know you've been watching her for a long time. Take her home with you, Chuck!"

"Oh, stop it," he said shaking his head. He looked at Tiffany, "Go on and go so I can talk to my sister."

"Gladly," she said as she put on her coat and stepped out the door.

"What do you want, Chuck? She'll clean your house for you. That's one step closer to marrying her. You'll have to fight Dane for her, though."

He sat down in the chair near her. "We have a problem. The Marshal, Matt Bannister, showed up today to investigate that robbery and the murder of Louis Eckman. Herb gave them a name, 'Dall.'"

"Dall? He had nothing to do with that!"

"I know. But the Marshal's going to talk to him tomorrow if we don't..."

"Kill him," she said quietly and shook her head. "What are me and my girls going to do then, Chuck? He isn't bringing much money home as it is, so maybe I won't even notice he's gone. But how am I going to survive, huh?"

"Troy, Devin, Dane, and I will help you and the

girls until you find another husband."

Danetta shook her head slowly with bitterness showing on her snarled lips. "I could prostitute that little wench out too. Her father won't be here to protect her then. Well, do what you have to do."

"I'm sorry, Danetta. We didn't know Herb said anything to them."

She looked sharply at her brother. "You tell that John Mattick the next time he shoots to kill someone, to make sure it's a killing shot! This is his fault!" She paused to shake her head with a snarl. "I'm not paying for Dallen's funeral. You are!"

"I'll take care of it." Chuck stood up. "He won't be coming home. I hope you said goodbye this morning."

"It doesn't matter," she said shaking her head.

"And there were three other men with him when he robbed that coach. Can you think of anyone you'd like to see gone?"

"Tiffany. You know she likes that Author James quite a bit. It might break her heart to have him killed too."

Chuck sighed. "Her hearts going to be broken when I come back. That's probably enough for today. I have three vagrant miners up on Dutch Creek that we can round up. I'll send the boys after them while Troy and I ride out to see Dallen. I'll be back with some bad news later. Until then, you should be nice to Tiffany. And like always, it's just between us."

"I'm always nice, and it's always family first."

5

Dallen's green eyes once shined bright and danced with life, but now they were dim and tired as Dallen was a broken man. He had labored his whole life for dreams of a comfortable and happy home, but every turn seemed to only lead to bad luck and poverty. He knew some of his choices along the way were foolish, but he had done his best to provide for his family. It wasn't for lack of trying or a willingness to work that there was very little food in his cellar. The last of the deer he had shot would be cooked in a stew tonight. His credit at the store was past due, and he had no money to buy a single ounce of flour or a carrot if he desired one. Cabbage...it was all that was left in his cellar, jars, and jars of home-canned salted cabbage. It was always an abundant harvest of cabbage in their garden, and it preserved well through the winter when food was hardest to come by. However, there was a bit of a mistake this past summer as he planted a row of cabbage and asked his new bride, Danetta, to plant two rows of potatoes. She misunderstood and planted two more rows of cabbage and one row of potatoes. Dallen had traded some heads of cabbage for other goods, but not everyone wanted to trade cabbage for potatoes or zucchinis. Now they had three shelves full of jars of finely sliced cabbage soaking in saltwater in quart mason jars. But then again, he was thankful they had something to eat. The food from their garden had not lasted near as long as he had hoped, and it was only mid-November.

Like every day except for Sunday, Dallen had spent hours shoveling soil from Happy Jack Creek into his sluice box, but once again, other than a few small grains of powdered gold; he found nothing of value. It was a wasted day, and his desperation to feed his family was wearing him down. It was getting too cold to be getting this wet to find nothing that could pay his bills. Jobs in Prairieville were hard to come by, and nobody quit their job when they found one. Dallen applied everywhere he could think of for a paying job, but without moving to a larger city where jobs were more plentiful, he was out of luck. He could've been hired as an Aurora County Deputy Sheriff under his brother-in-law, Chuck Dielschnieder. However, Dallen didn't like his wife's brothers well enough to work with them. He would sell out and move to Branson or maybe even the mining community of Galt up in the Blue Mountains where they were finding gold, but Danetta refused to leave Prairieville where her family was. He was willing to leave his family for six months to go to Galt and try his luck in the goldfields, but Danetta and Tiffany both argued against him leaving. He was stuck working along the cold water of his claim seeking the gold that once showed well, but now rarely showed a flake of any decent size. He sat down, defeated on a log near the fire of his camp, and rested his head in his hands. His depression only deepened with the thought of going home and being questioned by his wife about another day of failure to provide an income for his ladies.

"Lord," he prayed quietly, "I have always worked my hardest to get ahead, and I can't seem to do it. Timmy O'Brien lives in the most sinful ways, and he found a nugget bigger than my fist! He doesn't care about you, and yet he prospers in his life. I can't get ahead no matter how hard I try, and I don't understand why. My family is poor, and we have no food. And I don't know what to do. I'm thankful Danetta and Tiffany are getting along better, but Danetta is getting tired of being poor and eating cabbage. My Princess Tiffany is getting older and so beautiful, and I can't afford to buy her a decent dress to wear to church. The younger girls either. Jesus, I don't feel much like a man. I try to be honest, hardworking, and obedient to your Word, but I don't see any financial blessings. I know that isn't a promise, but Lord, what a blessing it would be for me. All I've done is work, try to raise my family, and please you. Forgive me for even saying so, but for what?"

"Praying again, Dallen?" Chuck Dielschneider asked unexpectedly.

Dallen stood up startled and turned around to face him. Chuck and his brother Troy were on their horses looking at him. Dallen smiled as he wiped his eye dry from the frustration he was feeling. "Yeah, you caught me in mid-prayer. What are you two doing here? Is everything okay at my place?" he asked anxiously.

"Fine. We have a problem," Chuck said coldly.

"What's that?"

Chuck frowned and paused before answering, "Unfortunately, Herb gave one name before he died. He said, 'Dall.' That means you, and the marshal is here to collect on that name."

"Me?" he asked, surprised. "Oh... no. You two can't pin that on me. I have nothing to do with that robbery! I've never been involved in that kind of thing and you both know it."

Troy sighed. "Dallen, it's you or us, and we're the only ones with guns," he said while pulling out his revolver and pointing it at him.

"Wait a minute," Dallen spoke, holding up his hands nervously. "I'm married to your sister. I've always treated her right and raising your nieces like my own daughters. We're family," his voice began to quiver. "Chuck, you know I'm all Tiffany has in this world. She's already lost her mother and sisters, please. You know how much it would mean to her for me to walk her down the aisle when she gets married someday. You don't have to do this. There's got to be another way. Chuck, we're family and family comes first, right?" he asked desperately.

Chuck sighed. "Dallen, how should I say this...

you're not family. Danetta doesn't even like you. I told her you wouldn't be coming home today, and she was fine with that. And don't worry, I'll take care of Tiffany," he said with a slight grin. "If she won't marry me, then Danetta had a great idea of starting a whorehouse for Tiff to bring in some money. The choice is Tiffany's. Which one do you think she'll pick?" he finished with a sadistic grin.

Dallen's eyes lost their fear and hardened. He stepped forward as he spoke with a depth of anger that took both men by surprise, "You stay away from my daughter! Or I'll kill you both!"

Chuck pulled his revolver and pointed at him and pulled the hammer back. "How are you going to do that when you're dead, Dallen? I'm just curious?" Chuck asked with a slight shrug. "Now," he said in a hardened voice, and he and Troy both fired their revolvers and hit Dallen twice in the chest. They watched him fall back to the ground with widened eyes staring into the sky while he tried to grab at the dirt beside him with his right hand.

"You can't answer that, huh?" Chuck asked with a short laugh.

Dallen stared at the sky above him and whispered as a tear fell from his eye, " Jesus, protect my baby."

Troy dismounted and walked over to Dallen, aimed his revolver at his head and pulled the trigger. "Yeah, he's dead. Throw me that gun belt, and I'll put it on him."

Chuck cursed as he dismounted his horse. "Why don't you shoot him six more times, Troy? I'm sure the marshal will believe none of those shots killed him! Put this belt on him and get him on the horse!" he shouted and threw an empty gun belt towards Troy.

Troy caught the belt. "Oh, calm down. He's not going to question how many times he was shot. It was a gunfight! Matt's had them before. I'm sure he'll be happy to take Dallen's body and leave town."

"Let's get him back to the Crowe's farm and wait for the boys to return with the other three bodies. We'll run those up to the Marshal tonight, and maybe he'll go home tomorrow. And I sure hope so, Troy, because the last thing we need is him and a couple of Pinkerton's poking their noses around here." The Crowe family farm was five miles outside of Prairieville along the Blue Mountains. It was a commonly used meeting place for the sheriff and his deputies and other outlaws and thieves of various kinds as well. The Crowe Brothers were notorious for their brutality and occasionally teamed up with the sheriff and others, such as their blood cousins, the Sperrys, and the Helms. Their farm was a hideout for anyone running from the law, and for a fee, a wanted man could hide in a mine shaft they dug into the mountain hidden from sight for as long as they wanted to pay for their mineshaft room and board.

Troy answered, "Just stick to the plan, and all will be fine."

Chuck took a deep breath. "Now, I need to figure out how to tell Tiffany without her thinking it was our fault."

"Tell her he was drunk and shot the other three men. She's young and dumb; she won't know the difference."

"Yeah, she will. She might be young, but she's not dumb. She knows her father didn't touch alcohol."

Troy looked at his brother, skeptically. "It doesn't matter much what she thinks. Danetta's going to break her down to nothing but a shell anyway. If she doesn't kill her first, that's going to start tonight. You can bet your life on that."

"Well, maybe one night with Danetta unleashed from her father will be enough for her to want to move into my place. We'll find out tomorrow," Chuck said, raising his eyebrows up and down.

Troy shook his head. "Twenty dollars says she's dead or forced down to selling herself within three days, but she won't be making your dreams come true. She's not even marrying age anyway, Chuck. Beside's that, you know Dane's the one set on marrying her. And you do realize we're talking about her over her dead father's body, right?" he said with a slight laugh. "Well, you go shatter her world, and I'll take him out to the Crowe's farm. I'll see you out there."

"Yeah, okay. See you soon."

"Hey, just to stay on her good side, tell her I'm sorry too."

6

Matt went to the Grand Lincoln Hotel and check-in for the night. The hotel was nothing more than a two-story clapboard building in the middle of town containing eight small guest rooms upstairs. Downstairs the hotel had a foyer with three tables set up for guests' meals, a counter used as the front desk, and behind the counter was a door leading to the owner's home; which filled the rest of the space of the first floor. William had already gotten his room, and Matt hadn't seen him since they parted ways while entering town. He figured William, like himself was probably tired from the trip and resting. Matt laid down on the bed in his small room and closed his eyes. An hour later, a knock on his door woke him up from a deep sleep, and he opened up his eyes slowly. He recognized William's pattern of knocking and slowly stood up and went to the door.

"Time for supper. Come on, we have a couple of fella's waiting for us," William said with his usual enthusiasm when Matt opened the door.

"Who?" Matt asked as he walked over to the bed, where he had left his moccasins.

"Those Pinkertons. They're waiting for us at a saloon no better than the one in Willow Falls. I never thought I'd ever find another outhouse for a saloon, but they have one here. Now, the Blazing Bull Saloon has got some life in it, but those Pinkerton boys wanted to eat and talk in the worst saloon in town. And you'll never guess the name of it." He waited with a slight grin for Matt to guess.

"No, I never will. What is it?" Matt asked tiredly as he slipped his moccasins on and tied the leather cords to tighten them.

"The Orvis Saloon. That makes sense, huh? Orvis, orifice, outhouse, crap. They couldn't have found a more appropriate name if they spent years thinking of one. Trust me; I made the rounds, and the orifice saloon is not where I want to be or the place I want to eat. I think when I get back over to Willow Falls, I'm going to stop in at the saloon and talk old Barney and Constance into changing the name from The Saloon to The Orifice Saloon." He laughed. "Yeah, that's what I'm going to do. Anyway, those boys are sitting down there waiting. I met them earlier, and they don't seem so bad. I think they want to be here about as bad as we do."

"They probably picked the best place to talk in semi-private. Well, let's go meet these gentlemen and see what they have to say."

Matt stepped into the Orvis Saloon and glanced around the saloon quickly before focusing on the two men who stood as he followed William to a table up against the far wall away from anyone else. The two men were dressed in pin-striped three-piece suits and had black derby hats that sat on the table. Both men wore a gun belt around their waist. One of them was a big man who put out his hand. He was just under six-foot-tall but weighed well over two hundred pounds. His black hair was cut short, and he had a full-faced beard that grew high up on his cheeks on his round face. He had narrow dark eyes revealed he was a serious man who seldom found a reason to smile. His grip was strong.

"Marshal," he said with a nod. "I'm Ivan Petoskey," he finished with a slight European accent to his voice.

"Ivan," Matt said as he shook the man's hand. Matt turned to the other Pinkerton and shook his hand.

"Nice to finally meet you, Marshal. My name's Pete Logan." Pete was shorter than Ivan, thinner, and less opposing. He had short brown hair and a clean-shaven oval-shaped face. His eyebrows were thick and nearly came together over his cold, lifeless brown eyes. A large cold sore scabbed the corner of his lip. His grip was firm despite his smaller frame.

Pete continued, "Here, sit down. We've already met your cousin. We weren't expecting him, but we've had a good time chatting with him." He smiled slightly as he sat down. "Let's order some food and talk over dinner."

"Very good. Call me, Matt, gentleman. I'm afraid I'm not one for idle chit-chat, you'll have to talk to

William for that." he said with a grin. "Well, you know what we're here for and know as many details as I do. Have you two been here in town long?"

Pete shook his head. "Let's order some food first. Hey," he hollered across the saloon, "We're ready to order. Sorry, gentlemen, I'm hungry," he explained to Matt and William. After they all ordered their dinners, Pete continued, "To answer your original question, Matt, we arrived yesterday. We took the train up from Sacramento to Portland and then over to The Dalles. It took us about four days of hard riding from there to get here on horseback. Working for the Eckman's, you can bet we prefer to take the train when we can. But the train only goes so far for now. And this is about as rural as I've ever seen. It's been a long journey."

"Two and a half days for us. Branson's about fifty miles north of here. Prairieville is a pretty poor area unless you're one of the large ranchers or farmers spread out in Aurora County. In town here, there are no big businesses like we have in Branson, so the economy is pretty low, especially with winter approaching. As you know, Mister and Misses Eckman were set up and preyed upon for having some money. I advise you two not to wear your suits, or it may happen to you."

Pete looked at Ivan with a smirk and then at Matt. "I think we'll be okay. So, what do you think about us poking our nose in the saloons tonight and see if we can't find this Dall character and his gang? We were telling William earlier that we want to get this case solved and get back home where it's a bit warmer. I don't want to make that ride back to The Dalles in the snow. I'll be honest, Matt, Ivan nor I want to be here."

Matt smiled slightly. "We might've gotten lucky because I talked with the county sheriff when we arrived, and I told him the driver named someone called 'Dall' before he died. Just so happens the sheriff's brother-in-law is named Dallen. He wanted to confront his brother-in-law himself. So, we all may be going home sooner than we hoped if he arrests his brother-in-law and his friends."

"Really?" Ivan asked with a surprised expression and looked at Pete. "Well, that would be great."

"Yeah, it would," Pete agreed. "But we'd still have that long ride back to The Dalles, and I'm still a bit saddle sore. We don't usually ride long distances on horseback. Like I was saying, we take the train most of the time down in California. We work mostly in one city or another."

William offered, "Well, you boys wouldn't have to leave this paradise all too soon if it snowed. You could lounge around the orifice saloon for the winter and drink until the ladies look good, huh?"

Ivan smiled slightly.

"No," Pete answered plainly. He looked over at Matt, "If we haven't got anything to do except wait for the sheriff, then I say we enjoy each other's company and have some fun tonight. This might be the easiest assignment we've ever worked after all."

"How long have you two been working for the Eckman's?" Matt asked.

"Five years for me and three for Ivan. Technically, we worked for them but answered to Carnell Tallon. He was the one we worked for, really." Pete frowned and lowered his eyes for a moment before continuing, "Sebastian told us what happened in Branson. We miss our boss, man, but I think Ivan and I understand that Carnell didn't give you much of a choice but to kill him. Carnell was personally invested in the whole search for Catherine and seeing her with Nathan..." He shrugged. "I don't know; maybe it just drove the common sense out of him. You probably wouldn't know it, but he was a good man."

Matt nodded. "I wish it had worked out differently."

Pete nodded. "Ivan and I have both been in those situations and understand. The man we want is Dall; he is the one who murdered Louis. We also want the man who killed our friend Tom Picard. He was the guard riding next to the driver who was killed without warning by the first shot. He was a good man with a wife and three young kids, and whoever shot him didn't give him a chance to live. I want the man who shot him maybe even more than Dall. Let me ask, if the sheriff brings Dall and his gang back alive, what are your plans with them? Are you sending them back with us?"

Matt shook his head slowly as he sipped his coffee. "No, the murders were committed in Aurora County, so I would leave them to the local authorities to jail and prosecute."

Ivan frowned. "Have you looked around, Marshal? Justice shouldn't be chanced on a jury from

here. This man's friends could be on the jury, and
any justice for our friends would be tossed out the
door like a muddy rug. Or his friends could persuade the jury members to let him go. It's not that
hard to intimidate the folks on a jury to get the ver-
dict you want from them, no matter how strong the
evidence is. We've seen it happen a few times now."

Matt realized from what Sebastian had told
him about these two men that he was looking at
men who had personally intimidated juries of the
legal system as just another part of their job. Matt
said, "We'll talk to the sheriff and see if he has any
concerns of that sort. If so, we'll ask for the trial to
be moved to Jessup County. But Dall or whoever is
arrested will not be going back to California with
you gentlemen, no."

Pete smiled slightly. "You can't blame us for hoping, though, huh?"

Matt continued, "This murder has drawn a lot of
attention, and the trial will no doubt be well covered by the newspapers with reporters hounding
the lawyers and everyone else involved. I did not
want to get involved with this either, but I already
am. If it weren't for me, Carnell would be down
here investigating this instead of William and me."

"That's true," Pete said with no doubt in his facial expression.

"My point," Matt added, "is that there won't be
room for any back-door politics, intimidation, or
favors with this trial. It will be too well covered."

"Or…" Ivan spoke slowly as he took another
drink of his glass of whiskey, "we could kill them

all and save everyone a bunch of trouble. We know Dall's guilty, so why not?"

William said with a casual shrug, "That's what I say. Killers need to be killed before they can kill again."

Ivan nodded. "That's two votes to one, Matt. Three to one actually, because I know Pete agrees with me."

Matt raised his eyebrows. "Well, fortunately, this isn't an election. If the sheriff brings Dall in, he'll stay in jail, and we'll track his gang down. I suggest we wait for the sheriff and see if he brings Dall in or not."

7

Matt didn't feel like going to the loud and rowdy Blazing Bull Saloon with William and the two Pinkertons, so he went back to his hotel room to relax and enjoy the quiet. He read a few chapters of his Bible, and then in the middle of his praying, a knock on the door got his attention.

Sheriff Chuck Dielschneider's voice spoke through the door, "Matt, come on down to the street. I have something for you. Do you hear me?"

"Be right there," Matt said loudly.

"Alright, I'll meet you down there."

Matt pulled his moccasins back on, his gun belt, and slipped into his buffalo coat before stepping out of his room. He walked down the hallway and then down the stairs through the foyer of the hotel and outside onto the front porch. In front of him stood Chuck, his deputized brother, Troy, deputy Charles Hammond and two other men with badges who held the reigns of four horses with four bodies tied over their saddles. Matt frowned unexpectedly, taken back by the size of the crowd that had emptied into the street to see the four dead bodies. Nearby, he could see William standing with the two Pinkertons. His voice spoke louder than the gasps and murmuring of the crowd as he joked about it being a wasted trip now that he had no one to kill.

Chuck spoke casually with a hint of sadness, "Well, Marshal, let me introduce you to my brother-in-law, Dallen Foster." He slapped the thigh of a blonde-haired man draped over the horse beside him. "Dallen tried to fight it out when I confronted him. Troy and I had no choice but to lay some bullets into him to save our own lives. We all knew he was a little crooked here and there, but no one suspected him of doing something like murdering Louis Eckman. I couldn't believe he tried to shoot Troy and me either! We're family, you know." He sounded quite sad about the outcome.

His brother Troy added, "And those three men are his pals, Archie Blackwell, Clay Johnson and... Burt Jones." He took a deep breath. "None of them were willing to surrender either. We tried to take them alive, but you know."

Chuck added quickly, "They're all poor miners working dead claims you know, and they were all friends with Herb. He must have arranged the robbery in desperation after Herb told them about some rich guy, and things got out of hand maybe. I don't know. Anyway, here they are. You can either take them back with you or leave them here to be buried. But tonight, we're putting them up in front of the saloon as a warning to other would-be thieves and murderers. Is that fine with you?"

Matt shrugged. "I'm not taking them with me, so what do I care. It's your town. That's him though, huh? You got them all?" His eyes scanned over the four bodies that were carelessly flung over saddles and tied to stay on. There was nothing to cover the deceased, just their clothing and blood still draining from the bullet holes with consistent drops onto the street. The body of the one named Burt Jones wore a pair of boots so badly worn out that leather tie strings from a saddle were cut off and used to tie around the toe of his boots to keep the sole on. All four men were poorly dressed, ragged, and unshaved.

Chuck raised his eyebrows as he said, "As far as I know. I don't think he had any other good pals, did he?" he asked his brother Troy.

Troy shook his head slightly. "No, this is it. I'd say this is the four that robbed that carriage."

"Marshal," Chuck asked, "is there a reward for this I might be able to collect on? I hate to even ask with him being family, but my sister has a family to raise, and it would help her. By the way, these are my other two brothers, Devin and Dane. They didn't go with us, but they're here now."

Devin was in his late twenties to early thirties and was a deputy as well and wore a badge on his gray flannel shirt under a brown coat. He was about the same height as Chuck, just under six feet, stocky and quite muscular. He had long red hair that reached his broad shoulders and a red full-faced beard about four inches long on his square face. His blue eyes were as hard and as tough as his brother Troy's. Devin Dielschneider carried a gun belt as well and appeared to be a no-nonsense kind of man. Devin looked at Matt with no expression and nodded quietly.

On the contrary, Dane Dielschneider was the youngest and looked to be in his mid-twenties. He came up short in the bulk of his brothers. Dane was much shorter and scrawny compared to his three brothers. Dane had dark red hair that was neck length and a thin pale face covered with freckles. Unlike his brothers who had blue eyes, Dane had dark brown eyes that almost looked black in the lamplight of the hotel's lanterns hanging on the porch. Dane's thin lips maintained a strange grin that never wavered as he stared at Matt.

Matt frowned at the awkwardness of Dane's grin and nodded to him. "Gentlemen," he said without much interest. His attention went back to Sheriff Dielschneider. "You would have to talk to Mister Pete Logan or Ivan Petoskey over there to answer your question about a reward. They work for the Eckman's, not me."

"I will," Chuck said. "Boy's take these bodies to the livery stable and get a hold of Dixon for the caskets. I want those bodies in front of the Blazing Bull as soon as possible," he said to his deputies, who he didn't introduce Matt too. "Marshal, come on over to the saloon with us and have a drink or two. I imagine you'll be leaving tomorrow, and we'd all like to get to know you a bit."

Matt shook his head. "I don't drink, Chuck."

"You don't have to drink. If you're afraid, all we have is some homemade mountain brew, you're partly right, but we have lots of the good liquor too. Why not come join us for a bit?"

The deputy Charles Hammond added, "It's not often we get someone interesting around here to talk to."

Troy Dielschneider smiled slightly. "Come on, Marshal. Come enjoy yourself with us."

Dane Dielschneider, still staring at Matt seemingly without blinking or moving his eyes a fraction of an inch, asked through his frozen grin in a soft toneless voice, "Are you scared?"

Matt looked at him, taken back by the oddity of the way he asked.

William stepped up onto the hotel's porch and patted Dane on the back as he passed him. "Being surrounded by a patch of carrots isn't frightening, son. A cluster of radishes either. Are the strawberries ripe? It's a little too red for my taste around here, but not scary. I'd hate to see your twin sister." He turned to Matt. "Come on, Matt, let's go visit with this bunch of fellas and take their money in a game of poker. We came all this way for nothing, so we might as well take one night to have a little fun and make some new friends, huh?"

Matt looked at William doubtfully. "Talking to people the way you just did isn't going to win many friends, William," Matt said softly.

"Matt, let's go!" Chuck hollered as he had walked away with Troy and Charlie. A large part of the crowd followed him while others walked away towards their homes.

"Matt, come on!" Ivan Petoskey yelled with a wave of his hand as he and Pete followed the group to the Blazing Bull Saloon down the street just a few buildings down and across the street.

Matt's attention went back to the young man named Dane, who continued to stare at him with his haunting eyes and uneasy grin. Dane spoke with the same soft voice, "You're not yellow, are ya?"

Matt narrowed his eyes as he looked at the odd freckled-faced young man who looked fragile enough to be broken in half with one hit. "No, I'm not yellow."

"I think you are," Dane said with the strange smile on his lips.

"You do?" Matt asked. "Maybe you can tell me why you think so? Or are you just going to stand here repeating yourself like a hungry meowing cat?" Matt replied, sounding irritated.

Dane's lips pulled a touch upward, increasing his grin. He spoke in the same soft voice without any changes to his tone, "Come on over and find out. Or are you too scared to see?"

"See what?" Matt asked with an irritated grimace.

William had been watching with a humored half-smile on his face. He shook his head in wonder. "Boy, you need to join up with one of those freak shows and change your name to the Talking Tomato and get out of this town and go see the world. Get some damn sun for sure and get a girlfriend, maybe. You're one creepy kid."

"Dane!" Devin Dielschneider called loudly, "Let's go." He was standing on the street with his profile towards them. His right hand was near his gun, and as he glared dangerously at William.

Dane's smile faded as he looked slowly from William to Matt. "Prove to me you're not scared. Come on over, or are you too scared to?" he said as his grin took form again. He turned away and walked to his older brother on the street. "Come on, Marshal. Or are you a scaredy-cat? Meow-me-ow," Dane said with an eerie giggle as they walked towards the Blazing Bull Saloon.

Matt shook his head with a dumbfounded grimace. "Meow-meow? What the?" He looked at William strangely.

William laughed lightly. "I don't know. I think the boy has been trapped in this town for too long. But unless you're a scaredy-cat? Maybe we should go find out."

Matt took a deep breath. "I suppose I should just so that kid doesn't think I'm afraid to. I don't know of what exactly, but something must be scary. Shall we go to the saloon?" he asked William.

William nodded. "Well, we're leaving tomorrow, right? So, we might as well go face your fears."

From the doorway of the Blazing Bull Saloon, Ivan Petoskey stepped outside with a deep laugh and a glass of alcohol in his hand. "Marshal, Matt Bannister, you have to come see this!"

"Shall we go see what's so funny?"

"No, you're too scared to, remember?" William

said as they began walking down the street towards the saloon. "What a creepy kid. You better lock the door to your room tonight because you don't want to wake up in the middle of the night to see him staring at you. He might ask if you're scared. And if that happens…just say yes and make him happy."

Matt laughed lightly. "That would scare me."

William shook his head with a smile. "He's so red and white, if he wore some blue, I'd swear he's a flag." He imitated Dane's soft monotone less voice the best he could, "Because you're yellow, aren't ya?"

8

Danetta Foster could hear her two daughters, Thelma, and Lynn trying to comfort Tiffany as she wailed in their bedroom. Tiffany's cries were deep and painful at the news of her father's death. Danetta had already told Tiffany to be quiet and the younger girls to get to bed, but Tiffany kept sobbing. For Danetta, it was simply a fact of life. Dallen was gone and wouldn't be coming home. He was a decent man, but he didn't supply all that she had expected, and his usefulness had expired when the gold faded out. It was family first, and if her brothers thought it was necessary to do away with him, then it probably was. She could live without Dallen, but she didn't want to live without her brothers and their protective nature over her. Her padded chair sat next to the hallway to their bedroom door, and she leaned over the side of her chair to yell towards the door, "Shut up! Or I'll come in there and give you something to cry about! Thelma, you and Lynn get to bed, or I'll whip you too!"

Thelma, Danetta's nine-year-old daughter, came out of the room with tears in her eyes and looked at her mother. "Ma, Tiff's really sad. Pa died," she said with a wavering bottom lip. She had bright red hair like her mother, but it was unbrushed and matted together as it hung down to her shoulders. Her young blue eyes grew more desperate and thicker with tears. She waited, expectedly for her mother's comforting words.

Danetta's hardened eyes softened just a touch. "Come here and listen to me," she said as she helped Thelma sit on her wide lap. "Thelma hon, he wasn't your father, and he wasn't even your Pa, and you shouldn't think of him like that. I never wanted to tell you this, but Dallen never liked you and Lynn. He only liked Tiffany. Do you want to know a little secret? He wanted me to give you and Lynn away because he didn't like you."

Thelma's face expressed the hurt the words brought into her little heart, and tears slid down her cheeks. "Why?" she asked with a shaking voice. "I loved him, Mama. Why didn't he like me?"

Danetta sighed. "Because some people only like their own children and no one else's. Even if they marry their Mama like he did me, he still didn't like either of you. He told me Tiffany was his princess, and you and Lynn were just warts on his feet that caused a lot of trouble and pain. Sweetheart, remember he always called Tiffany his princess, not you. It's Tiffany's fault really; she always told him what bad things you two girls did, even if you didn't do it. She'd always lie to keep his love all to herself. And that's why she's so sad. She's selfish and a liar. So, don't waste your love on him, sweetheart. He's not worth a single tear either. Look at me, see? Not one tear. I know what a piece of rubbish he was, and now I don't have to worry about him giving you and Lynn away. I think we're lucky Uncle Chuck and Uncle Troy had to shoot him because he was going to give you and Lynn to the Chinamen. You know your uncles would never allow that. They'd never do anything to hurt us, and they were watching out for us. Now, you get on to bed, as I said."

"Mama, is that why Uncle Chuck and Uncle Troy shot Pa?"

"Dallen, is his name, dear. Not pa anymore, okay? They shot him because he did some bad things, and Marshal Matt Bannister came to town to look for him. In fact, the Marshal's staying at the hotel and will be leaving tomorrow. So, I'm going down to the saloon with your uncles to meet him. Who knows, maybe I can get you a new daddy tonight," she laughed lightly. "Now, get to bed so I can go."

"Okay, Mama," Thelma said and climbed off her lap to walk back to her room. She stopped. "Hi, Tiff. Are you feeling better?"

Danetta leaned forward and turned to look back down the hall and seen Tiffany standing there, glaring at her. Her face was wet with tears, and her eyes were reddened by crying. A thin clear line of drainage fell from her nose to her top lip. She placed her hands-on Thelma's shoulders to hold her near her. "You…are such a liar. My father loved these girls just as much as he did me. You had him murdered just like you did your first husband, I'm sure. You are an awful person, and I hate you!"

Danetta's eyes narrowed as a slight smirk came over her face. "Thelma, go on to bed, sweetheart."

Thelma nodded anxiously and went on into her room.

Danetta stood up and turned to face her fourteen-year-old stepdaughter. "You think I had your father killed?"

Tiffany nodded slowly. Despite the rage she was feeling towards her stepmother, her fear of Danetta was showing in her eyes.

Danetta pressed her lips together and shook her head slightly. "Well, I didn't. I liked your Pa, I didn't love him, but I liked him. He shouldn't have killed that Eckman fellow, and he'd still be here talking to his Princess and ignoring me!" she snapped bitterly.

"He didn't kill anyone! He wasn't even there. That happened on the day I was helping him at the claim. Or do you not remember? Someone is lying, and it's you and your brothers. I'm going to tell the marshal the truth, and you're all going to pay!"

"You'll have to get by me first, if you can," Danetta challenged her by raising her eyebrows questionably.

"Fine! I'll go when you're sleeping."

Without any warning, Danetta doubled up her fist and swung her right arm as hard as she could towards Tiffany's face. It connected with her cheek, and Tiffany flew into the wall and then collapsed to the floor. She held her cheek in pain but was more surprised by the unforeseen blow. Danetta reached down and grabbed a handful of her blonde hair and dragged her across the floor into the kitchen while she screamed and tried to pry Danetta's hands from her hair. Thelma and eight-year-old Lynn both came out of their room, yelling for their mother to stop. Danetta ignored them and grabbed a knife off the counter, bent down, and put it to Tiffany's throat. She sneered through a hate-filled grimace, "You will do no such thing, or I will kill you right here and now! If you say one word about this to anyone, either I will kill you or one of my brothers will! You have no choice but to do what you are told from here on out, or you will be sorry! I could cut a line across your pretty face so hideous that no one will ever look at you twice, Princess!" she spat out bitterly. "You will do what you are told to do to bring money into this house! Aren't you?" she asked, pulling her hair back to expose her throat more to the knife. "Aren't you?" she demanded an answer.

"Yes," Tiffany whispered through her choking tears.

"You won't refuse whatever I tell you either, will you?" Danetta asked with a cold tone.

"No...."

"As soon as the Marshal leaves town, you're going to become the most popular little prostitute in town, Princess!" She doubled her fist over and hit Tiffany again in the face before pulling her up by the hair and pushed her towards her family room.

"Get to bed! And stop crying!"

Tiffany went into her room and fell onto her bed, facedown. Blood flowed out her nose onto her thin pillow. Her stepsister Thelma followed her in and sat down beside her. "Tiff, are you okay? You shouldn't make Mama mad."

Tiffany sat up and pushed her off the bed. "Go away!" she yelled through her turmoil.

Thelma fell to the floor and looked up at her with a hurt expression.

It was the heavy footsteps walking towards the bedroom that caused Tiffany to stand up when Danetta entered the room. Danetta was holding a leather belt with the buckle end hanging down. She immediately swung the belt, and it wrapped around Tiffany's ribs as she reached up to protect her face. The buckle whipped around her side and slammed into her back. Tiffany cried out in pain and arched her back painfully. Danetta swung it again as she hissed like a viper, "Don't ever yell at my girls again!"

Tiffany screamed in pain as the buckle hit the back of her head. She dropped to her knees near her pillow and held her head with both hands where a knot was forming on her skull. She could feel the blood coming through her fingers, and she moved a bloody hand in front of her face to see if the wet warmth she felt was blood. Just then, the buckle hit her back again, and she fell forward with a loud cry. She landed in front of the small table separating the two beds and saw her black-handled calligraphy pen with its fine steel tip that her father had gotten

72

her for Christmas, setting in its pen case near her bottle of ink. She used it for writing poetry and drawing pictures in a paper tablet kept under her bed in a small lockbox. She took hold of the pen in her right hand and spun around desperately on her knees and drove the dip pen deep into Danetta's side a few inches above her hip. Danetta stepped backward while dropping the belt and reached down in a panic to pull the pen out of her side. Tiffany ran by her and out of the house, sobbing without her shoes or a coat on.

The metal point entered Danetta's flesh easily, and she felt the shock of the pain as the black handle stuck out of her with blood running down her dress. She didn't care about Tiffany running outside; she was more concerned with pulling the pen out of her side and any potential harm it caused inside of her. She grabbed the handle with her hand and slowly pulled the pen out. It had left a decent sized puncture wound that bled steadily. She spoke in a panic, "Oh, my lord. Thelma, go get Chuck and have him bring the doctor! Tell him; Tiffany stabbed me. Tell Troy and Devin to bring me her head on a platter. Hurry up and go!"

9

Matt and William entered the Blazing Bull Saloon to a loud unexplained applauding and cheering. Everyone seemed to be excited, including Troy Dielschneider, who held a glass of alcohol in his hand. He was looking at Matt with a large expectant smile.

"Marshal, I told you, I was the fighting champion around here, and that's true except for one other guy I won't fight. And I think you might know him," Troy said loudly as the crowd of men in the saloon waited expectedly.

A man with his back intentionally turned to Matt, turned around. He was around five foot ten inches tall, well built with a muscular frame, and had short curly brown hair and a wide oval-shaped face with strong cheekbones. He was clean-shaven except for a well-groomed goatee. His eyes were blue and narrow below his brown eyebrows. He wasn't a bad-looking man, but his eyes were cold and menacing. He wore a deputy's badge on his left shirt lapel and a six-gun on his waist. John wore black pants and a light blue button-up shirt with the sleeves rolled up. He smirked smugly while he quickly looked Matt over.

"John?" Matt asked, surprised. He smiled slightly. "How are you?" he asked, staring at his old friend.

John held his hands out to his side and pressed his lips together with a slight shrug. "Great. And you're looking more Indian than ever. Still think you are one, huh?" he asked, noticing the moccasins on Matt's feet and his buckskin clothing and long dark hair that was in a ponytail that went to the middle of his back. The last time he had seen Matt, his hair was still ear length.

"I am in part," Matt said as he stepped forward to shake John's hand. "How long have you been around here?"

"Too long," he answered as he shook Matt's hand firmly. "I hear you're in Branson now. You've done well since our days in Boise City." His eyes looked at Matt with a certain tenseness, yet behind the tough exterior, there was a touch of uneasy fear in John's eyes.

Matt frowned as he looked in John's eyes and realized why the fear was there. "Yeah, I'm in Branson now. So, you're a deputy here?"

"Yep. Who knew we'd both become lawmen, huh?"

"That we have," Matt agreed, looking at his old friend.

Troy stepped near the two of them and said, "Come on, you two, let's see a rematch. John, take him outside and whip him again."

John smirked and lowered his head a bit. "I told them how I whipped you back in Boise City."

"Oh…" Matt said, suddenly understanding why Dane was saying what he did and why the sheriff and his deputies wanted him to come to the saloon. "I see."

Troy continued, "Let's go outside and see who wins. Don't you want a rematch, Marshal? Or are you going to declare John as the tougher man?"

William Fasana spoke pointedly, "Matt's never lost a fight!"

"He did too!" someone in the saloon yelled. "John whipped him like a pup!"

Ivan Petoskey yelled out, "I have ten dollars on the Marshal!"

Troy answered, "Your bet's taken. I got John for ten dollars!"

"Two dollars on John!"

"Whip him again, John, and take his badge!"

"Come on, John!" the men in the saloon were yelling out over one another, encouraging John to take Matt outside and beat him up.

Devin Dielschneider stood near his brother Troy as he said, "I'll take John. And if Matt's yellow-haired cousin jumps in, he's mine! Right, Goldie?" he asked William bitterly."

William looked at Devin, who stood a few feet away. "Well, well, well, that's quite a tempting invitation. How about we forget about them and step outside and see what you have, Big Red?"

Devin raised his eyebrows sharply. "Let's go!"

"No!" Chuck yelled, stepping in front of Devin to stop him from going outside. "There's only one fight I want to see, and that's between John and the Marshal. Come on, John, quit talking and take him outside!" he ordered.

"That's embarrassing," William said to Devin. "Big brother doesn't want you getting hurt apparently, so you better listen to him and be in bed by ten."

Devin stepped forward and pushed William with both hands. "I'll fight you right now! I'll knock your golden head right off!"

"Devin, shut up!" Chuck ordered as he once again intervened between the two of them.

"He was making fun of Dane! He was calling us all strawberries and stuff like that! Let me knock him around a bit, Chuck."

Chuck looked at William with disdain. "There's only one fight I want to see and this one ain't it. John, take him outside, and let's see a rematch."

William put his index finger in his nostril to pick his nose and said, "How disappointing. Embarrassing for you, Big Red, but disappointing," William said with a slight laugh and looked at the green dried mucus on the tip of his index finger. He then flicked his finger towards Devin.

Devin brushed off the front of his coat with an infuriated grimace and lunged towards William. "You want to fight, let's go right now! Get out of the way, Chuck!"

Chuck pushed his brother backward. "Knock it off, Devin!" he yelled. "It's not your fight tonight."

"He flicked a booger on me!"

"I don't care! Now shut up!" He glared at his brother harshly. He looked at William, who was snickering under his breath. "And you better watch yourself before I let my brother knock you silly!" Chuck shouted at William.

William furrowed his brow sarcastically and then raised one brow. "Please do."

Chuck looked at Matt. "Control your cousin before my patience wears thin!"

Matt put his hand on William's shoulder. "William, that's enough. Sheriff, I'm sorry to disappoint you and these other folks, but I'm going to my hotel room." He looked back at John with hardening eyes. "It's good to see you, John, but I'm not going to fight you for their entertainment."

John shrugged with a small smirk. "I understand. You don't want to get beat again now that you're a big-name marshal."

Matt looked at him evenly. "Oh, we'll cross paths soon enough, John. You can trust me on that."

"Well, you know where I am when you're ready to try to beat me again; if you ever have the guts to," he added quickly and glanced at his friends with a smile.

"That I do. See you soon, old friend. Let's go, William." Matt turned around and began to leave the saloon. He was insulted by disappointed men calling him a coward, among other things, as he stepped out of the saloon. Matt gritted his teeth with humiliation and anger as he stepped out onto the saloon's porch and saw Dane Dielschneider standing there leaning against the support beam of the roof. He had a cigarette in his hand and put his fixed gaze on Matt. He grinned. "I told ya you'd be afraid. John scares ya, huh?"

Matt glanced at him irritably and walked past him wordlessly.

"The Marshal's a coward," Dane said with a slight chuckle.

William stepped off the porch and turned back towards Dane. "Join a freak show, I'm telling you, you'd make a fortune!" William turned back towards Matt and asked as they walked across the street, "Would you like to explain why we are walking away from a perfectly fair and exciting fight?"

"Later,"

"No, not later, now. You just walked away from a public challenge; do you know what that's going to do to your reputation?" William asked sharply. He grabbed Matt by the shoulder and turned him around to face him. William was serious and had no humor on his face. "You can't walk away like this! You have to fight him, or you're going to be challenged from here on out by everyone who thinks they're tough. There's a time to be nice and walk away, but there's also a time where you can not afford to walk away, and this is it! If you walk away from that guy, you might as well hand your marshal's badge over to Truet and go be one of Tim Wright's deputies because you'll leave here with the same reputation of being a coward that he has."

"Ouch," Matt said lightly.

"Yeah! Now get back in there and whip his hide

so we can leave here with our pride intact."

Matt frowned and looked at his cousin. "Sometimes, it's better to use a little more wisdom than brawn. Trust me, now's not the time."

John walked out of the saloon in a hurry taking off his gun belt and handing it to Troy as he stepped off the porch. "Matt Bannister! I'm calling you out right now! Fight me now or leave town with your tail tucked between your legs like you did last time, you damn coward!" He was followed out by the large crowd of men from the saloon. All were making bets and encouraging John to force a fight.

"You can't walk away now," William said softly. He made eye contact with Devin Dielschneider and spoke loudly to mimic Devin's own words in the saloon, "And if Big Red jumps in, he's mine!" He grinned as Devin took an angry step towards him and was held back by his brother Chuck again.

John walked quickly towards Matt and pushed him with both hands. "You're going to fight me now, or I'm going to beat you like a whimpering dog anyway!" His face was enraged and must have been severely harassed or threatened one way or another to force Matt to fight.

Matt shook his head as calmly as he could. "I'm not fighting you tonight, John. You already know that."

"What? Are you scared to fight me?" he asked loud enough so that everyone could hear.

"Fear has nothing to do with it. I don't like to fight my friends."

"Friends?" John scoffed. "We ain't friends! We

haven't been since I whipped your hide! And we aren't going to be friends either!"

Matt looked at him, squarely with a slight upward curl to his lips. "Yeah, that's probably true."

Chuck ordered loudly, "Hit him now, John!"

Matt grimaced and shook his head slightly. "Have a good night, boys," he said and turned his back to John and stepped towards the hotel.

"Get him!" Chuck yelled while others yelled similar words. John stepped forward and shoved Matt's back, forcing to stumble forward a couple of steps.

Matt turned towards him with hardened eyes. "Stop pushing, or I'll hurt you in front of your friends. And you know I can. Last time it was my own fault, I won't make the same mistake twice. Try me and see!"

"Yes. It's going to happen!" someone said excitedly along with other cheers of anticipation and echoed through the crowd of men. Many of the men who wanted to see the fight waited with childlike glee on their faces for the first punch to be thrown. They were a bit dismayed when Matt turned around once again and took another step towards the hotel.

John, feeling the pressure from his audience, followed Matt, and reached forward to grab Matt's ponytail. "Don't walk away from me!" he demanded as he pulled the ponytail.

Matt grimaced with anger, and without turning around, he kicked his left foot back up into John's crotch. The bottom arch of his foot connected brutally with John's testicles. John let go of Matt's hair and dropped to his knees while holding his crotch. Matt turned around and grabbed John's goatee with his left hand to lift his chin while his right fist was clenched tight, ready to break John's jaw with a solid right. He hesitated while looking at his old friend. "I told you the time's not right, but it's coming fast. Real fast!" He shoved John's head back, pushing him back to his side. He curled up in a fetal position holding his crotch.

Troy Dielschneider stepped forward angrily. "What are you, a girl? Kicking a man in the jewels is a woman's fight! Why don't you try doing that to me? Come on, fight like a man! I'm right here!" His chest was pushed out, and his back slightly bent back as he puffed out his chest.

"Get lost," Matt said as his attention went to a young red-haired girl running quickly towards Chuck.

"Uncle Chuck!" she cried out with tears running down her face. She was out of breath from running.

Chuck's face suddenly grew concerned as he went to the girl and knelt to meet her on her level. "Thelma, what is it?" he asked urgently.

She pointed back towards the way she had come from and spoke through her deep breaths, "Tiff... she stabbed Mama!"

"What?" Chuck exclaimed. "What do you mean she stabbed her? Did Tiffany stab your Mother?"

Thelma bit her fingernail and nodded her head as she fought from crying.

Chuck shouted severely, "Dane! Watch Thelma.

Troy, Devin, let's go!" he said and began jogging down the street, followed by his brother Devin.

Troy pointed at Matt. "Next time!"

"Anytime, rooster!" William called out with a smile. He looked at John, who was struggling to stand up. "You better rest up and rethink your strategy. Because I don't think Matt is playing with you this time."

Matt pointed his finger at John. "See you soon. Let's go, William."

10

William asked Matt as they entered the hotel foyer, "Do you mind explaining to me who that guy is, and when did he ever beat you in a fight?"

Matt paused at the bottom of the stairs. "That is my old friend John Mattick. When I left Willow Falls as a teenager, I went to Boise City and found work at a feedlot. That's where I met John. Like myself, he was out on his own, too, and we became fast friends. He was a great guy until I discovered he'd been stealing money from me and my pocketknife as well. I confronted him, and one day, while building a corral, we got into a fight. I was knocking some sense into him at first, and then he went kind of crazy and just started swinging with both arms like a wild man. I stepped back to create a little more space, and there was a stack of boards behind me; I tripped over them. I tried to get back on my feet, but he kneed me right square in my nose, and it stunned me pretty good. I didn't recover fast enough, and he followed it with a series of kicks and knees and left me bleeding and dazed on the ground." Matt sighed. "He won. I left Boise City right after that and never seen him again until tonight. He's apparently bragging to people about that," Matt said with an embarrassed smile.

"Apparently," William agreed. "Well, it wasn't much of a show, but I guess you showed him. Maybe we can get out of here early tomorrow, huh? I want to get back to the Monarch Hotel and into some nicer clothes."

"No."

"What do you mean, no?"

"Let's go to my room." Matt led William to his room and closed the door behind him. "Have a seat."

William sat down in a chair, asked through a yawn, "Now, why are we not going home tomorrow morning?"

Matt took a deep breath and exhaled. "What was it the man said before he shot Louis Eckman?"

William shrugged. "Dall?"

Matt shook his head. "No. He said his father was killed by debris from a tunnel explosion while working for the railroad."

"And?"

"John's father was killed working for the railroad. I remember him telling me that his father was killed by a rock that came flying out of a tunnel explosion and hit him in the head. Sound familiar? Do you think it's a coincidence, or did the sheriff kill the wrong man?"

William narrowed his eyes with a perplexed

grimace. "That would mean John shot the stage-coach driver who helped set it up the robbery. So, they know each other, right? Then why would the driver say his name was Dall and not John? They're both one syllable, and it would be just as easy to say John as it is to say, Dall."

Matt raised his eyebrows and tightened his lips in thought. "I don't know. What I do know is John would be the one that shot Louis Eckman, not the man the sheriff brought in tonight. Unless being killed by flying debris from tunnel explosions was so common that two men in this town have that much in common at least. Maybe they do, I don't know. But we might stick around and learn more about the sheriff's brother-in-law Dallen and his three friends to find that much out anyway."

William leaned back in his chair. "Oh, you're thinking the sheriff's dirty, aren't you?"

Matt frowned. "Have you ever met another sheriff who encourages his deputy to fight? He delivered those four dead bodies relatively fast, considering they're some of the most wanted men in America right now. And he seemed a little too cheerful in the saloon for killing his brother-in-law an hour or two before, don't you think?"

"Maybe he was a bad husband."

"Or maybe the sheriff lied to protect his deputy. Either way, I say we do a little investigating and see how much we can aggravate the sheriff and his deputies tomorrow. They don't seem to like us much now anyway, do they?"

William smiled as he ran his hands over his long

blonde wavy hair. "Not a bit." He had trimmed his blonde goatee and mustache down from a few inches long to an inch long where he liked it keep it since working at the Monarch Hotel.

"Tomorrow, we'll talk to the two Pinkertons, Ivan, and Pete, and let them know our hunt's not quite over yet. Maybe I'll let them talk with the Sheriff and his deputies while we go find the dead men's families."

"Sounds fine..." William yawned. "I'm going to bed, Matt. I'm afraid it's been a long few days, and I need to get some sleep."

"Me too. See you in the morning, William."

William yawned and nodded his head. "You know it's not even late, right? I don't think I've gone to bed this early since I was seven, maybe, and that was only after getting whipped for not going to bed!" he chuckled. "See you in the morning, Matt."

After William left, Matt locked his door and sat down on his bed. He was tired and wanted to get some sleep as well. He put out his oil lamp and laid down. Thirty minutes later, there was a soft knocking on his door. He listened to make sure the knocking wasn't coming from down the hallway. The soft knocking sounded again, and he stood up, grabbed his revolver, and went to the door. "Who is it?"

"Claudia Richmond. I own the hotel, Marshal Bannister. Could I speak to you for a minute?" she spoke softly to keep her voice down.

Matt opened the door carefully and looked out in the dim hallway to see the small gray-haired lady who had registered him into the hotel at the front desk. "Can I help you?" he asked curiously.

She spoke in a whisper with an urgent tone, "Can you come to the office, please?"

Matt frowned, judging her anxiety correctly. "Sure. Let me get my moccasins on, and I'll be right down."

***

The Grand Lincoln Hotel was owned and operated by Harry and Claudia Richmond. It ran parallel to the main street, but the Richmond's lived on the ground floor under the guest rooms. The entrance to their home was behind the front desk in the foyer of the hotel. Matt knocked on the door, and Claudia answered it silently and waved him inside their home in an urgent manner.

"Marshal, I'm glad you're here. We have a bit of an emergency that I don't know how to handle," Claudia explained as she led him through their home.

"How can I help you?" he asked as they entered a small family room where her elderly husband sat in his chair, smoking a pipe. In a chair near him was a young blonde-haired girl wrapped in a blanket who had been crying and looked to be beaten up. Matt nodded at her with a growing empathetic expression.

"Marshal," Harry said as a greeting. He continued, "Claudia, why don't you tell him what's happening here?"

Claudia motioned towards a wooden chair for him to sit down. She sat in her rocking chair and sighed. "This young lady is Tiffany Foster. Sheriff Dielschneider murdered her father this evening. Her stepmother is the sheriff's sister and beat her with a belt buckle and threatened to kill her if she told anyone. You should see her back! That woman deserves to be put in jail for treating this child that way and the key thrown away! Tiffany is very afraid if she goes back home, her stepmother will kill her. She held a knife to Tiffany's throat earlier." She looked at Matt with an anxious expression before she continued carefully. "Tiffany had to stab her step-mother with her ink pen to escape. She's terrified of being found by the Sheriff or any of his brothers because her stepmother is their only sister. They'll hurt her, Marshal. Can you help her? She came here because she was freezing and had nowhere else to go where they might not find her. But they will come here looking for her too, and we can't protect her from them. This hotel is our home and only source of income. If they caught us hiding her here, our whole life could be taken away from us one way or another."

It was clear to see the elderly Richmond's were very nervous about her being there but also concerned about her welfare. The young lady was visibly shaken up by the loss of her father and the abuse she had suffered. She held the blanket tight around her body, and her hands shook with fear. Her eyes revealed her tortured soul, and she reminded Matt of a beaten puppy, that only wanted to be loved. He noticed the red stain of blood in her hair from the belt buckle, he assumed. He could see her reddened dirty bare feet from running through the cold streets without shoes. The Richmond's had her covered in a blanket immediately to help her warm-up, and there was a cup of hot tea sitting next to her that she hadn't touched. Her right eye was swollen and turning black along with her swollen cheek that would turn into a nasty bruise.

Matt's heart went out to the young lady. "Hello," Matt said to her gently. "My name's Matt Bannister. I need to ask you, is your father's name, Dallen, by chance?"

She nodded and dropped her face into her hands and began sobbing. Her sobs were deep, painful, and uncontrollable. Matt frowned as his heart broke for the young lady. He let her sob for a few minutes while Claudia tried to comfort her. He leaned forward, placing his elbows on his knees and spoke softly, "I need to ask you, did your father have anything at all to do with the stage robbery two weeks ago? Is he friends with John Mattick and your mother's brothers?"

Harry spoke bitterly, "That Mattick's nothing but trouble!"

Tiffany looked sharply up at Matt. "She's not my mother! I don't have a mother; she married my father!"

"Okay. I won't refer to her like that again. Do you know if your father was friends with the people I mentioned or if he was involved in that robbery?"

"I was helping my father the day of the robbery

down at his sluice box. I can prove that because my journal is under my bed. It's the day I told my father that Danetta was beating on me." She paused as her face grimaced with pain and fought from sobbing. Her lips squeezed together tightly, and her eyes filled with what looked to be a quart of water. Her voice became high pitched as she said, "My Pa never would've hurt anyone or stoled a thing. He was an honest man. Chuck, Troy, and the rest of them never liked him because he never wanted to be around them. They didn't blend, my Pa would say. He was a Christian, Sir. He wanted nothing to do with them."

"Well, that's why they didn't blend. Sometimes, people don't want us Christians around because we don't blend. We don't fit in, and we're not much fun when we don't partake or approve of their life-style. Occasionally, those folks can get a bit bitter because we aren't like them. And sometimes those people can become so embittered and hateful they are willing to kill the Christian. And that might be what we have here, because the Sheriff, Chuck Dielschneider was not bothered at all by the death of your father." Matt paused before continuing, "Tiffany, I believe you, but the stagecoach driver, Herb Johnson, was shot and killed too. Before he died, he gave one name 'Dall.' Why do you think he would name your father as the man who shot him?"

Tiffany looked at Matt strangely and shook her head slightly. "Are you sure he said Dall and not Dell, as in Dielschneider?"

Matt's eyes widened as he inhaled. "No, I'm not

sure. Are the Dielschneider's...?" He looked at Harry Richmond questionably.

Harry answered pointedly, "Rotten to the core, every one of them. The sheriff is one of the worst. But you won't hear people say that around here because people disappear. And this young lady will too if you don't protect her from them. I can't because I have no place to put her, and I'm too old to fight them, boys. They'll be looking for her all night, and they will be coming here. She stabbed the Dielschneider's sister, and that won't go over well."

"Marshal Bannister," Claudia said, "The only way this young lady is going to have a chance to grow up is if you protect her."

He looked at Tiffany and rubbed his beard thoughtfully. "You're going to have to sleep in my room and stay there no matter what, or for however long we're here. No complaining and no leaving the room unless it's safe to do so." He looked at Claudia. "Do you think whoever comes looking for her will search my room?"

Claudia shook her head, unknowingly. "I don't know."

"Then, from this point on, you know nothing more than she came here looking for me, and you refused her access to see me." He paused in thought. "Tell them my cousin William Fasana was downstairs and told her I don't buy whores, but he offered her a dime, and she left crying in the street, and you haven't seen her since. Understand?"

Claudia spoke incensed, "Marshal Bannister,

that is horrible! I will not refer to her in such a vile way!"

Matt nodded. "It is horrible. And that's why they'll believe it. If you want to save this young lady, then you had better tell them exactly what I just told you. Otherwise, they won't believe a word you say and push you out of the way and find her. Now can you do that?"

They both nodded. "We can if it will keep her safe."

"It will. Do you folks have an extra mattress or cot I could use? She can have the bed."

Claudia answered, "We can give her one of our empty rooms. I don't think it's appropriate for a young lady to share a bedroom with a grown man out of wedlock, do you, Harry?"

"Misses Richmond," Matt spoke quickly. "It's very easy to live in a black and white world of moral rights and wrongs, but there are occasions when the world turns gray, and all those presupposed notions are not going to work. Not everything's so black and white in a world full of lawlessness and life and death; especially when you're trying to fight wickedness on its terms. If you put her in her own room and those men see the light in five rooms lit up and know only four rooms are rented, what do you think they're going to do? How about we put aside your personal beliefs and let me do my job? I might know how to do it better than you. My ways may seem a little odd to you, but when you are dealing with men who see nothing but the color in a lawless world, a black and white view of the world will get you, or someone else killed when you're dealing with men like that. I like to think my job is to right the wrongs of others, bring people to justice, and protect the innocent. Please, if those men come here, tell them exactly what I told you to say despite your moral convictions, and let's put her in my room despite your personal judgments. And no one, absolutely no one is to know she is here. Not your Reverend or your children, no one! Are we clear?" he asked firmly.

"Yes, I understand," Harry said. "And Claudia does too."

"Do you, Claudia? Because they're going to come to you."

"If it saves her, I'll do it."

"Good. That's why I am doing it that way. Let's move a mattress into my room before those Pinkertons come back from the saloon. And by the way, that means them too. They don't need to know she's here either. And I insist you charge me the full price for her staying here too. We're taking a mattress out of one of your rooms, so it's only right to pay you for it." Matt knew any extra bit of income might help them get through a tough winter when travelers were rare.

11

Chuck Dielschneider burst through the door shouting, "Danetta!" He saw her sitting in her chair, holding a rag over her side. An expression of horror was on her face as the fear of being stabbed deep enough to pierce a vital organ constantly ran through her mind. "Danetta, are you okay?" he asked quickly.

"No! Did you bring the doctor?"

"Not with me, but Troy went to get him. Where'd you get stabbed? How serious is it? Move that rag so I can see."

She moved the rag, which revealed a torn hole in her dress surrounded by blood stains about three inches wide by six inches long on her side. The bleeding had slowed considerably but still seeped out of the hole in her skin. "I told Thelma to tell you to bring the doctor!" she said bitterly.

"I didn't have time, Danetta!" he answered sharply. "Now, how long was the knife she stabbed you with?"

Danetta sighed irritably and spoke through a raised voice, "She didn't use a knife; she used her writing pen!"

"A pen?"

"Yes, her pen! Now is there anything there that can kill me?" she asked worriedly. "I don't want to die, Chuck." The fear of internal injuries scared her far more than anything else in her life ever had. Her heart pounded, and her head felt light and a bit nauseous from the anxiety that was overwhelming her.

Chuck shook his head slightly. "I wouldn't think a pen could reach deep enough to do too much damage. It's not bleeding much anymore, which is good. On the bright side, it did bleed out, which should wash all the ink and bad stuff out. A stitch or two wouldn't hurt either, though. Why'd she stab you?"

Danetta looked at Chuck with indignant eyes. "She was threatening to go tell the marshal about you . She was with Dallen the day the stagecoach got robbed, and she didn't take killing her father well. I was beating some fear into her when she stabbed me and ran out of the house. She was going to find the marshal! Chuck, I don't like how this is turning out. You boys have got to go stop her."

Chuck took a deep breath and groaned under his breath. "Devin, go back to the Blazing Bull and gather the men. We need to find her before she gets to the marshal." He looked at his brother. "But do not go near the hotel or the marshal, his cousin

William Fasana, or the two Pinkerton men. Do not even talk to them; I'll address them when I get there. Take the boys and scour this town inside and out. Start at the Reverend's house and everywhere else she might go. If you find her, take her to jail and hold her there. I'll deal with her myself."

Devin nodded. "Don't worry, Sis, we'll find her. And you'll be fine. You're too tough to be killed by a writing pen." he said with a comforting smile and left the house in a hurry.

Danetta shook her head slowly. "I don't ever want to see her again; do you hear me, Chuck?"

He nodded. "It's unfortunate, but Tiffany might disappear before daylight. She might just be found hanging in your barn with a suicide note by morning."

"That's fine. Just get rid of her! And I want Dallen and her both buried at first light in the morning without any notices or witnesses. Just bury them!"

Chuck nodded with understanding. "They probably have Dallen's body up in front of the saloon by now. If she sees him leaning there, we might hear her start wailing.. It's kind of like setting a bait trap, isn't it?" he grinned. "I probably need to get going though so we can split those boys up and find her. I'll make sure Dallen's buried before the sun's up and Tiffany, too, if we find her." He paused to look at his sister. "You'll be okay until the doctor gets here, right?"

"As long as I'm not dying, I'll be fine! But I want the doctor to look me over and make sure. I'm too young to die; I tell you! Chuck, do me a favor and spit in Dallen's face for me before he's buried, will you? He left me in a poor house with that horrible daughter of his. And it's his fault for not joining up with you."

"Well, what's done is done. Dallen's playing the harp somewhere heavenward, and he's probably not good at that either. In the meantime, we need to find his daughter and let her know how bad he misses her. She'll be joining him in the harp quartet of his family soon enough."

Danetta chuckled and then grimaced. "Don't make me laugh," she said painfully. "Just get to her before she gets to the marshal. We don't need that trouble."

"He's just one man. My concern is those two detectives. I never dealt with those kinds of people before. They were drinking pretty good before I left, though."

"The Marshal too?"

"No, he had nothing to drink. We had to work hard to persuade him to even come to the saloon."

"Hey, did John and him fight?"

Chuck shook his head. "No. The marshal chickened out like a frightened hen."

Danetta looked surprised. "John must've really licked him good back then, huh? Maybe the Marshal will leave town first thing in the morning for good, and we'll be done with him."

"I hope. We don't need him hanging around. I'm going to the hotel and talk with the Richmond's and see if Tiffany came by there."

"They might lie even if she did. They aren't

beyond trying to protect her. That whole church group in town help each other out a lot. She's like one of their own," Danetta said.

"It doesn't matter. The Marshal's pretty easy to get along with and doesn't seem too interested in anything other than Dallen. He won't get involved in domestic problems; I don't think. Sit here and relax until the doctor gets here. You'll be fine, Danetta. I'll take care of Dallen and Tiffany."

12

Matt laid the extra mattress on the floor of his room, which left very little room for walking or sitting anywhere but on either of the two beds. "Okay, Tiffany, I'm going to take the bed, and you can sleep on the mattress on the floor. You're a lot younger, you'll understand. Okay?"

She stood by the door uncomfortably and nodded silently.

"I'm not going to hurt you. So, you can relax and sit down if you want. We're going to go over some rules, though. First and foremost, do not look out the window no matter what. We'll always keep the curtains closed. Do not leave this room no matter what. There's a chamber pot right there for you to use when you need it. I'll step outside when you need to use it. I know it's uncomfortable, but for now this is what we have, okay? Do not touch my guns, saddlebags, or other things. Respect my privacy, and I'll respect yours, fair enough?"

She nodded quietly.

"Very good. Do you have any questions for me?" he asked and sat down on his bed.

She shook her head.

"Are you scared?"

Her lips tightened, and she nodded her head slightly as tears filled her eyes again.

"I understand. Listen, why don't you lay down and I'll quit asking you questions until you're ready to talk. I know it's been an unimaginable evening and a lot to take in. So, you just lay down and cry if you need to. I know it's almost ridiculous to suggest, but try to keep the crying quiet if you can. I will not complain myself, but we are trying to keep you safe and don't want anyone hearing you. Tiffany, you don't know me, but I'm here to protect and help you. If there's anything I can do for you, let me know. I will not harm you, okay? And I won't let anyone else hurt you, either. You are safe here."

She sniffled. "Thank you."

"You're welcome. So how old are you?"

"Fourteen."

Matt frowned. "And your mother is where?"

"Heaven. My younger sisters and my mother died of Diptheria in California seven years ago. My pa and I came up here two years ago, and he met Danetta last year. That's when they got married." She sounded bitter. "I wish he never met her. He'd still be alive if he didn't." Her body began to jerk in heavy silent sobs.

Matt stood up and went to her and put his arms around her. "Go ahead and cry," he said as her arms went around him, and she broke into heavy sobbing with her face buried in his chest. He could feel her body convulsing as she sobbed, and he bit his bottom lip emotionally as tears filled his own eyes. "Shhh," he whispered as her sobbing became uncontrollable. He let her weep with her wailing muffled against his chest. The love she had for her father was obvious in the depth of pain that came through her tears. There were no magic words that would take her grief away or soften the truth that her father, the one man who had cared for her all her life would never be there for her again. There was nothing Matt could say to ease her suffering; all he could do was hold her and let her grieve. "Lord, I pray that you'll fill this young lady's heart with peace even in the midst of her suffering tonight. Let her take comfort in knowing her father is with you in Heaven. I know Tiffany is hurting and scared, so I ask that you'll let her know that she is safe, not because of me, but because of you. Give her the strength and courage to get through this terrible day and every day ahead of her. It's going to be a hard road for her, so Lord, I ask you will pour your grace and blessings upon her. May your favor be upon us and your will be done to bring justice to those who hurt this child of yours. Thank you for bringing Tiffany here tonight. Let her rest peacefully and repose her hurts onto you. Thank you, Jesus," he prayed softly as he held her.

She began to regain control of the sobbing but did not let go of Matt. She just held him and let her tears run down her face in silence as she stared at the wall. "I love him so much," she whispered painfully. "I love him so much."

Matt closed his eyes and held her. "I'm so sorry you have to go through this. I really am. But…" He reached for her chin gently and lifted her face to look at him. When her blue eyes connected to his, he said, "You will get through this. And one day you will be able to smile again. I promise you that. For right now, though, it's okay to mourn for your father."

A gunshot startled him as a series of gunshots were being fired outside on the main street. Matt quickly broke from Tiffany's grasp and went to the window. He peeked out onto the street and seen a group of men standing around Ivan Petoskey and Pete Logan as they fired their pistols at the body of Dallen Foster. Dallen's body was propped up in a casket on the Blazing Bull's front porch next to the other three bodies in their pine caskets. The men who were standing around them were laughing and challenging them to hit certain targets on his body.

"Oh, my Lord," Matt said and closed the curtain. He looked at Tiffany with hardened eyes from the anger that was rising within him. He jabbed a pointed finger towards her forcefully. "You stay away from the window! Do not touch the curtain or the lantern. Lay down and stay down no matter what!" He pulled his gun belt off the nightstand and wrapped it around his waist in a hurry. "I'll be back. Lock the door. I'll have the key to get in."

"What is it?" she asked anxiously.

"Just stay put and do not look out the window!"

Matt walked quickly out of the hotel and towards the crowd of men. He could hear the Pinkertons' laughing as they shot Dallen's body in varying places where the group of men placed bets on where they could or couldn't hit their next target. They were all having a good time by the sound of the cheering and laughing. Matt pulled his revolver and fired a shot into the air as he approached.

"What the hell do you think you're doing?" Matt yelled as he burst through the crowd to face the two Pinkertons with his gun in his hand. "Who is the undertaker here? Someone get the lids on those caskets and get them out of here! The rest of you get back inside or go home!" he yelled at the crowd. He turned back to Ivan and Pete. "What are you doing? This is just...Why?" he yelled in disgust.

Pete looked at Matt indignantly for interfering with his fun. "Go back to the hotel, Marshal. This is our time."

"Your time? I don't even know that means, Pete. I'm telling you both right now to put your guns away and either go back inside or go to bed. But you will not be shooting up these bodies!" His rage was far deeper than he expected it to be. He wanted to beat the hell out of both men for shooting Dallen's body. His breathing was heavy, and his hands shook with anger.

Ivan spoke in a slow and even manner, "He shot the boss, we're just getting our due justice in."

"Justice has already been done. What you're doing is sick! You work for me right now, and I'm telling you, this isn't how it's done on my time!" he spat out at Pete.

Pete was quick to reply. "We work for Divinity Eckman, not you! And let me tell you, she'll be glad to know that we had the chance to shoot him. The job's done! And you mean nothing to us. Now get out of the way before we decide to shoot you!"

Matt raised his eyebrows. "That choice is yours to make, but this is ending right now."

Ivan leaned towards his friend and spoke something Matt couldn't hear. Matt's revolver was pointed downward, but he casually pulled the hammer back until it clicked. He didn't like the way the two Pinkertons were acting. The alcohol they had been drinking had taken effect, and if there was anything more unpredictable than a drunk gunfighter with a short fuse, Matt didn't know what it was. There had been too many men killed over meaningless arguments under the influence of alcohol, and Matt for one wasn't going to chance being shot by two drunk roughnecks with a fake Pinkerton badge.

Pete smirked wickedly. "We have our guns cocked and in hand too. You killed my friend, Carnell Tallon. You shouldn't have done that, but Miss Divinity might reward me for killing you too. You can't kill us both, Marshal."

Matt noticed the crowd backing up a little bit. "I hope it doesn't come to that, Pete. Again, that's up to you and Ivan."

William Fasana walked up behind the two men with both of his revolvers pulled and had one pointed at each of them. "I can," he said and pulled the hammers back on both of his revolvers. They were inches from the back of both men's heads. William continued, "Between Matt and myself, I don't think you boys have a chance. But if you're drunk enough to try it...go ahead," he said plainly.

Ivan and Pete both turned their heads back and saw the barrels of William's two .45's pointing at them. Pete turned back to Matt and spoke with a dangerous snarl on his lips. "You're lucky tonight," he said as he put his revolver into his holster. Ivan had already holstered his.

"I'm sure I am. Now get out of my sight!" Matt turned towards the crowd and yelled, "Where's the undertaker or someone to put the lids on those caskets? Get these men off the street now!" He turned back to the two Pinkertons who hadn't budged an inch. "Leave now, or I'll leave you lying in the street!"

Ivan shook his head slightly and spoke easily, "We don't take to being threatened, Marshal. We do the threatening, not take it. And for a man who won't fight a challenge, well, we don't feel too threatened."

"Told you," William said from behind the Pinkertons. He still had his guns pointed at the two men.

Matt stepped forward quickly and kicked Ivan in the chest with his right foot. Ivan fell to his back with an awkward fall that knocked the wind out of him. As soon as he landed, Matt had his revolver pointed an inch from Ivan's face with the hammer locked back and ready to fire. Matt's eyes were furious and showed no fear what-so-ever as they glared down at Ivan. "I'm not threatening you! I'm telling you to get off this street, or I'll hurt you! Do you understand me?" he shouted.

"Yes," Ivan said, surprised by Matt's speed and the ferocity of his eyes.

Matt glanced at Pete, who was standing still with William's revolver pressed against his head. William winked at Matt.

"Sheriff," Matt said, "You never should've allowed this to happen! But for now, I want you to take these men's guns for the night. They won't be needing them anymore this evening." He reached down and took Ivan's revolver with his left hand and tossed it to the ground near where Sheriff Dielschneider stood. "You can pick up your guns tomorrow when you're sober," he said to Ivan.

Sheriff Chuck Dielschneider bent down and picked up Ivan's gun and handed it to his brother Troy. He waited for Matt to take the gun out of Pete's holster. Once he had Pete's gun, the Sheriff said loudly, "Gentlemen, let's ah…break it up. We're all supposed to be on the same team here. You men can pick up your guns at my office tomorrow morning. In the meantime, let's go in and have some drinks."

Matt holstered his revolver and looked at the sheriff with a disdain that he couldn't help. "Get those bodies off the street now!"

"Sure," Chuck said uneased by Matt's tone. "Steven, Mark and Howard, get these coffins closed and back to Joe's for the night." He turned back to Matt. "No problem."

Troy Dielschneider smirked as he watched Pete help Ivan up off the ground. "If only you could do that to John. Maybe then you'd get the respect around here you used to have. But running away like a coward doesn't bring much respect. I know, because when I say jump, this whole town jumps! But I don't ever run away scared." He chuckled.

"From what I've seen so far, I wouldn't say that's much to brag about," Matt said as he watched the two Pinkerton's walking disdainfully towards the saloon door.

Troy's smirk disappeared. "I have fifty dollars that says John can whip you right here, right now! Do you think you have the steel to take that bet? Or are you going to run back to your hotel room like a scared pup?"

Matt looked at Troy with annoyance and sighed. He looked at his old friend John Mattick and asked, "Do you want to fight, John?"

John looked a bit skeptical of Matt as he said, "I'm in. I'll whip you again," he said as he began to unbuckle his gun belt.

"Not tonight, John. You've been drinking, and I want you at your sharpest. Right here tomorrow at noon, you and I will square off again. No interruptions, no help, and no ending until one of us can't fight any longer! Let's see if you got lucky or if you can do it again. I'll be here tomorrow, but tonight I'm going to bed. And I don't want to hear any more shooting! Agreed?" He asked loudly and looked around at the men who still stood around them.

Chuck answered for them. "Of course, he'll be here! Hey everyone, the fight's on for tomorrow at noon!"

"I asked him, not you," Matt said pointedly as the crowd began to cheer excitedly.

John smirked. "Are you still calling me a thief?" He pulled out a pocket knife with a rosewood handle with a willow tree skillfully carved into the wood. It was the pocketknife John had stolen from Matt years ago. The knife was a Christmas present sent to him by his father when he was young. The knife had belonged to his Grandfather Fredrick Bannister. John flipped it in the air and slid it back into his pocket.

Matt's lips turned upwards just a bit. "That and more. I'll see you tomorrow, John."

John smiled. "See you then."

Chuck laughed and clapped his hands with excitement. "I'm going to make some money on this fight!" He looked at William, "Hey! Claudia told me what you said to that young blonde girl that was looking for Matt. That was hilarious! She's our local insane girl named Tiffany. She's very pretty, though; I would've offered her a dollar or two, not a dime." He laughed shaking his head.

Matt waited with a deep sinking feeling for William to answer. He said a quick, silent prayer as his whole plan was now dependent on William's response.

William laughed lightly with the sheriff. "I thought it was kind of funny too. Do you think I should've offered two bits?"

The sheriff laughed along with Troy. "It wouldn't have hurt. Hey, did you see which direction she went to? Her mother's worried about her."

He pointed down the street. "That way towards the stables, I believe. She was pretty, but I'm a cheap guy. I figured with all the poor folks around here; a dime might do it," he said with a smile.

Chuck waved his hand towards the stable at the other end of town. "Charlie, you and Fred go check out the stable and take her to the jail if you find her." He looked at Matt and explained, "She's just a confused kid. Her mom thinks a night in the jail might do her good. She's a pretty blonde fourteen-year-old named Tiffany. Have you seen her, Marshal?"

Matt shook his head. "I haven't seen her. I was trying to sleep when I heard the shooting and came out here. I'm going to bed now, Sheriff. I'll see you tomorrow." He said and began walking towards the hotel.

"Oh, wait up, I'm going to," William said and joined Matt's side. When they were far enough away, he asked, "I know it's probably none of my business, but what do you know about a blonde girl?"

"Thank you for playing along as well as you did," Matt said appreciatively. "I'll explain and introduce you when we get inside."

William laughed. "And you were afraid I was going to start some trouble here."

13

"Sheriff, how about you give us our guns back?" Ivan asked Chuck inside the saloon.

Chuck shook his head uncomfortably. "Sorry fella's, I already had Devin take them to my office for the night. You'll get them back tomorrow." He laughed lightly. "We don't want any accidental shootings tonight, now do we?"

Pete Logan sneered as he looked at the sheriff. "It wouldn't be accidental."

"Yeah, and that's what I'm afraid of. If you men shot the Marshal and his cousin, why, we'd have to arrest you two, and we don't want to do that."

"You wouldn't be able to arrest us," Pete said with a scowl. "We've been on our best behavior so far, but we're about to let loose and do what we are best at. And that Marshal is in my sights first and foremost," Pete said as he wandered up to the bar to order another drink.

Ivan smiled slightly. "Pete has had too much to drink tonight," he explained to Chuck. "We'll be heading out tomorrow after the fight, Sheriff. Let me ask before we leave; you're sure there's no one we're overlooking who helped kill Louis Eckman and my friend, Tom Picard? Tom was the guard carrying the shotgun. All the attention has been on Louis, and we were sent here to find the man who killed him. No one seems to care who killed my friend, and I'm taking it upon myself find that killer too. Do you know which one of those dead men it was that shot him?"

Chuck frowned noticeably and shook his head. "I'm sorry, I don't know who shot him, but it was one of the four we had outside. Either way, the man you're looking for is dead."

Ivan nodded as he took a drink. "It's too bad you didn't allow me and Pete to question those men before you killed them. We would've got some answers from them. Quite frankly, I only cared about finding the one who killed Louis and the one who killed Tom. The other two don't matter."

Chuck glanced at Ivan quizzically. "That's a little odd for Pinkerton's, isn't it? Don't you normally arrest anyone who was involved in a robbery?"

Ivan smiled and motioned toward Pete. "We're not that kind of Pinkerton. We're the bloodhounds if you will. Meaning we come for blood, not arrests."

"Oh. Well, we got them for you, anyway," Chuck said with a slight hint of uneasiness in his voice.

Ivan shrugged disappointedly. "We came a long way for nothing. By the way, did you find Misses Eckman's wedding ring and jewelry? I imagine the bums spent the money, but the jewelry must still be around somewhere."

Chuck leaned back and shook his head slightly. "We haven't searched their homes yet. Dallen may have hidden it so his family wouldn't know he stole it. He was married to my sister, you know, and she wouldn't put up with thievery like that. A good Christian lady like her wouldn't have anything to do with a killer like him."

"Maybe we better go looking for her jewelry tomorrow morning so that I can take it back to Divinity. Are you okay with that?"

"Sure. I have no problem with that."

"Good. Because I don't think I can go back without that ring and keep my job. It's worth more than any of us can make in ten years. I hope you're not planning on keeping it for yourself if you find it, are you?" he chuckled good-naturedly.

"As I said, we haven't even had a chance to look for anything yet."

"Tomorrow, we will." He saw his buddy Pete stumble over to a table where Troy Dielschneider, John Mattick, and a few other men were sitting. "Excuse me, Sheriff, I gotta go keep Pete out of trouble." He carried a chair over to the table where Pete sat down in the last empty chair without asking to join them. "Mind if we join you?" Ivan asked, setting his chair down at their table.

"Not at all," Troy said. "You gentlemen got the raw end of the deal earlier, huh? If it weren't for his cousin, Matt wouldn't have had a chance. Don't worry, though, my man John is going to hurt him tomorrow. You two are sticking around to watch the fight, aren't you?"

Ivan nodded. "Of course." He looked at John Mattick seriously. "He's fast. Much faster than you'd think for a man his size. Strong too."

John nodded. "I know. I've fought him before."

"Years ago, when he was nothing more than a pup. He's come a long way since then."

John smiled as he took a drink of his glass. "So have I."

"Here, just in case you start losing," Ivan said as he reached into his pocket and pulled out some black painted brass knuckles and handed them to John. "They'll lay out the toughest man with one hit. Those aren't brass; they're cast iron. They'll break a skull open as easily as cracking an egg open with them. Trust me, I know."

John took hold of them and slipped them onto his fingers. "It wouldn't make it a very fair fight, would it?" he asked with a hesitant grin.

"It won't be a fair fight anyway. I don't think you'll beat him without those."

"Whoa!" Troy yelled loudly. "How much do you want to bet? I can take anyone around here, but I wouldn't want to fight John! I've seen him destroy people with his fists! Matt hasn't got a chance! Did you see how scared he was earlier? John's already got him beat!"

Ivan smiled slightly. "I saw no fear, just a man who wasn't interested in, as he put it, fighting an old friend for other people's entertainment. Trust me; your friend will lose without those knuckle busters."

John leaned back defensively and glared danger-ously at Ivan. "You know, you sure talk tough, but he sure knocked you on your butt, didn't he?"

Ivan chuckled for the first time. "Yes, he did, and I didn't even see it coming. You won't either is my guess. My money's on Matt if you don't use those. And yeah, I like to think I'm pretty tough, I get paid to be anyway. My employers must think I am too because they pay me quite a bit to hurt people."

Pete Logan sat silently in a chair next to Ivan with his eyes getting heavy, and his head slightly weaving from side to side. "Don't kill him...I am."

Ivan laughed. "Yes, you are, Pete." He looked at the others around the table. "In the morning, he's going to apologize for sounding like a drunk fool. Well, gentlemen, I'm going to bed. We have a long day ahead of us tomorrow." He nodded at John, "You keep those just in case you need them. If not, give them back to me clean after your fight. But I wouldn't mind if you handed them back to me bloody either."

"I thought you were betting on Matt?" Troy asked quickly.

"I said he'd win. I didn't say I liked him." He paused in thought. "Winning a fight means nothing. Have you ever broken someone's arm? Ever broken someone's leg? Or their neck in a fight? If you hit him in the forearm, shin, or back of his neck with those, you will. And you might like it. I'm not in-terested in seeing him lose a fistfight; I'm interested in seeing Matt Bannister in pain, crippled or dead. Can you do that?" he asked quietly.

John stared at Ivan, stunned. "Why?"

"Of course, he can!" Troy stated quickly. "A fair fight that accidentally went wrong...we can't go wrong with that! Right, John?"

John nodded slowly. "Right. I could do it, but what's your reason for wanting him hurt so bad?"

Ivan shrugged slightly. "He kicked me. Why else would I?"

"I thought you all were working together to find those heathens?" John asked.

"He doesn't matter to me. I could gun him down, and fifty dollars says I'd walk away unscathed. The Eckman's money, attorneys, and men like me have a way of convincing juries and judges to let a lot of things go. Don't let anyone tell you the judicial system isn't corruptible; I assure you it is if the price is right." He smirked as he stood up. "Even the most incorruptible judge wants to live another day. Yes, I would say Pete and I are tough men with... some valuable experiences. One thing I know is how much steel is in a man's soul; how much he can take and how fierce his temperament is. Watch out tomorrow. Use those knuckle busters; you're going to need them." He tapped Pete's shoulder. "Come on, Pete, let's go."

When they walked out of the saloon, Charlie Hammond asked, "Why'd he tell us that? Do you think they're catching on that it was us?"

Troy raised eyebrows questionably and shrugged his shoulders. "I don't know, but I liked the advice. Put those things in your pocket and use them if he starts to get the best of you."

John chuckled lightly. "I won't need them, but I'll keep them anyway."

14

Unlike the Blazing Bull Saloon, the Orvis Saloon made most of their money from meals served throughout the day. They opened early to serve breakfast and closed earlier than any other saloon. Some saloons had a reputation for lively crowds and becoming a town favorite to drink, gamble, and carouse in, and in Prairieville, The Blazing Bull was the place for wildness and fun. The Orvis was known for good food and a quieter crowd who wanted to have an easy-going night. The food was tasty, and Matt and William were both glad of that on this cold morning. They had both slept soundly and felt much better than they had the night before.

"Here they come," William said as he took a bite of his fried potatoes. "I suppose you're not going to let them in on your secret blonde friend?"

"Not after last night, nope." Matt paused and waited for Ivan Petoskey and Pete Logan to enter the saloon. Matt nodded as they made eye contact with a nod and went to their table away from Matt and William and sat down.

"I don't think they like us anymore," William said.

Matt shrugged and took another bite of food.

"You know, I kind of like this marshal thing. I think when we get back home, I'll join up with you."

"Think so?" Matt asked with a slight smile.

"Yeah. I don't mind traveling, and I don't mind the mysterious nature of people when you come around. Kind of like Little Red out there peeping his red dot of a head around the corner to keep his eyes on you." He nodded out a window towards the corner of the local store. It was a lapboard two-story building with a fake front that had one big painted word across the front of it, STORE.

Matt glanced up just in time to see the dark red hair of Dane Dielschneider peek around the corner to see what Matt was doing. Matt shook his head. "Déjà vu. He's not wearing a gun belt, or I'd suddenly feel like I'm right back in the McDermott's Mercantile in Willow Falls."

William chuckled. "Someone should tell him red is a rather bold color to be sneaking around with. I think I'll encourage him to join the Pinkerton's instead of the freak show." He looked at the two Pinkerton Detectives who were ordering their breakfast from an older woman who owned the saloon with her husband. "Hey, you two, you have a new recruit trying out for a job over by the store. Maybe you could give him a tip or two on his dream to be a Pinkerton Detective when you leave here. What do you think?"

Ivan peeked out the window. Pete glared at William as he sipped his coffee slowly. It was Pete who spoke with an unfriendly tone, "If you ever point your gun at me again, we will square off with them. That goes for you too, Marshal. If you ever get in my face again, we'll have an issue to deal with."

Matt raised his eyebrows as he swallowed his food. "From what I saw last night, that may not be as easy for you as shooting a dead man."

"We'll find out," Pete said quietly. He turned his attention back to Ivan.

"Hope not," Matt stated while staring at him. "Hopefully, we can part ways on friendly terms despite what happened last night."

Ivan nodded and looked over at William and Matt. "I agree."

"Good. Do you two want to join William and me at the Sheriff's Office after breakfast? I think it might be of interest to you."

"Why?" Ivan asked.

"I have some questions for him. You might find them intriguing as well."

William smiled to himself and then leaned forward towards the two men with a serious expression on his face. He spoke slowly and clearly, so there would be no misunderstanding, "Intriguing is a big educated word for interesting, Pete. Just so you know."

"Knock it off," Matt said sternly.

Pete glared at William irritably and looked away without saying a word. He wasn't feeling good from the night before.

William chuckled to himself.

Pete then spoke, "I think I'll pass, Marshal. If you don't mind me saying so, I'm looking forward to seeing that deputy John bust you up today. And your big mouth cousin isn't going to be able to help you either." There was a threatening tone to his voice.

Matt lifted his head back slightly to make eye contact with Pete. "By the sounds of it, I should be betting on John too. Unfortunately, I'm not a betting man. William is though. Are you betting on John too?" Matt asked William.

William sighed exaggeratingly. "If I wasn't trying to get a deputy marshal's position with you, I would be, yeah. But as it is, I better stay on your good side and bet my last hundred dollars on you." He looked at the other table. "Do either of you want to make a bet? If you haven't got a hundred dollars, I can go with whatever you want." He whispered across the room, "I just want my boss to think I believe in him is all."

Pete answered, "A hundred dollars? Let's see your money, and you have a bet."

Ivan shook his head. "I wouldn't."

Pete waved Ivan off with a slight motion of his hand. "I think John's got this one."

Ivan shook his head. "Fools and their money. So, Matt, I'm meeting up with the Sheriff anyway so we can search the homes of those killers for Misses Eckman's wedding ring and jewelry. I'll head over there with you after I eat."

"I'll just sit here and drink some more coffee and watch that young man Dane playing peek-a-boo with me. Odd kid." Matt furrowed his brow as Dane once again peeked around the corner.

"He's probably wondering if you're scared," William quipped.

Ivan leaned over and looked out the window again. He shook his head. "I heard the boy isn't as simple-minded as you'd think. He's just ...different somehow."

The older lady came out of the kitchen carrying two plates of food to deliver to their table. She volunteered, "Dane Dielschneider is a thief. His fingers are like glue. We wouldn't have a table or chair if we allowed him in here. He's probably waiting for you all to leave so he can sneak into your rooms and rob you blind without you seeing him go inside."

A nerve wakened in Matt's back as a chill ran down his spine. He had left Tiffany in his room to remain hidden, but if she was discovered and the news got back to the Sheriff and his brothers, things could end badly. Matt was confident that John Mattick was the one who killed Louis Eckman and Herb Johnson, but as to who killed the Pinkerton guard Tom Picard was anyone's guess. He knew the sheriff and his deputies were guilty of killing the four men who laid in their caskets, but he couldn't prove the sheriff and his brothers took an active role in the robbery or intentional murder to cover up their own crimes. He could suspect, but he couldn't prove it. The last thing he wanted was to get into a heated fight with the Dielschneider family and their friends without absolute proof that they were what he was beginning to suspect them of being. He had a plan, though it wasn't solid and had a lot to be desired. He was tempted to share his thoughts with the two Pinkertons, but for some reason, he was reluctant to trust them enough to do so.

Ivan spoke, "If I catch him in my things. I'll snap his neck like a twig."

"Don't worry about him, I'm going back to bed for a while," Pete said. "He won't come to our rooms."

Matt put his elbows on the table and rested his chin on his folded hands. He spoke softly to William. "Do not let him near my room when Ivan and I go see the Sheriff."

William frowned. "I was looking forward to questioning the sheriff, but I'll watch Tomato head and see what he has planned." He looked at Matt, sincerely. "You know the sheriff's brothers may not react well when you beat John." He nodded towards Pete. "Him either when he hands me his money. What I'm saying is keep your gun close."

Matt nodded. "And don't you encourage any trouble either. Leave Pete and the Dielschneiders alone. I need you to keep an eye on Tiffany today. I have a feeling they'll be searching everywhere for her."

William nodded slowly. "You got it. Do you have any idea what you're going to do with her when this is all over?"

Matt shook his head. "Let's get through today.

I'm sure someone will take her in around here."

"Are you afraid of losing the fight today?"

Matt shook his head. "No. But we'll see what happens."

"You don't sound very confident. Do remember I bet a hundred dollars on you, so let me know now before I show Pete my money and make the bet official."

Matt smiled slightly as he finished the last drink of coffee. "You're a gambler…it's a gamble."

15

When Matt and Ivan walked into the sheriff's office together, Sheriff Dielschneider, his brothers Troy and Devin, along with deputies Charlie Hammond, Fred Johnson, Rocky Culp, and John Mattick all looked up from where they were sitting around the dining table. They all had a serious expression on their faces.

Troy Dielschnieder was the first one to speak, and he did so sarcastically, "Are you running out of town before the fight happens, Marshal? Did you come to say goodbye while you still can?"

John smirked as he sat back in his chair. "Running away already, Matt?"

Matt smiled slightly at the sour greeting. "Not quite. I'll be there at noon. No, this is business," Matt said, leaning against a desk.

"Oh?" Chuck asked. "How's that? Coffee's over there if you two want some." He leaned back in his chair and put his arms behind his head to listen to Matt.

"No, thanks, Sheriff. Ivan mentioned you were going to search the homes of those dead men for some jewelry. It got me thinking, and I never asked, did you find any of the money those men took?"

Chuck frowned and shook his head. "We haven't had a chance to look. That's what we're doing today. You're more than welcome to come if you'd like."

Matt shook his head. "No. I am curious, though. Last night when I was looking at those bodies, I noticed all four of them were dressed like they were working their claims. Were they?"

Chuck nodded slowly with a thoughtful frown on his face. "Yeah, they were. I wasn't with my deputies at the cabin, but Dallen saw us coming and got defensive. When we asked about the robbery, he went for his gun. We had no choice but to shoot him."

Charlie Hammond volunteered, "Basically, that's what happened to us too. We're lucky none of us were shot."

"Especially John, because then he wouldn't be able to fight, huh?" Matt asked with a slight grin.

John nodded. "Right."

Chuck asked, "Is that what you came in here for, Marshal, to ask if they were miners?"

Matt shook his head. "I knew they were miners. I'm just curious why they didn't spend any of the money?"

The Sheriff lowered his arms and sat the chair back down. "I don't know why they didn't spend any of the money. Maybe they knew we would be suspicious if they suddenly wore suits and bought the nicest house in town." He sounded irritated by the question.

"If they were smart, they would take it easy on the spending," Matt agreed. "Even a half-wit deputy should figure that out. Ivan, what do you think? If you were them, would you spend some money on needed necessities?"

Ivan shrugged thoughtfully. "I don't know. It depends how bad I needed something and how much it costs, I imagine. I wouldn't buy a new suit and a house, though."

Sheriff Chuck Dielschneider sounded frustrated, "I couldn't tell you why they didn't spend any money. But we're going to look for it today. That and the jewelry Ivan is needing to find."

"How much money was taken, Ivan?" Matt asked.

"Over two thousand dollars and Divinity Eckman's jewelry. And like I told the Sheriff yesterday; I need that jewelry found, and Pete and I aren't leaving until it is. Everyone knows Divinity Eckman doesn't need the money, but the jewelry is personal to her, and she wants it back."

Troy sounded slightly sarcastic as he said, "Well, there's no place for them to sell it around here, so it's gotta be around somewhere."

Matt watched the facial expressions of the men sitting at the table, and there was no doubt in his mind that they were all uneasy talking about the jewelry and money. There was also no doubt that if trouble were to come, it would begin with Troy Dielschneider. He may have been a tough man, but he was emotionally weak and unable to control his impulsive nature. He would be the one Matt would have to watch out for first and foremost. He took a breath. "So, they stole over two thousand dollars of cash money, split it up between four or five of them and still, didn't buy a single thing. Not a steak from the butcher, not new pick or shovel or new trousers."

"They might've, we have no idea!" Chuck said sharply. "Matt, I'd appreciate it if you just got to the point."

Matt looked at the Sheriff evenly. "The man you called Burt Jones was wearing boots held together by strings. The sole of his boot was falling off, and he wouldn't spend six dollars to buy new boots? He could find six dollars' worth of gold in a few days' effort, yeah? No one in any town would think twice about a man buying new boots to work his claim. But he didn't. I find that odd for a man with over, let's say almost five hundred dollars in his pocket. Don't you?"

"Maybe he just didn't get to it yet?" Troy offered with a scowl on his face.

"Maybe. But if you were him, wouldn't you? I notice you have good boots on. You all do. I wear moccasins in the winter," he said raising a foot for everyone to see. "Our feet are awfully important, and I'm thinking if Burt had the money, he would spend just enough to cover his feet and keep them warm and dry in the cold weather. I'm no Pinkerton Detective, but I know just enough to know that doesn't make any sense. I don't think he was one of the robbers."

"Are you calling us liars!" Troy yelled with a cold rage in his face.

John Mattick's eyes opened just a bit wider with a cold chill of panic.

Charlie Hammond grimaced. "You're wrong. They did it, or they wouldn't have a reason to shoot at us!"

Devin Dielschneider glared at Matt dangerously.

Sheriff Chuck Dielschneider raised his hands and ordered his deputies to quiet down. "Matt, you must think we made a mistake identifying the leaches who robbed that stage? Please explain if you do because, as you can tell, my boys take their job quite seriously. And any accusations can be quite offending to these boys and me as well."

"I don't mean to offend anyone or toss out an accusation, but the fact remains, I believe that man, Burt Jones, would have bought boots if nothing else if he had the money. I think you got the wrong man."

"Then why'd he shoot at Devin?" Troy asked harshly. "I can promise you these are the right men! Dallen named them, you..."

"Troy, shut up!" Chuck shouted.

"I didn't know that," Matt said with interest. "Well then, if they didn't spend any money, it should be easily accounted for when you find it. Over two-thousand dollars should be easy to find. Right, gentlemen?"

The deputies all looked at Matt with hardened eyes and bitter scowls. Chuck nodded. "Yeah, if we can find it, it should be there. However, we don't know if they spent any or not," he said with a shrug. "We can't promise to find much. We might find it all or nothing at all. Hell, those miners are vagrants, they might've sent that money back home to their families for all we know. As I said, we haven't even looked for it yet. But today we're going to try to find every penny of it. Will that satisfy you, Marshal?"

Matt smirked slightly. "Ivan will be more interested in that than I am. It is his boss's money and personal property, not mine. I hope you find something to prove those men did it, or there might be an investigation into the killing of an innocent man."

Troy spewed out a few carefully picked curse words towards Matt. "You have no right to come in here and accuse us of killing someone for no reason! You are a piece of work, and I can't wait to see John bust your head open! No one wants to see that more than me! And when he's done, I may just step in!" His eyes glared into Matt with great hostility.

Devin shook his head and spoke calmly, "I think you and your cousin need to go back where you came from and stay out of our area for good."

Chuck bit his bottom lip in thought. "Marshal, we're not going to listen to any more of this. And I think my brothers are right, after today's fight; we want you gone. The case is solved, and you're no longer needed here. As a matter of fact, forget the fight and just leave our town right now!"

Matt took a deep breath. "I'd like to myself, but now you gentlemen have me wanting to avenge a fight I lost years ago. I'm sorry, gentlemen, but in my opinion, you got the wrong men. Until I'm proved wrong, I will continue to think so and assist you in finding the right men. That's where I'm standing gentlemen, like it or not; that's the way it is."

"I'll prove you wrong!" Troy stammered as he stood up. "I'll prove you wrong today!"

Matt shrugged. "Prove me wrong, and I'll go home. Until then, I'm going to go explore around your town, talk to a few people, and get a feel for your community." He looked at his old friend, John. "I'll see on the street at noon, my old friend."

"I told you, I'm not your friend," John said with contempt.

Matt stood up from the desk. "So be it. Have a good day, gentlemen. Ivan, I hope you find your jewelry." He walked outside of the office.

"Ivan, why don't you go get your horse ready and meet us back here. We have to finish up our morning meeting, and then we'll catch up with you," Chuck suggested.

Ivan nodded and left the office.

Chuck took a deep breath and exhaled. "Like I was saying before, they interrupted us; we have to find Tiffany. Our plans have changed a bit this morning, but Dane's out there looking for her too. Devin, when the rest of us ride up to the cabin, I need you to go to Danetta's and put the jewelry in the barn somewhere. Don't let Danetta see it! And then keep looking for Tiffany. I have a feeling the Marshal may have her or talked to her at least. She must be somewhere, and he's very confident about us having the wrong men. Now we know, next time put new boots on the dead men." He chuckled spitefully. "John, I want you to go home and rest up for your fight. I want you to cripple him or kill him if you can. The rest of us will keep his cousin from interfering. You keep hitting him until his brain is dead. I'll pay you an extra thousand dollars if you do. Do you understand me?"

"I do."

"Good. Devin, if you find Tiffany, take her to my place and tie her to a chair. If anyone gives you any trouble, say you're arresting her for the attempted murder of Danetta. She stabbed her, right? That's all anyone needs to know. Gentlemen, we have a busy day and not much time. So, let's get moving."

16

Danetta Foster wasn't surprised when her brother Chuck knocked on the door a few times and stepped inside. "Danetta, I'm sorry to come by unexpected, but I need to search your place for some stolen property. This is…"

"Matt Bannister?" she asked abruptly with a hint of excitement to her voice.

"No. This is Ivan. He's a Pinkerton Detective."

"Oh," she said disappointedly. "So, what are you looking for? Obviously, not Tiffany."

"Hello, Miss," Ivan said. "We are looking for a significant amount of money and, more importantly, some jewelry that was stolen from Misses Eckman. If you have any knowledge of its where-abouts, now would be a good time to say so."

She smiled and flicked her hair out of her face, "You'll have to forgive my appearance; my step-daughter ran away last night after stabbing me in the side. That's why I won't be standing up and showing you around our house. It's also why the house is a mess. I'm worried sick about her and would appreciate your help as a Pinkerton Detective to help find her. She was quite upset about her father being killed yesterday, of course. She left to go speak to the marshal. She won't accept the fact that her father could do this to us." She began to cry. "I tried to help her to understand."

Chuck explained, "We just came back from searching his partner's cabin up on Dutch Creek and found nothing. I think the money must be here somewhere. On the way back here, we went into town and ran into Devin, and we decided to get you one of Joanne's cakes. Devin," he hollered, "bring it on in."

Devin stepped inside of the house with a comforting smile. "Hey, Sis. We got you a carrot cake, just the way you like it. I sure am sorry about Dallen, but as they say, thieves never prosper. I guess that explains why he never wanted to be a deputy with us, doesn't it?" He handed the cake to her in her chair.

She wiped the tears from her eyes. "Would you cut me off a piece, please."

"What? Not just a fork, this time?" Chuck teased with a laugh.

"Shut up, Chuck. And get to searching if you are. I'll tell you right now I don't have a thing to eat in this house and have two mourning girls to raise on my own now. If that idiot hid money from me, I don't know anything about it. But if he hid a bunch of money from us while I'm eating cabbage soup,

133

I'll kill him myself!"

"That would seem a bit redundant, wouldn't it?" Devin asked with a grin. "Let me cut you a piece of cake."

Danetta looked at Ivan with a flirtatious gaze and spoke sweetly, "Ivan, sir, if you find some of that money, could you spare some of it to help my girls and me? We're barely surviving as it is. It would be a nice Christian thing to do."

Ivan shook his head, unmoved by her plea. "No, it's not my money. And quite frankly, my employer would have me shot for giving her money to the family of the man who killed her husband. I won't be doing that. Sheriff, do you mind if I start looking?"

"Yeah, let's start looking," Chuck said and gave Danetta an indignant scowl after Ivan walked down the hallway to search the farthest bedroom. "Devin, why don't you go check the barn?"

"I will go in a second," he said and brought Danetta a plate with a large slice of cake on it. "And I have been looking for Tiffany. She went to the hotel to find the Marshal, but his cousin mistook her for a prostitute and told her Matt wouldn't be interested in seeing her. His cousin then offered her a dime for her services, and she ran off crying. Which makes me laugh," he chuckled. "No one has seen her since."

Danetta grimaced at the mere mention of her name. "She has nowhere else to go. Did you search the Reverend or the church's house? Did you search everyone's house who goes to that church including the hotel? They have rooms upstairs; did you check those?"

Chuck answered, "Ivan is staying in the hotel. Hey Ivan, have you seen or heard a fourteen-year-old blonde-haired girl around the hotel?"

"No," came his voice from the back room. They could hear him in the room searching in the drawers.

"Well, then I don't know where she could be!" Danetta said loudly. "But you find her!"

"Oh, eat your cake. I'm not Dallen; you don't scare me much, Sis," Devin said and walked outside to search the barn.

"When does Bad Shot John fight the Marshal?" She asked Chuck while he half-heartedly searched through her family room.

"Noon. I suspect we might have one retired marshal by the end of it. John has no intention of taking it easy on him this time."

"Is the marshal handsome? I heard somewhere that he was." She added when Chuck looked at her oddly, "I'm looking for a new husband!"

Chuck laughed lightly and went back to looking. "Any luck back there?" he shouted to Ivan.

"Not yet."

"You know," Danetta said loudly, "you probably won't find anything in here. We have two little girls who get into everything. So, if he didn't hide it in the barn, then he may have hidden it out at his claim or buried it somewhere until all the hubbub is over. Dallen wasn't the brightest candle, but even a dimwit like him could think a bit. If it's not here, then I'd search his claim and start digging, because that's where I think he'd put it. He always talked about buying a farm in Northern California in some town he fell in love with years ago. I don't remember which one though. I never listened to him really because we couldn't afford half a dozen eggs, let alone a farm."

Ivan left the back room and entered the girls' room. "I'm not finding anything," he said irritably.

"I told you, you probably wouldn't."

Before too long, Devin stepped into the house, holding a white pearl necklace and a large wedding ring. "I'm assuming these are them, Ivan."

Ivan came quickly out of the bedroom to see what Devin found. "Where'd you find these?" he asked while taking them into his hand.

"The barn. It's all I found, though."

"Where in the barn?" Ivan asked.

"On the top shelf of a cabinet."

"Can I see the ring?" Danetta asked, intrigued. "As you can see, I don't have a ring. I've been married three times, and not one of those so-called men could afford to buy me a ring!"

Ivan held out his hand for her to see. She picked the ring up and was amazed by the beauty and intricate design of such an elegant piece of jewelry. It had a gold band with the largest diamond she had never seen surrounded by a dozen small red rubies. "This is breathtaking!" she said in disbelief. "My word, I didn't even know they could make such a beautiful ring. I can understand why she would want it back so bad. How much do you think this is worth?" she asked Ivan with widened eyes.

"A lot," Ivan answered. He held his hand out to take it back from her.

She hesitated and tilted her head flirtatiously as she fluttered her eyelashes over her big, ice-blue eyes. "What would you do if it got stuck my finger and wouldn't come off?"

Ivan answered with no humor in his voice, "Ma'am, I'd take out my knife and cut your finger off without any hesitation at all. I wouldn't put it on if I was you and hand it back to me."

"Oh," she said with a stunned expression and handed it back to him. "I hope you don't talk to your wife like that."

"I'm not married," he answered shortly. He looked at Chuck. "Let's go search the barn for the money."

"I'll be right behind you." After Devin and Ivan went out to the barn, Chuck turned to Danetta. He kept his voice low, but his anger was quite evident in his hissing tone, "Don't you ever do this again! Now we're going to be out at Dallen's claim looking for money that's not there for most of the day! Next time keep your mouth shut!"

"Did you bury Dallen as I asked?"

"Yes, he's buried," he said bitterly.

"I want that ring. Get it for me."

"How am I supposed to do that, Danetta?" he asked sharply.

"With a bullet to the back of his head!" she exclaimed with widened eyes.

"He's a Pinkerton Detective! Forget it."

"I want that ring!"

Chuck sighed and shook his head. "Well, good luck getting it. Besides, we have more important things to worry about, like just getting him, his partner, and the marshal out of town!"

"Fine. Just go search the barn," Danetta said irritably with a wave of her hand.

Chuck left the house and went out to the barn to help search for money that he knew wasn't there. He had given the ring and necklace to Devin that morning to run out to Danetta's and hide them in her barn. Chuck had planned to meet Devin at the Sheriff's office when they came back from searching the cabin up on Dutch Creek. The trip into town was under the premise of promising to buy his sister Danetta a cake before going out to her place. Ivan didn't seem to have a problem with that, and the other deputies had gotten wet searching for the money on the other side of Dutch Creek. They needed to go home and warm up after traveling home in wet clothes in the cold weather. Devin just so happened to be available to ride out with Ivan and Chuck to search for the missing money and jewelry.

"Finding anything?" Chuck asked as he entered the barn.

"Not yet," Devin said, lifting a burlap sack that had been tossed aside on the ground.

Ivan grunted as he tossed aside a few boards that were beside the tall cabinet. "We still have the room with the saddle, the hayloft, and the corral to look through. It's got to be here if the jewelry was!"

Chuck moved into a small room with a workbench where Dallen kept his saddle on a board bolted to the wall. "I'll look in here. Did you already search his saddlebags?"

"I did," Devin said.

"Well, let me look around here," he said, moving some things around.

"Did you boys find anything yet?" Danetta asked as she entered the barn.

Chuck looked out of the room at her. "What are you doing out here?"

"It's my barn. I can come to watch you fella's sift through my husbands' things, can't I?" She was wearing a blanket wrapped around her shoulders being held on by her left hand around her neck. She had no shoes on.

"It's too cold to be without shoes, isn't it?"

"My feet are so callused they won't know it for a week." She stepped further into the barn. "Ivan, would you like to come over for dinner tonight? I'll make us a fine dinner," she asked flirtatiously.

He glanced back at her and smirked slightly. "No, thanks." He turned back to what he was doing without any interest in her.

"Oh! Well, I'm not looking my best right now for sure, but I clean up like a swan. Do you like pork? I have a roast I can make up that'll be like candy, it's so good. If you don't have other plans with a lady, maybe you should come on over for dinner?"

He sighed and spoke without turning around. "I'm not interested in coming over, Ma'am."

Danetta's eyes narrowed. "Are you sure?"

139

Chuck interrupted, "Yes, he's sure. Danetta, go back inside and let us search this barn. There's nothing we're going to steal in here," he said with a grin and stepped back into the room to act like he was searching.

"Well, maybe Ivan should say so. He's the one I'm asking," she said bitterly.

Ivan snickered while shaking his head. He turned to look at Danetta. "I just said I'm not interested in coming over for dinner or you. Okay?"

"Okay," she answered. When Ivan turned around Danetta brought her right hand up out of the blanket with an already cocked revolver. She pointed it at the back of Ivan's head and pulled the trigger. He dropped to his knees and fell forward, hitting his head on the base of the wall to the small room beside the cabinet.

Devin spun around and gasped. He just stared at his sister with the gun in her hand, standing over Ivan's dead body. He was too stunned to speak.

Chuck came quickly around the corner of the room and yelled, "What in the hell are you doing? What...Why? He's a Pinkerton, Danetta!"

She lowered the gun and stepped forward to reach down into Ivan's pocket. She pulled out his money clip and jewelry. She looked up at her brother. "I told you I wanted this ring. And now I have money to eat on for a while too."

Chuck's face was full of concern. "You just killed a Pinkerton Detective who was with Devin and me, how in the hell are we going to explain this, Danetta! Did you think about that? No, you didn't, you just acted on impulse! You're going to get us all hung! You're going to be hung! Do you think he's not going to be missed?" he shouted and kicked the dirt in anger. "His partner is going to be asking where he is as soon as we get back to town! Matt Bannister is already suspicious of us, and now you killed the one man who was going to clear us! You are so stupid, Danetta! My lord, you're stupid! What are we supposed to do now, huh?"

Danetta shouted, "You figure that out, Chuck! You figured out how to get away with robbing the Eckman's, now figure this out and quit crying about it! He's just a man! Kill his partner and kill the marshal too. Tell everyone the same people who robbed the stage did it!"

"They're already dead!" Chuck screamed in her face. "Oh, my lord!" He turned away from her and threw his hat across the barn angrily. He turned back to Danetta. "I should take you in and throw you in jail! There's no getting out of this one! No one's going to believe it was an accident. You just cut our lives short, Danetta. Thank you!"

She began to cry. "I just wanted the ring! Do you think it's easy not having anything to eat except cabbage? My girls are starving! I have no money, and you killed my husband! How am I supposed to raise my girls on nothing? Do you want me to feed them, hay? We haven't got any!" she screamed. "I'm going to have to kill our horse for food."

Devin shook his head. "He rejected her, that's why she shot him! Not everyone thinks you're a swan, Sis. But we can't leave him lying here either.

141

I'll grab a shovel, and we'll bury him in here and toss some straw over the dirt."

"Well, hurry up before my girls get home from school."

"It's not even noon yet. We have time."

Chuck sat down on a wooden box and ran his fingers through his hair. "I don't know what to do or what I'm going to tell his partner. I think we're in some deep trouble."

Danetta spoke sharply, "You do stuff like this all the time, but when I do it all of a sudden it's a problem? We're family and family comes first! Use your damn noggin and figure it out!"

He glared up at her with a dangerous expression. "I plan things before I do them! I arrange and set up alibis! You shoot to kill and say, 'help me, big brother.'" He rolled his eyes in anger. "I don't know if I can help you."

Danetta kicked some dirt towards Chuck. "Well, are you going to sit here and cry about it or try to come up with something? Because when you leave here, his partner and the marshal will be asking about him!" She pointed at Ivan's body.

Chuck stood up and pointed his finger at her. "I know! You crossed the line!"

Danetta raised her eyebrows questionably. "No, maybe you did when you killed my no-good husband. And Tiffany's still not been found."

Devin spoke, "I'll bury him here, and then take his horse a couple of miles out and shoot it where no one's going to find it right away. You... No, wait," Devin said thoughtfully. "Who's that guy who lives way out past Dallen's claim?"

"Dewayne Gobles," Danetta said. "And he does think I'm a swan!" she added bitterly to Devin.

"Why?" Chuck asked.

Devin answered, "We could kill him and take both bodies back into town. And say we went out to Dallen's claim like Danetta suggested, and while looking, Dewayne shot Ivan and tried to shoot us. Because he wanted the money for himself."

"Dewayne's pretty well-liked by the church folks in town. He's an old man with an honest reputation, do you think anyone will believe that?" Chuck asked skeptically.

He shrugged. "Does it matter? The only ones who need to believe it are the other Pinkerton and the Marshal. Unless you have a better idea?"

Chuck shook his head. "I like Dewayne. Well, let's go get this done."

Danetta smiled. "See, I knew you two could figure something out. And I have my dream ring!" she said, admiring it as she put it on her finger.

"Get that off, and I better never see you wearing it either!" Chuck warned. "I hope it was worth it."

She smiled. "Oh, yes. It's worth every penny."

17

"Are you ready?" William asked Matt inside of his hotel room. "It's about time to go down and," he paused to imitate Dane Dielschneider's soft-spoken flat monotone, "face your fears."

Matt nodded. Despite his many experiences since leaving Boise City years before, he felt an uneasiness in the pit of his stomach. He was about to face his old friend in another street fight, one that he had lost last time they fought. He tied his moccasins tighter on his feet and looked at Tiffany as she sat quietly on a chair in the corner. "Are you doing okay?"

She nodded. "John is a mean man. Be careful, because he is mean and fights dirty, I'm sure. I've heard Troy talk about watching John fight. They make it sound like he can't lose. If you get hurt, I'll help take care of you," she said sincerely with worry showing through her eyes.

Matt smiled gently. "I'll tell you what, if I lose,

I'll only want you taking care of me. But you know what, I've fought him before, and he wasn't unbeatable. I assure you; I'll be okay."

"Promise?" she asked with a slight thickening of her tears. "Because if you're hurt, who's going to protect me from them? Danetta will kill me if I'm taken back home."

Matt frowned. "I promise. I'm not doing this alone, Tiffany. William is here to protect you too. Isn't that right, William?"

William leaned against the wall and looked at Tiffany and nodded. "Like a niece or nephew, you bet."

"Listen, I know you're scared, and do you know what you should always do when you're scared?"

"Pray?" she asked.

Matt nodded. "How about we pray together and trust the Lord to protect us both, okay?" He got on his knees in front of her and took her hands in his and prayed. When he finished praying and opened his eyes, he looked at her, a tear was slowly falling down her cheek. "You'll be fine. But I don't want you peeping out that window even for a second no matter what you hear, okay? Because if you do and someone sees you, they'll try to get you. I don't want anything to happen to you, so can you promise me you'll stay away from the window?"

She nodded quietly.

"And most important, do not open the door for anyone, but me or William. And it's one knock only, right?"

She nodded with her eyes locked onto Matt; they

glossed over with heavy tears. There was something about her expression that caused Matt's eyes to moisten unexpectedly. It was the desperation that only a child has in the innocence and depth of their hurting heart and confusion of an uncertain future. Matt reached his arms out for her. "Come here."

She quickly wrapped her arms around him tightly and began to sob. "Please, don't go! They killed my father, and I'm afraid they're going to kill you too! Please don't leave me, Matt," she wept.

From outside came the voice of John Mattick shouting, "I'm here, Matt! Are you coming down or cowering out? I think he's scared, folks."

Matt pulled away from Tiffany. "Remember we prayed? I'll be fine and will be back up here in an hour or two. In the meantime, you read the Bible and trust what your reading like it was the words of God because it is. Trust him, Tiffany."

"Are you going to arrest Chuck and Troy for shooting my father?"

Matt frowned and nodded slightly. "Eventually. But for right now, John's the one I want." He stood up and looked at William. "Are you ready?"

William nodded quietly. "It sounds like they're getting impatient out there."

Matt nodded as they left the room. He locked the door behind him and then said as they walked down the hallway towards the stairs, "You know I wish we would've brought Truet and maybe Uncle Charlie to even up the odds a bit if things go bad."

William raised his eyebrows quickly. "You need

to start hiring some experienced gunmen and get away from hiring office maids. You just said it yourself, you're other two deputy marshals aren't experienced enough to help when the firing pin hits the powder, are they?"

Matt shook his head as he went down the stairs. "No. I'm glad you're here, William."

"And think you didn't want me coming along at all."

"I'm glad you did." He paused at the front door of the hotel and looked at his cousin. "Are you ready to cause some trouble?"

William smiled slowly. "I live for it."

Matt grinned. "Then let's go do it."

18

John Mattick was standing in the middle of the road facing the hotel when Matt stepped outside onto the porch. John was dressed in brown trousers with suspenders over his dirty white long sleeve long johns. Behind John in a semi-circle was a large crowd of men of various sorts and a few saloon girls who were excited to see the fight. They had seen John fight before but had never had the opportunity to watch him fight the one man that had made John a local legend of sorts. He had beaten the famous U.S. Marshal Matt Bannister in a fist fight, and to anyone's knowledge, he was the only one to have done so. Now, they had the opportunity to watch it happen again. For those who enjoyed the local entertainment of no rules bare-knuckle fighting in the street, John was the man to beat, and the biggest fight possible would have been between him and the only other unde-feated fighter, Troy Dielschneider. However, they were not only sheriff deputies, but they were also best friends, and everyone knew that fight would never happen. But beating Matt Bannister was the one thing that made John notable above all others. Now that Matt was in town and the old foes were fighting again. The excitement the rematch caused within Prairieville was unmatched to anywhere else except in the prizefighting ring. It made sense in a sick kind of way since there was nothing else to do in town for entertainment except drink and fight. The combination of the two went together like a matching pair of gloves everywhere in the world, but in Prairieville, it was a pastime and a fun way to gamble.

John smiled as Matt stepped onto the road, followed by William. Both men were dressed in their buckskin pants and shirt to stay warm in the cold. "It's about time!" John said loudly. "I was beginning to think you were going to show yourself as a coward. After the beating I gave you last time, it wouldn't have surprised me."

Troy Dielschneider began to laugh and spin around to face the crowd with a display of over-excitement. His loud voice of encouragement and emotional euphoria was annoying. But by no means was he alone with the cheers, excitement, and laughter.

Matt's eyes scanned the crowd quickly and then focused on John. "I told you I'd be here."

John smirked. "I'll tell you what I'm going to do, Matt. When I knock you out, I'm going to cut your ponytail off and hang it on my wall. Isn't that what you so-called Indians do? Scalp your victims?" he asked as his friends laughed.

Matt looked at him with no humor on his face. "John, if you can knock me out, I'll let you cut my hair. And I won't even shoot you for it. You got my word on that. But you won't win, and you sure as hell won't knock me out. But give it a try. Because I'm going to hurt you." Matt handed his gun belt to William and began to pull his buckskin overshirt over his head when John stepped forward quickly..."

"Watch it!" William said quickly.

Matt's head and arms were caught in the vulnerable position of being mid-way over his head when he heard William. He moved his left leg back to twist his body away from whatever was coming from his front — John's foot connected with the inside of Matt's thigh missing its mark by an inch. Matt tried to pull the buckskin off his shoulders before John could get another easy blow in. John reached in through the head hole of Matt's shirt and grabbed his ponytail, making it impossible to pull the shirt off. John pulled Matt's head down and brought his knee up, ferociously towards Matt's face. Matt tucked his chin down as far as he could to protect his exposed face from a direct blow. The knee was blocked partially by the top of Matt's forehead, meeting the tip of John's femur bone just above the knee. The blow was still jarring, but not near as devastating as a blow to his nose would have been.

Matt grimaced in anger and pushed his arms back through the sleeves to free his hands. John pulled his knee back to bring another devastating knee to Matt's head and grunted as he brought his knee up as hard as he could. Again, Matt tucked his chin down despite the pain of his hair being pulled and wrapped his arms around John's leg as the knee landed against his head. Matt took the blow and tightened his hold on the upper leg of John. With a great effort, he stepped forward into John and straightened himself up, lifting John off the ground by one leg. Matt picked John up as high as he could and then slammed him back down to the ground as hard as he could. John let go of Matt's hair as he fell. The back of his head and upper shoulders landed first on the hardened ground. Stunned by the hard slam to the ground, John laid on the ground momentarily as Matt stood up quickly and pulled his buckskin shirt off in a hurry revealing his red long john shirt underneath. Matt looked at John with a rage-filled face.

"Get up, John!" Matt ordered with his open hands ready to fight. "Don't quit on me now! Get up and show your friends how tough you are!"

"Now you've done it!" William laughed lightly to John.

John stood up, rubbing the back of his head. "Let's go," he said. He put his fists up in a fisticuff position and jabbed a right fist. Matt blocked it easily. He jabbed again with the same result. He went to throw an overhand left, but Matt blocked it with his right hand and struck John in the face with a quick left. John's head popped backward. Matt followed it with a right cross as he stepped forward with his left foot. And then a quick left jab to John's chin. John's hands went up to cover his face and block any more hits. Matt lowered his hips just a bit and struck John in the diaphragm with a solid right, followed by a left hook to John's kidney.

John gasped and stepped back in pain. A look of worry filled his expression. He wiped his nose with the back of his hand while taking a deep breath and stepped forward again. He faked a right jab, to watch Matt's reaction. He faked another right, but as soon as he pulled his hand back, Matt faked a left and followed it with an overhand right that landed squarely on John's jaw. He stumbled back a few steps and shook his head.

Troy yelled, "Get him, John!"

John ran forward to tackle Matt, but Matt spun to his left, tossing John on past him. Matt turned to face him. "Getting desperate, John? Just like last time, huh? I won't trip over boards this time."

John stood up with an angry expression. He ran towards Matt with his head up and tackled Matt to the ground. On the way down, Matt turned his body while pulling John's right arm in towards him while forcing his left arm out away from him. Instead of Matt landing squarely on his back, they landed on their sides with the momentum rolling John to his back and bringing Matt on top of him. Matt straddled John's body and clenched his left arm around John's to hold him in place. He threw two quick hard right fists to John's face upon hitting the ground. Matt paused and looked down at John.

"No, I'm not finishing this right now." He got up off John. "Get up! You've been talking about me for a long time. You're making this too easy for me in front of your own crowd. Now stand up and fight!" Matt shouted with his eyes burning with an intensity that even quieted Troy down when he looked over at him.

John stood up with a reddened area under his left eye from the two quick hard shots he received on the ground. He clenched his fists and approached Matt with more caution than he had before.

"Are you going to try taking me down again or fight like a man?" Matt asked with his open hand defense. "My hair's right here, come earn it."

"Yeah, I got it!" John said and spat out a bit of blood from a slightly split lip. He faked a kick, and when Matt's hands lowered, he threw a hard-over-hand left that connected to Matt's jaw that made him stumble a bit. He followed it with a right elbow that Matt was able to avoid by moving his head back and stepped to John's right. Matt then kicked his left foot ferociously through John's right ankle, lifting his leg upward waist-high, and John fell to his back quickly on the ground. Looking up, he saw Matt inviting him to come at him with his fingers.

John hit the ground with his fist and yelled in frustration. Matt smiled slightly. It had been what Matt was waiting for. The most careless fighters were the most frustrated or those blinded with anger; either way, Matt knew he could now pick him apart. John stood up and came at Matt swinging in anger with his left hand and then his right hand looking for one to land. Matt ducked under a wide left and threw a vertical fist straight into John's diaphragm and followed it with a left hook to the kidney. John bent over as the wind was knocked out of him, and as his chin came down, Matt brought up a hardened right uppercut that landed under John's chin and sent him back to the ground.

John rolled to his hands and knees and spat out a mouthful of blood and two teeth he had lost from the uppercut. He looked at Matt dangerously with an infuriated groan and came at him again, swinging with both arms. Matt stepped his left leg forward just a touch and threw a straight overhand right between John's fists and landed squarely on the bridge of John's nose. John collapsed and rolled to his stomach as his nose burst open with blood.

Matt sighed as he looked at his old friend. "Are you done?" he asked as the men who had crowded around stood stunned to see their champion lying in a growing pool of his blood so quickly.

John turned his body so Matt couldn't see and reached into his pocket for the knuckle busters that he put on his fingers. He began to stand, keeping his hand slightly behind him. He looked at Matt tiredly. Blood covered his face, and his left eye was swelling up. "I'm not giving up," he said, and with a mighty swing, he brought his fist around with the brass knuckles. Matt moved his head back just enough for the iron knuckles to miss his forehead. He stepped back and brought his hands up to protect himself. John regained his fighting posture and stepped towards Matt again.

Matt knew if John connected with the iron knuckles that he would most likely be knocked out or seriously hurt at least. They were a potentially dangerous weapon and could break a bone easily as hard as John had swung his fist. Caution overwhelmed him as he knew it was suddenly a fight where his very life was on the line.

John threw another wild left hand as hard as he could, and again, Matt backed up to let the knuckles pass by his head. As soon as the fist went by, Matt changed levels with his hips and stepped in quickly to drive his right shoulder up underneath of John's left arm as it met its full extension and drove John upwards and back down to the street. John landed on his side with his left arm trapped between their two bodies. Matt lifted just enough to allow John to pull his arm back across his body to hit Matt with the iron knuckles, but Matt was expecting John to do just that and wrapped his right arm around John's arm in an over hook locking his elbow straight against Matt's body. Matt sat up just enough to grab his right wrist and pulled his arm inward, dislocating John's elbow socket. John began screaming from the pain of his separated elbow.

Matt grabbed John's arm roughly and pulled the knuckle busters off John's fingers and tossed them towards William.

"Get off him!" Troy Dielschnieder yelled angrily and stepped towards Matt aggressively.

"Back off!" Matt yelled.

William put his left hand on his revolver as he

spoke to Troy and the others who would try to force Matt off John. "He said back off. I think I would if I was you."

"What's this? You beat him!" Troy hollered at Matt. "You won fair and square! Get off him. He needs a doctor! You didn't have to break his arm!"

Matt looked up at Troy. "Do you have any shackles on you?"

"What? No. Why?" he asked.

"That's fine. William?" he called and held out his hand.

William handed him a pair of wrist shackles.

"What are you doing?" Troy shouted. "It was a fair fight! You can't arrest him for this!"

Matt forcefully pulled John's right arm behind his back and tightened one side of the shackles onto his wrist. John did not put up a fight as he grimaced in pain from his dislocated left elbow. Matt took hold of his left arm and began to pop the elbow back into place as John screamed in pain. It popped back in place, and Matt bent it back to shackle it to his other wrist. John cried out in pain with a horrible grimace.

Matt stood up and pulled John up to his feet. He reached into John's pocket and took the pocket-knife that John had stolen from him years ago. "I'll be taking this back. You won't need it where you're going. And by the way, I've had many tougher fights than you." He faced the crowd that had begun yelling at him for making John suffer so much for no reason what-so-ever. He raised a hand to quiet down the crowd. "Listen up! John Mattick is under arrest for the murder of Louis Eckman and Herb Johnson."

"What?" someone yelled as the crowd gasped and argued.

"The sheriff already got the killer!" someone else said.

Matt ignored the many complaints and watched Troy stare at him in silence. "Let's take him to your jail."

Troy shook his head. "You can't be serious?"

"I am very serious."

"He's a deputy sheriff! He didn't do it, Dallen did!"

Matt looked at him harshly. "Let's go now."

The crowd began to gasp, and William said, "Hey Matt."

"What?" He looked where William nodded towards, and he saw Sheriff Chuck Dielshnieder and his brother Devin riding near the crowd with two dead bodies on the two horses they were leading.

"That's the Pinkerton, Ivan," William said as he stepped next to Matt. "I like this town less and less by the day."

Matt looked at the sheriff and then scanned through the crowd and squinted his eyes slightly as he noticed Dane Dielschneider standing against the saloon across the street by himself staring at him with his strange, uncanny grin. "I have a feeling it's only going to get worse. Give me my gun belt."

19

Sheriff Chuck Dielschneider didn't know how the town would react to him bringing in the body of Dewayne Gobles and the Pinkerton, Ivan Petoskey. He and Devin had discussed their best version of the story and would tell the same one. Still, there was the issue of character. Dewayne was a solid man of character and Christian values. He was non-violent, but one of the more eccentric men in the area. He was loved by many and helpful to a fault, but he lived far out of town in a small cabin and didn't want to be bothered by visitors. He was friendly and talkative, but hard to get to know and preferred to be alone when he wasn't in town. He had never married and lived mostly off the land. He hunted, grew a garden, preserved his food, and patched his clothes with cloth from older garments. He was an oddity, but a loved oddity at worst. Chuck feared no one would believe his story that Dewayne attacked them for stolen money. It didn't add up to Dewayne's character traits, and

Chuck and Devin both knew it.

On the other hand, robbing the Eckman stage wasn't in Dallen's character either, but so far, no one had questioned it openly anyway. Maybe that was because they feared the Dielschneider's, maybe it's because they feared the sheriff's deputies, or maybe it was because they feared the Crowe Brothers, either way so far the community had not questioned the sheriff's affairs. Maybe they just knew better for their own good, because there was a lot to fear if they got on the Sheriff's bad side. It took a lot to get on his bad side, though. He was an easy-going man who let a lot of things go under the bridge and did his best to keep a calm and peaceful town. However, if anyone raised a voice of concern, Chuck and his men would take it upon themselves to encourage them to accept it for truth.

He frowned when he saw the crowd in the street, and Matt pulled a bloody, faced John up off the ground. "We missed the fight, and it looks like John lost," he said to Devin with disappointment.

Devin squinted his eyes. "It looks like John's shackled, Chuck."

"What the...?" Chuck paused as the crowd walked towards them.

"Who is that, Sheriff? Is that...Dewayne? Is that Dewayne Goble? It is! What happened to Dewayne?" one man asked.

"What? Dewayne's dead?"

"That's the Pinkerton!"

"Sheriff, what happened?"

The questions came too fast and too many at

a time for Chuck to process as his attention was on Matt holding John in a pair of shackles. Matt stepped towards him, but it was the Pinkerton Pete Logan who grabbed the Sheriff's coat demanding the Sheriff's attention, "What happened to Ivan?" Pete's eyes burned into the sheriff like daggers.

The commotion was pulling Chuck's attention in a dozen directions as everyone wanted to know what had happened and continued to speak louder than the clamor that was already overly distracting.

"Tell me now!" Pete screamed in the Sheriff's face.

"Um, he was shot..."

"Shot by who?" Pete interrupted angrily.

Matt pulled John across the street towards the Sheriff. "Chuck, you can't talk out here. Let's go to the jail. Pete, let's talk to him there."

Pete glared at Matt and then nodded. He turned to the sheriff, "Let's go!" he said and then went to look at Ivan's uncovered body. He looked closely at the back of Ivan's head and then his distorted face.

"Pete," the Sheriff called as he handed his reigns to Devin. "Follow me. Marshal, unshackle my man!" he ordered Matt.

"We'll talk in your office. Not here!"

"Devin," Chuck yelled out over the chattering crowd, "Tell them what happened."

Chuck unlocked his office door and held the door open as Pete Logan, Charlie Hammond, Troy Dielschneider, and Rocky Culp followed him in. "Don't worry, John. We're on your side," Chuck said as Matt guided John inside. Chuck closed the door behind him in the faces of those who wanted to listen in. "What the hell's going on, Matt? Why is my man in shackles? Is it against the law for him to fight you?" he shouted.

Matt ignored him and pushed John into an open cell. He loosened the shackles with a key and pushed John down on a bed.

"Listen to me when I'm talking to you! What do you think you're doing?" Chuck shouted, standing near the cell door.

Matt looked at him and spoke pointedly. "He's under arrest for the murder of Louis Eckman and Herb Johnson."

"What?" Chuck exclaimed. "How do you figure that? We already got the man responsible. Herb named him, Dall! In other words, Dallen Foster! John, come on out of there and go home," Chuck said irritably.

Matt shouted, "He's not going anywhere! And we're going to talk because he's your deputy and he led the ambush on the Eckman's. My question is, who else knew about it and helped do it? But first, why is Ivan dead, and who is the other body you have out there?"

Pete Logan shook his head as he stared at the Sheriff. "No, Matt. I want to know why you're so sure the deputy killed Louis. What evidence have you got?"

"Yeah," Chuck answered, "What evidence have you got against my man and to accuse me of wrong-doing? That is what you're doing, right?" Chuck asked as he walked away from Matt and sat down behind his desk.

Matt looked at John lying down on the bed, holding his nose. "My evidence is John and I were friends years ago. He might've forgotten, but I never did. The man who led that ambush and shot Louis Eckman said his father was killed by debris from a tunnel explosion while working for the railroad." He nodded towards John. "So was John's. Now either John did it, or there are two men around here whose fathers were killed in the exact same way. And I doubt that."

"It could have been someone else. A lot of men died building the railroad." Troy Dielschneider suggested with a shrug of his shoulders.

"Yeah, but it's not!" Matt shouted unexpectedly. "Pete and I could have Misses Eckman come here and have five men say the same words in their normal voices and I bet she will identify John as the one. Twenty-five men, fifty men! Pete, could we do that?"

Pete nodded. "It will take her some time to get here, but yes. And she would come if I asked her too."

Matt continued, "There's no doubt in my mind who did it, and I will stay here indefinitely to see to it that justice is done. She will identify him, from his size and build, his voice, and maybe even his boots. Add that to the way his father died, and he will be convicted. No Sheriff, he is not walking out of here. And if he does, I will come after you!" he said with a hardened tone. "Now I'm going to ask you point-blank, did you or any of your deputies assist, help, have any knowledge of or suspect John of this or any other crimes?"

"Hell, no!" Chuck yelled. "And I don't believe he did it anyway! But I'm curious why you would even suggest we had anything at all to do with that?"

Matt hesitated and then spoke softly, "The driver, Herb Johnson supposedly said, Dall, but what if he was misunderstood and he said Dell, as in Dielschneider?"

Troy shouted, "Oh, for crying out loud! You are crazier than a loon if you think he said our name!"

Chuck shook his head. "I won't even respond to that."

Pete spoke with a rage burning just under his calm demeanor, "Then maybe you'll respond to how my friend died?"

Chuck sighed. He began telling him how they had searched for the money and jewelry and couldn't find it. However, Danetta mentioned Dallen would have hidden it on his claim because the nosy girls in his home would've found it. They had gone to the claim and began looking when Dewayne showed up and questioned them. Dewayne shot Ivan unexpectedly and propositioned the sheriff about sharing the money with him. Chuck and Devin attempted to arrest him for the murder of Ivan, and that was when Dewayne tried to shoot them too. Unfortunately, Dewayne was killed. "So, we brought them both into town. I am sorry about your friend. It happened most unexpectedly," he said quite honestly.

"How'd this Dewayne know about the money

anyway?" Pete asked.

The Sheriff shrugged. "I'm not sure. It's possible he was part of Dallen's gang."

"That should be easy to find out," Matt said and went to the jail cell and pulled John up and forced him over to the sheriff's desk and sat him down in a chair. "John, I know it was you who killed Mister Eckman. It won't do you any good to deny it. You probably heard me talking earlier, right?"

John nodded. "I heard."

"Good. Let me ask, did you lead that gang during the robbery?"

John glared up at Matt. "I said I heard, but you have to prove it was me!"

"Okay," Matt said and grabbed the hair on the back of John's head and jerked his head back and grabbed John's nose and began squeezing his broken nose. John tried to fight him, but the pain of Matt's grip was too much to bear. "Did you lead that gang, John?" he shouted.

John screamed. "Yes! Let me go! Please!"

"Yes, what?" Matt yelled and pinched his nose harder.

John screamed, "I led the gang! Yes, it was me!"

"Who else was with you?"

"Stop! Please stop! Okay, I'll tell you!" John cried out desperately.

"Let him go!" Chuck yelled and stepped around the desk quickly to grab Matt and break his grip on John. Troy joined him, and they pulled Matt off John and pushed him away from the chair John sat in. "Don't touch my friend again!" Chuck yelled over Troy's threats.

Matt shoved the Sheriff back. "Back off! I'm questioning my prisoner! If you don't like it, leave!"

"It's my jail! And he's my friend."

John smirked as he took a painful breath. "Dallen and the other three men. And Dewayne as well. He was the shooter in the trees," he said as he bent over, holding his face to ease the pain. "That's who was with me."

Chuck acted surprised. "What?" he yelled, stunned. "John, I can't believe you could do something like that! I would have hung you myself if I had known that! I have stood by you through thick and thin, and this is how you represent the law we swore to defend? I am appalled!" He sat back down at his desk, shaking his head. "I am just sickened!" He motioned for Troy. "Throw him back in jail."

"I'm sure you are," Matt said, sounding more sarcastic than not.

Chuck looked up at him. "What?"

"Sickened."

"What's that supposed to mean?"

"Nothing. Did you ever find that girl you were looking for? Or are we going find her dead out in the brush somewhere?"

Chuck glared at Matt, refusing to answer the question. It was Deputy Charles Hubbard who spoke calmly, "No, Marshal, we never did find her. She's Dallen's daughter and is a bit upset right now. I'm sure she's safe somewhere and hiding out until she calms down."

"That would be a nice thought, because if she

ends up dead, then I'm going to think something isn't right here. Too many people are dying, and they all seem to have one thing in common, you gentlemen."

Troy spoke coldly, "That's a funny statement coming from you. You've killed more people than anyone I know of. People don't want to go to jail; you should know that."

"I do know that. But I've arrested far more than I've shot. We now have five bodies since I arrived here and not one arrest. But you never had a single suspect until I arrived. And now five suspects are dead and one Pinkerton. I think that's a little suspicious. Wouldn't you think so, Sheriff?"

"We never had the information we needed until you told us," Chuck said irritably. "And I am offended, no, I'm insulted that you would have the audacity even to think we were covering up a crime that was so horrible and needless. Now, I'll admit, I'm ...shocked one of my deputies may have had a part in that! I'm embarrassed by that and John can stay in jail! But do not accuse me of being a part of it, Matt! I'm telling you now, you're barking up the wrong tree, and I won't put up with it! If you have any evidence that I'm guilty in any way, please lay it on the table. Otherwise, shut the hell up!" he spat out angrily.

Matt nodded slightly. "Okay." He turned to Pete Logan. "Pete, do you have any questions for the Sheriff before I leave?"

Pete asked one question, "Why did that man shoot Ivan?"

Chuck widened his eyes as he shrugged exaggeratedly. "Because he was a Pinkerton is my guess. It must have scared him; I don't know. And we didn't wait around to ask."

Pete nodded. "You didn't ask him why he shot a man he didn't know?"

Chuck shook his head. "No. We didn't have time! He turned his gun on us, and we had to shoot him."

"How many shots did he fire at you?"

"It happened so fast I didn't count. One, two, maybe three."

"He isn't wearing a gun belt. Where is his gun?"

Chuck's eyes widened just a touch before he sighed heavily. "He wasn't wearing one. He had a revolver in his hand."

Pete nodded. "So, Ivan turned his back on a man that held a gun in his hand?" he asked carefully.

"Yes. Detective, you can question me all night if you want to, but the fact is Dewayne showed no hostile signs while we were talking to him. None of us suspected or imagined he'd do what he did. It was an absolute unexpected action that left your friend dead, and ours too ultimately. What's done is done, okay?"

Pete rubbed the scab on his lip slightly. "I suggest you take your men and go find that money and Misses Eckman's jewelry now that you know about where it is."

Chuck shook his head with frustration. "Sure, we'll go try to find it. You're welcome to come along if you want."

Pete shook his head. "No, just find it and get

it back to me or like the Marshal, I'll be sticking around until I find it myself."

Matt said, "I'm going back to the hotel. But before I go, I have one question."

Chuck sighed. "What?"

"If this Dewayne shot Ivan and then turned around to start shooting at you. At what point did he offer to split the money with you?"

"What?" Chuck asked with a grimace on his face. "He asked before he shot Ivan."

Matt frowned in thought. "So, he asked if you all wanted to share the money. You all said 'no.' Then he shot Ivan and shot towards you without hesitation at close range and missed?"

"Luckily so, yes."

"Very lucky, indeed. That means those three men in the coffins, Dallen and now Dewayne all shot at you at close range, and not one of you got hit, right?"

"Correct. Believe it or not."

Matt smirked as he looked at the Sheriff. "I don't. But that doesn't mean it didn't happen that way. People are strange and unpredictable sometimes." He paused to point at John. "Keep him in jail. I will talk to you later. Pete, are you done for now?"

Pete nodded. He pointed at the sheriff. "Find that money and jewelry. That's a warning!"

As Matt and Pete left the building, Matt asked, "Do you believe him?"

"No. Do you?"

Matt shook his head. "No. He's lying. But we have to prove it before we can move any further along. Come on up to my room for a minute. I have something to show you."

20

Dane Dielschneider peeked in the front window of the Grand Lincoln Hotel and couldn't see either Claudia or Harry Richmond at the front counter. The door to their home was closed, so Dane slipped inside and went behind the counter. He looked at the guest registry and saw Matt was staying in room number two. Ivan Petoskey was in room one, Pete Logan was in room three. William Fasana was staying in room number four. The other four rooms were empty. Dane pulled out his jackknife and manipulated the lock that held the key drawer closed. He opened it and took one of the two keys to room number eight. Dane closed the drawer and went back around the counter to the foyer and walked quietly up the stairs. He paused in front of room number two for a moment. He listened through the door keyhole but couldn't hear anything. He moved down the hallway to room eight, unlocked the door, and stepped inside.

He had been in all the rooms before. It was not

the first time he had snuck into the hotel and taken a key or two to search through the guest's things. Dane had stayed in the hotel for five consecutive days once before the Richmond's discovered him. That particular time was during the Independence Day Celebration, and he was found only because someone rented the room he was staying in. Dane was a thief and a very good one. He was small enough to squeeze through small spaces, limber enough to climb the sides of buildings if it was at all possible and smart enough to know when and when not to enter a home or business. He had been in many of the homes and businesses in and around Prairieville. Most of the time, no one even knew he was ever there.

He heard someone walking up the stairs and opened his room door just enough to hear clearly. He heard one knock on Matt's door, and it was unlocked and opened from someone inside. William stepped into the room and closed the door behind him. Dane smiled. He had been watching the fight outside when a slight movement caught his attention from the corner of his eye. He watched the window of Matt's room and saw the slight moving of the curtain and the slightest glimpse of Tiffany as she peeked out the window to see who was screaming in pain during the fight. No one else apparently saw her, but he did. Now it was up to him to take her out of the hotel and back to his brother Chuck's office ideally, but with the Marshal and the other Pinkerton there, he would have to take her back to Danetta's. He couldn't take her out of the room with Matt's cousin there though; so, he would wait. He would wait for as long as it took for Tiffany to be alone again.

Dane didn't carry a gun; guns were bulky and inconvenient for a man of his profession. Dane preferred slender agility, silence, and a knife that he carried at all times. It wasn't a long knife; it was a simple three-inch blade jackknife that he kept folded in his pocket. It had two blades, one was short and had been filed down to use for locks. The other blade was three inches of thicker steel sharpened to a near razor's edge. He wasn't worried about what anyone would say to him if he forced Tiffany out of the hotel and down the street because she had stabbed Danetta and was wanted by the law. Dane wasn't a deputy or a lawman of any kind, but everyone knew who his family members were. No one would question his authority or stop him, without facing the wrath of his brothers, other deputies, or his friends, who all watched out for him. Dane had no fears, except for being caught by either Matt, his cousin or the only surviving Pinkerton so far.

Within half an hour, the door opened, and he heard William tell Tiffany he'd be back in a few minutes. Dane peeked out the door and watched William's long blonde wavy hair descent the stairs and heard the front door opening and closing behind him. Dane moved quickly down the hall and paused in front of Matt's door. He knocked one time just as William had.

The door unlocked, and it opened just a touch. "What did you forget?" Tiffany was saying with her back turned towards the door as she walked back over to a chair to continue to read the Bible.

Dane stepped in and closed the door behind him. He giggled with a soft eerie tone. "Hi, Tiff."

She spun around in terror and screamed in reaction to seeing him in her room with his uncanny grin. His dark eyes roamed over her like a man buying a horse. He seemed to be looking at everything all at once and approving of the stock he had found.

He moved quickly to her with his jackknife in his hand. "Shut up!" He sneered under his breath and went to grab her and accidentally stabbed her in the arm.

She cried out in pain mixed with the fear she had as well.

"Oh! Oh no! I'm sorry, Tiffany! I didn't mean to cut you," he said anxiously, as he looked with concern at the blood coming through the dress sleeve of her upper arm.

"Get out!" she yelled through her tears. "Get out of here!"

"Shut up!" he sneered through a wicked grimace that had taken over his face. He brought the knife up to her cheek. "I will cut you where you can never hide the scar! Now sit still and shut up! If you scream again, I'll split your cheek wide open."

She covered her face with her hands and began to weep quietly. She had been found, and the consequences she would face by the Dielschneider's would be painful and severe. She spoke softly through her quivering bottom lip, "Dane, please, don't tell anyone where I am. Please! If you ever liked me at all, then please help me. Danetta's going to kill me, Dane."

Dane smirked as he looked at her. He spoke with his unnatural monotone, soft emotionless voice, "You never wanted to be my friend before. So why should I care about you now?"

"Dane, please!" she begged. "Danetta is going to kill me, and so is Chuck. Will you please just let me go? You're the only one I can ask to help me. Please, Dane. I'll do anything, don't tell them where I am."

Dane's grin slowly spread to a smile. "Are you going to marry me?"

"What?" she asked horrified.

"Let's go get married right now, and they won't hurt you because you'll be family."

"No!" she said shaking her head. "Please, just leave me be, and don't tell anyone I'm here, please."

Dane closed his eyes as he spoke more aggressively, "Danetta, said a few months ago that when you came of age, she'd make you marry me. Now your father's dead, so you're of age! You're going to marry me whether you like it or not! Danetta and Chuck will force you to. So, you either marry me today or I'll tell them where you are! And I'll go get them right now." He turned towards the door to leave.

"Wait!" she called out suddenly. "What if you can't protect me from them? Danetta hates me." Tiffany knew William had gone down to the privy for a bit and would be back in a short time. If she could keep Dane talking for a few minutes more, she knew William would come back and save her from Dane.

Dane smiled softly and knelt in front of her. "I know they wouldn't hurt you because you'd be my wife. Danetta will love having you as a sister. We'd be family, and in the Dielschneider family, family comes first. Now, get your boots on and let's go see the Reverend."

"I always wanted a big wedding. You know, with lots of guests and a pretty dress."

Dane's voice became a touch harder, "Get your boots on. We have to go."

"Where would we live?" she asked to take up more time.

"Where I live now. I have my own bed. After today we will... have a bed," he said slowly with his uncanny grin. He looked at her like she was the greatest joy of his life.

Tiffany said a silent prayer for William to hurry up and return. "You never even said you loved me or anything. How can you expect our marriage to be a happy one if you can't say that at least once before we get married?"

Dane's head tilted to the left slowly. "I love you, Tiffany. I always have. That's why I asked Danetta if I could marry you before Chuck does."

Tiffany grimaced with repulsion. "Chuck's an old man! I wouldn't marry him."

"He's only fifteen years older than me, and I'm Twenty-Seven. That's not too old. Would you rather marry him or me, because we're your only two choices in town? Troy and Devin like other girls, but Chuck and I like you. Anyone else who likes you will be dead; I promise you that." He handed her boots to her. "Put those on, and let's go!"

He heard someone coming up the stairs and pointed at Tiffany with an intense expression on his face. "Don't say a word!" He looked quickly around the room and saw Matt's scabbard for his rifle leaning against the corner wall. He went to it and quickly pulled the rifle out of the scabbard and stood beside the door.

"Please don't shoot him! I won't marry you if you do," Tiffany said with a shaking voice with her nervousness showing in her eyes.

He put a finger over his lips with his dark eyes burning into her. There was one knock, and then one knock more. The doorknob turned, and the door opened.

William stepped in, saying, "I thought you locked the door...What's wron..."

Tiffany pointed behind him and began to yell when Dane slammed the butt of Matt's rifle into the back of William's head. William fell forward, reaching for his gun with one hand and the back of his head with the other. He hit the floor with his elbow and face landing on the foot of Tiffany's mattress on the floor. Blood was already seeping through his hair.

With a devilish grin, Dane raised the butt of the rifle and slammed it down again on the back of William's head. He collapsed on the mattress with blood spilling out of his head.

Tiffany screamed. Dane quickly aimed the rifle

at her. "Shut up! Put those boots on now!"

Petrified, she slipped her feet into her worn-out white leather boots that Claudia had given her to cover her feet. She began lacing them up through her compressed sobs.

Dane cursed and tossed the rifle down on Matt's bed. He reached over and grabbed her arm and roughly pulled her out of the chair towards the door. "Stop crying! You don't even know him. Wipe your eyes and be quiet as we're leaving. If you cause a scene, Chuck will find you before we get married, and then you're in trouble. It's best for you to marry me and be safe, at least. Come on," he said as he dragged her out the door with her boots still untied.

She looked back at William and saw that he was breathing even though the amount of blood soaking her mattress was considerable.

21

"Our job coming here, Marshal Bannister was to find the man who killed Louis and take care of him. Now my partner's dead, and so is the wrong man for killing Louis! And in my opinion, so is the wrong man for killing my partner. This town's corrupt, Marshal. I hope you know that," Pete said as a matter of fact. "We just have to prove it."

"Come upstairs, I believe I have the proof we're looking for," Matt said as they walked into the hotel. "But you do know I can't let you kill John Mattick without a trial. He was alive when I arrested him, and I expect him to be alive to face a jury."

"From what I know about you, you're not too opposed to private justice."

Matt smiled despite himself. "It has its moments. But since he's in jail, that's where he needs to stay. Here come on in," he said and put his key in the door. "Hmm, it's unlocked." He opened the door and seen William lying face down on the bottom part of the mattress. "William!" He went to him quickly and looked at the wounds on his head. "William, hey William," he said, turning him over. He looked up at Pete. "Go tell Claudia to fetch the doctor quickly. I don't know how bad he's hurt. William," he said, trying to wake William up again. Matt glanced around the room and seen his rifle lying on the bed and noticed Tiffany missing immediately. He grit his teeth as a wave of fury ran through him.

William moaned and reached for his head. "My head's pounding."

"I don't doubt it. You're going to need some stitches. Who hit you?"

"That little red Dielschneider. He was behind the door."

"How'd he get in?" Matt asked irritably.

"I don't know. All I know is my head hurts, and it didn't before he hit me." He closed his eyes and laid on his side.

"Do you have any idea where he took her?"

William opened his eyes and looked around the room for Tiffany. "No. But give me a few minutes, and I'll help track Red down."

"You stay here and wait for the doctor. Pete and I will go find him and bring her back."

"Well…" William said as he sat up and leaned against Matt's bed. "Save him for me, would you?"

"You bet, I will."

Pete entered the room. "That sounds like personal justice to me, Matt."

William looked at him and then closed his eyes to keep his head from spinning. "That, it is, Pete. And if he hit you, you'd want the same thing."

"Who hit you?"

"Little Red."

"A Dielschneider. It figures. Any reason why other than to kill you? I'm thinking they're trying to do us all in one at a time."

William pointed at Matt as he held his head.

Matt explained, "That girl they were looking for is Dallen Foster's daughter, Tiffany. She has been staying here since last night. Dane must've seen her or found her by accident. But we need to find her because she is our only evidence that the Sheriff is lying. Dallen was never at the robbery, and I doubt those other men were either. Her journal will prove she was with her Father the day it happened at his claim. We need to find her and do it aggressively. Do you want to help me?"

Pete smiled slightly. "Absolutely. What's she look like?"

"She'll be the only blonde fourteen-year-old girl scared to death with a Dielschneider."

"That should be easy enough to recognize."

"I appreciate your help; let's go find my young friend."

***

Dane held Tiffany's arm firmly as he guided her hurriedly towards the Christian Church two blocks off Main Street. He was taking her to the church for an impromptu wedding. There was no appointment with the minister, nor did Dane know if the minister was at the church. All he knew was he wanted to marry the attractive young lady, and he wanted to do it now before his older siblings got a hold of her. The people they passed on the street looked at them with concern but dared not interfere with the youngest Dielschneider brother forcefully guiding the young girl down the street. Her eyes were filled with dread, and her step was reluctant as he pulled her along the side street. The people just walked by with uncomfortable expressions and continued to mind their own business.

As they neared the church, Tiffany stopped walking and said, "Wait, I need to tie my boots. They're hurting my feet. You don't want me to have blisters on my feet on our honeymoon, do you?" she asked with a fake smile.

He chuckled. "No," he said softly with a grin on his face and excitement in his eyes that bordered on obsession. He let her arm go and allowed Tiffany to kneel to tie her boots. He looked around the street and fidgeted impatiently while he waited. "I can't believe we're getting married today. Tonight's gonna be our honeymoon," he snickered softly while his eyes opened a touch wider as he stared down at her.

She laced and tied one boot slowly while looking around for anyone who could help free her from Dane. She knew the Reverend wouldn't marry them, but she didn't want to endanger the Reverend or his family by placing him in the position to reject Dane's petition to marry her. She knew all too well that Dane would make the Reverend and his family's life's hell until his twisted sense of justice was paid. She stood up and turned towards Main Street and knelt back down to lace and tie her other boot slowly. She looked up and saw a man and woman turn off Main Street and begin walking towards them. She looked up at Dane with a slight innocent smile.

Dane continued to stare at her with his fixed excited grin and childlike excitement in his dark eyes. "Just think in nine months our baby will look like a strawberry roan. You know, with the mixture of our hair." He giggled awkwardly.

Tiffany's stomach stirred with disgust. "Yeah, they will." She said as she stood back up. "Well, shall we go get married?"

"Yeah. I don't have a ring handy, but I can get one. One of the most beautiful rings you've ever seen. We're going to be so happy, just you wait and see."

"I can't wait," she said while glancing behind her verifying that the couple was still walking about a block away from her. "I never knew you liked me so much, Dane. Maybe I'm lucky you found me first. Do you think the Reverend is there?"

"I hope so. If not, we'll find him."

"Watch out! Snake!" She yelled urgently.

He screamed a high pitch shriek and jumped back with fright. He let go of her while putting his attention on the ground in front of him, looking for a snake.

Tiffany pushed him down as hard as she could and began running back towards the couple, walking towards her from Main Street. She ran as fast as she could and heard Dane curse and begin to run after her. She could hear him gaining on her quickly, and she began to cry out for help. Dane grabbed her by the back of her dress and spun her around and threw her into the road. She rolled a few times on the cold ground and laid there to get her bearings after being tossed. She began to get up slowly when Dane grabbed her by the arm and jerked her up harshly. "What did you do that for? I'm trying to help you!" he yelled in her face with an enraged expression. His yellow uncleaned teeth gave a foul odor that she couldn't escape.

Tiffany's eyes widened in horror as she stared at the dangerous expression on his face. She had never seen anyone's eyes turn as black and evil as Dane's were. His snarl revealed a rage that he had kept buried, but it was rising quickly within him. His grip hurt her arm; there was no gentleness in his grasp at all. She had always thought Dane was a bit creepy, uncomfortable, and weird. But she had never feared him until now.

"Hey, leave her alone!" the man said, leaving his lady on the boardwalk along the road. He was an average-sized man dressed in a checkered suit with a wool overcoat with a derby hat. "Let her go!" he demanded.

Dane looked at the man and said through a demented grin, "I know who you are. You're the doctor!"

The doctor, Jonathon Jones, hesitated. "Yes, I am. Now, you let her go her own way. It doesn't look like she wants to go with you."

"Do you know who I am?" Dane asked, still holding onto Tiffany.

"One of the Sheriff's brothers. I don't know your name, but how about you let her go?"

Dane raised his voice in reply, "How about I ask the Crowe Brothers to burn your house down? We're getting married today, so mind your own business!"

"Help me!" Tiffany yelled and spun her free hand around to slap Dane's face. The stinging slap to his cheek caused him to let go of her arm and take a step back. Tiffany immediately began running towards Main Street.

A sound like a growl from deep within came from Dane's sinister sneer as his eyes grew wild like a mad man's. His hand slid into his pocket and pulled out his jackknife. He opened his three-inch blade and started after her. Doctor Jones grabbed him by the arm. "Hey! I told you to leave her alone!"

Dane immediately swung the sharp blade towards the arm that was holding him. The Doctor let go of him as the blade sliced through the material of his overcoat. Doctor Jones ripped his coat off to see his arm. With a sigh of relief, the blade had not touched his skin. "Did you see that?" He asked his wife in shock.

Tiffany ran as fast as she could along the road with Dane right behind her. She ran out into Main Street screaming and tripped over a wagon rut and fell hard to the ground skinning her palms as she fell face first. The tip of her chin was scraped by the uneven ground. There was still a crowd of men loitering around the businesses in town after the fight and the news of the Sheriff bringing in the two bodies. If her running out into the road and falling didn't draw their attention, then Dane reaching down to grab her arm with a knife in his other hand did.

"Get up!" he yelled viciously. "Come on, get up!" he yelled, letting go of his grip of Tiffany and then kicked her.

"Hell, yeah, Dane, get mad!" A young man with neck length black hair yelled with a laugh while he stepped out of the crowd of men. Others joined him as he walked closer to where Dane and Tiffany were. "Kick her again, bud!"

"Break that mare!" another young man laughed. He stood next to the other man with neck length black hair. They looked like they could be brothers.

Tiffany screamed in terror while a crowd gathered around her watching Dane kick her repeatedly. "I told you to get up! You're gonna slap me?" he asked bitterly and kicked her again. "I was trying to help you! Now get up and let's go!"

"No," she whimpered through her terrified sobs.

Dane kicked her in the face and then kneeled over her and grabbed her hair with one hand, and held with the knife in his other hand for her to see. "Marry me or die!" he hissed.

Matt Bannister fired a shot into the air and pointed his revolver at Dane. "Touch her again, and I'll kill you!" he sneered. "Back away from her now!" he yelled. His eyes showed his fury, and his heart pounded with anger.

Dane stared at Matt, surprised at first, and his enraged expression softened to his normal unthreatening, odd grin. He closed his knife and spoke softly, "We're getting married. We're just having a pre-wedding quarrel. It's okay; you can leave."

The two men who had encouraged Dane laughed. "Yeah, Marshal, you can leave. Dane's just proposing." The man laughed along with his brother.

Dane had let go of her hair but remained kneeled on one knee over her as she laid on the ground sobbing. Matt stepped forward and kicked Dane in the face forcing him off her. He landed on his back and looked up at Matt as he wiped a bit of blood from under his nose.

"I said back away from her! And you better stay away from her!" Matt shouted. Tiffany got up quickly went to wrap her arms comfortingly around Matt.

Dane spoke in a threatening tone, "If you're smart, you'll give her back. We were on our way to get married, and you can't stop us."

Matt grimaced. "Your crazy engagement's over. Go home or do whatever you do but leave her alone." He gently guided Tiffany behind him and then put his left arm out and backed up slowly to guide her away from the crowd of men in case any of the men in the crowd attempted to grab her. He knew the Sheriff had set a twenty-dollar bounty for whoever brought her in. Technically she was rightfully wanted by the local law, and that knowledge made Matt more cautious and ready for any attempt to grab her. He was comforted, knowing Pete Logan stood near him with his hand near his exposed revolver.

Dane stood up and said in a raised voice with his anger was taking over. "You better hand her over before I have the Crowe Brothers make you disappear! And they will if I or my brother's ask them to!"

"Don't bring us into this!" the black-haired man who had encouraged Dane to keep kicking Tiffany said quickly. He held up his palms towards Matt and shook his head with a grin.

Matt raised his eyebrows with interest as he looked at the two men with black hair who had encouraged Dane to hit her. "I wasn't aware you all were so closely associated with the Crowe Brothers. That's nice to know," he said while looking at the two Crowe Brothers. He looked back at Dane. "Listen up, Little Red, if I ever catch you near my hotel room again, I won't give you a chance to say you're sorry. Do you hear me?" he asked pointedly with his eyes burning into him.

Devin Dielschneider pushed his way through the crowd, with his eyes glaring at Matt. He stepped in front of Dane, coming face to face to Matt. "Sorry for what, Marshal? If you think you and your damn cousin can come in here and harass my little brother, you're dead wrong! I don't care who you are; this is our town. And we won't back off for anyone, not even you! His name's Dane, not Little Red, or anything else your possum faced cousin called him last night. Do you hear me?" he shouted. "Next time, I won't be warning you and your cousin!"

Matt narrowed his eyes irritably. "I'm talking to your brother, not you. If you want to interrupt and be a big man, that's fine. But I think your brother gets the point. If not, then he better be prepared to feel some pain."

Devin looked back at his younger brother. "Leave him alone, Dane. Don't even go near him from here on out." He looked back at Matt to continue speaking, but he was interrupted by Dane.

Dane said, "Tiffany and I are getting married. She said we would!"

"No, I didn't!" she yelled from hiding behind Matt.

Devin looked at Matt squarely. "Your business here is done. You need to go back to Branson now and mind your own affairs." He nodded towards Tiffany. "She needs to come with me, though; we have a warrant for her arrest."

Matt shook his head slightly. "Not a chance in hell."

Devin smirked slowly. "I suppose you're going to stay in the hotel forever and hide her from the law, Huh? She stabbed my sister in the stomach, which is attempted murder. Now I can go get my brothers, and we will forcefully take her from you, or you can hand her over to face the consequences of her actions."

Pete Logan spoke for the first time, "Deputy, you and your brothers might be something special here in Nowhere-Ville, but keep in mind your threatening a professional gunman who has faced far more dangerous men than you."

Devin shifted his eyes over to Pete and scoffed lightly. He looked back at Matt. "Don't say you weren't warned."

Matt raised his eyebrows. "I'll keep that in mind. Let your brothers know I'm taking John Mattick and Tiffany back to Branson for a fair trial. We'll be leaving tomorrow probably. I have a few more things to check out before I go, though."

Devin lowered his brow. "You're not taking them anywhere."

"Sure, I am. Unless you're going to stop me here and now?" Matt challenged intentionally.

Devin paused and looked at Matt strangely. He smirked and shook his head slightly. "I'll let my brother know. You can deal with him."

"I plan to."

"Good. Dane, let's go."

"What about Tiffany?"

"What about her, Dane?" Devin asked in a raised voice. "Get over here! Let's go." He helped his brother up and pushed him lightly towards the crowd of men. Devin slapped one of the long-haired young men in the stomach gently and nodded for him to follow him. Both young men with black hair followed Devin. Dane reluctantly stepped forward as he was pushed ahead. He was looking back towards Tiffany.

Matt glanced at Tiffany. "Are you alright? You have a bit of dirt on your chin." He wiped her scrape off with his finger.

She nodded with a slight torn smile between

gratitude and terror.

"Who were those two young men?

She wiped her eyes dry. "Bo and Lorenzo Crowe. They're awful too."

"How many Crowe Brothers are there?" Matt asked, curiously.

"Five or six. Their sister is the youngest, and she's nice. But her brothers are bad."

22

"We have a problem!" Devin said as he entered the sheriff's office with Dane and the two Crowe Brothers. "Matt Bannister says he's taking John and Tiffany back to Branson with him."

"What?" Chuck asked, looking up from his desk. "Did he find Tiffany?"

Devin rolled his eyes. "Your brother was going to marry her."

"Huh?"

Dane spoke uneasily, "We were going to get married when the marshal interfered."

Chuck narrowed his eyes, growing irritable. "What are you talking about? What's going on?" he asked Devin sharply.

"I don't know where Tiffany came from, but she's with the Marshal now." He motioned to Dane. "I caught Dane kicking her on the street saying they were going to get married. That's all I know. I got there when Matt kicked Dane in the face and threatened to hurt him. We exchanged a few words, and here we are."

Chuck looked at his youngest brother. "Where'd you find Tiffany?"

"The hotel. She was staying in the Marshal's room."

Chuck closed his eyes and sighed. "That means he lied; he knew where she was all along. I don't know what she may have told him, but I'm sure she told him Dallen was innocent." He cursed loudly. He stood up and walked over to the jail cell, where John laid on the bed, holding a cool rag over his broken nose. "This is your fault for killing that man! If you had just robbed him as I told you to do, we wouldn't be in this mess! But you had to make it personal!" He turned to his other deputies in the room. "Well, now what? Danetta murdered a Pinkerton Detective! Danetta chased Tiffany into the arms of the Marshal, and Dane wants to marry her..." he paused and looked at his younger brother. "Why were you kicking her in the street? Were you bringing her here?"

Dane looked at his brother and slowly grinned and answered with a chuckle, "No."

"Dane, I am not in the mood for games. What were you doing with her?" he shouted.

"Getting married. Tiffany and me were going to get married so she wouldn't be arrested or get hurt by Danetta. She wanted to be part of the family. To-night would've been our honeymoon." He giggled awkwardly.

Troy Dielschneider laughed. "Dane, you wouldn't

know what to do anyway. You'd give her a little peck of a kiss on the cheek, and you'd think she was pregnant. You better let someone who's a man marry her for you. If she did wind up pregnant, I'd be suspicious and expect it to come out with black hair," he said, nodding toward Lorenzo Crowe. Lorenzo was the youngest of the Crowe brothers at twenty-two.

Lorenzo nodded. "Could happen."

Devin ignored the pointless chit chat and asked quickly, "Where was Matt's cousin? He wasn't anywhere around."

Dane's grin widened. "I killed him."

"What?" Chuck shouted with surprise . "How?"

"I hit him over the head with a rifle until he was dead. He was down and bleeding everywhere when Tiffany and I left." He giggled.

Chuck yelled, "What in the hell are you trying to do, start a war? They sent four men down here to investigate a robbery gone bad, and now two of the investigators are dead after we supposedly killed the robbers! You and Danetta are signing the warrants for our own hangings, you stupid damn runt! Get out of my office before I throw your ass in jail! Get, Dane! How stupid can you be? For crying out loud!"

Dane looked hurt by his brother's words. He spoke softly, "I had no choice; he wouldn't let me take Tiffany."

Chuck's face hardened, and he stepped forward and grabbed Dane by the coat collar and shook him. He slapped his face with his right hand. "Wake up,

Dane! Tiffany would never marry you! Never! She was lying to you! I'm assuming that's why you were kicking her, right? She will never marry you! How would you support her anyway? Stealing pocket-knives?" He let go of Dane and pushed him towards the door. "Get out of here. Go home and clean the house or something."

Dane's eyes filled with water but refused to fall. "She said she would."

"Get out of here before I tear your head off!" Chuck yelled furiously.

Dane glared at his brother for a few seconds and then turned around and left the office.

Deputy Rocky Culp spoke while shaking his head, "Good riddance. I hate to say it, Chuck, but your little brother gives me the heebie-jeebies."

Devin pointed his finger at Rocky. "Don't you ever say that again! He's a good kid with a good heart! I am tired of you all putting him down. Did you all know the Marshal and his damn cousin were making fun of him for having red hair? His cousin told him he should get a job in a freak show. And I don't think it's funny!" He spat out at Charles Hammond, who was trying to hide his laughter. "And you," he directed his attention to his brother, Chuck. "You have no business treating him like that! He's your brother. You treat your friends better than your own little brother. You just tore his world apart. Dane doesn't live in reality, and we all know it, but that's no reason to threaten to hurt him! He looks up to you, Chuck!"

Chuck looked harshly at Devin. "I don't care.

What I do care about is two of the people coming here to investigate us being killed on the same damn day! When they're placing ropes around our necks, Dane's going to be standing in the crowd with his stupid grin, and what are you going to say then? 'Well, at least we didn't hurt his precious feelings, Chuck?' Piss on that! He can either grow up or go cry somewhere, but not around me. You need to quit babying him, Devin. Maybe that's his problem; you're always coming to his rescue like a knight in shining armor. Let him experience some bruises in life, and it will toughen him up."

Devin waved Chuck off. "I'm going after Dane before he causes a scene. Someone's got to go calm him down." He left the office irritated.

"He'll get over it," Troy said simply. "Now what about the Marshal and the other detective? Dare I say we finish them off and dump their bodies in the woods?"

"No," Chuck said with a heavy sigh and sat back down behind his desk. "John's not going to tell them anything. And we can make up an alibi for him here in town. We can use our brains and win this battle; we don't need to kill anyone else. So, start talking, boys. We need a solid alibi for John on that day. And Tiffany?" he paused. "Well, she is just a kid still, herself. What she says is emotional babble. And I'm sure we can persuade Danetta to swear Tiffany is a liar and has a history of violence. We can have her locked up in the institution for the insane. Yeah," he said slowly. "I think we can do this and stay in the good graces of the Marshal and the Pinkerton."

"You forget one thing," Charles Hammond said, "He knows your brother killed his cousin. And if he doesn't, he will when he finds his cousin dead."

Chuck looked at him and cursed. He looked at Troy and paused. "What do you think?"

Troy shrugged. "I already told you. But if you arrested Dane and handed him over to the Marshal, it would show your honest intentions. That might negate any suspicion about anything else. The court of law would let him go with our encouraging the jury. You boys will help, wouldn't you?" he asked Bo Crowe.

Bo nodded. "In a heartbeat."

John spoke from the jail cell. " Dane would tell Matt all the things you are doing and have done. Matt will get it out of him. Your brother isn't the smartest pup of the litter. All Matt has to do is offer him a shiny bright frosted cake or his grandfather's pocketknife that I had, and Dane will talk like an excited child. I hate to say it, but you'd be safer if you took him out of the equation altogether. As they say, dead men tell no tales."

Chuck looked at John, laying on the cot with his nose covered. "That's something to think about, John. But he's our brother, and family comes first. Doesn't it, Troy?"

Troy stared his brother with a hardened expression and then smirked just slightly. "It's something we could think about, but he has never said anything before. He's never been a problem. The problem is at the hotel."

23

Matt glanced at Tiffany and couldn't help but to smile to himself as he saddled his strawberry roan mare, named Betty. They were going to be riding in the cold of a November evening, and she needed to be dressed warmly. She had come to the hotel in a light dress and no coat or shoes on her feet. She had been given a pair of high lace-up white leather boots from Claudia the evening she came to the hotel to keep her feet covered at least. For tonight's ride, she borrowed a pair of red and black check-ered trousers from Harry Richmond that were far too baggy even with the suspenders that were over a tattered green sweater that had seen better days years ago, also borrowed from Harry. Knowing those alone would not keep her warm enough, she borrowed William's black bear coat, which was too long and heavy for her to wear comfortably, but it would keep her warm. The hood, which had the bears face sown onto the top of it, covered her whole head, so only her chin showed underneath it. She looked a bit ridiculous, but the horrible ensemble was secondary to its need at hand as Matt wanted to see her father's claim and see if there was any evidence to back up the Sheriff's story.

Matt glanced at her again with a smile. "It's probably the Lord's providence that you're wearing white boots, or you'd be mistaken for a bear. I'll bet if you wanted to have some fun, you could crawl into the schoolhouse tomorrow on your hands and knees and scare a few kids. Maybe a teacher too."

She pulled the hood back with a slight grin. "That's mean. I'd scare those kids half to death."

"Maybe, but then you could say it was a lesson on bear safety. If the kids think you're scary, tell them not to go berry picking alone in the woods," he said with a wink. "Some of their parents might want to tan your bare hide, but until then, it might be fun."

She laughed lightly. "You sound like you might have been a naughty boy as a child, were you?"

He chuckled. "I got into some trouble here and there. Maybe a little more than I should've sometimes. But I was always up for an adventure and a laugh when I was a kid."

"And now?"

He frowned slightly and set the saddle on William's sorral mare named simply enough Ace. "I've had my fill of adventure and hope for more laughter to come along. Anyway, this is William's horse, Ace. She's a sweetheart, but a bit hardheaded at times. William doesn't ride her enough anymore to keep her from getting a wild idea occasionally. Do not let her get her way because she is going to test you to see if she can take control. Don't be surprised if she tries to wipe you off on a branch or start to buck a bit, but not so bad that I don't think you can't handle it. You're a horse girl, I can tell by the boots." He smiled.

"Ha...Ha...Ha," she said sarcastically.

"Seriously, just don't let her get her way stopping to graze or turning back towards the stable, and you should be fine. Everything starts with small things, right? Don't be afraid to use the reins on her, either. If she gets too rambunctious, we'll trade seats. Okay?"

"I don't think we'll have problems. She's a beautiful girl. Aren't you?" she asked Ace while she held her hand out for Ace to nuzzle. She then pet her neck softly. "I think we'll get along fine, what do you think, Ace? You're such a beautiful girl," she said, admiring William's mare.

"Well, hop on her and let's go before it gets dark."

They rode three miles outside of town to Dallen's claim on Happy Jack Creek. It was eerily silent except for the sound of the water flowing over the rocks. Matt hitched Betty to a tree and began looking over the ground for three patches of blood. According to the Sheriff, Dallen, Ivan, and the man who shot Ivan, Dewayne were all shot and killed on this claim. The wound on Ivan Petoskey was a close-range shot to the back of his head. The bullet exited through his face, which meant there should be a large patch of blood on the ground and quite possibly brain and bone fragments as well. There should've been blood almost everywhere with as much killing that supposedly happened there. Matt looked over a wide area and after forty minutes of looking, had only found one blood trail of droplets and a small pooling of dried blood near the water. It proved Dallen had been killed here, but there was absolutely no trace of a second or third murder taking place there that morning. Not a drop of blood from another body was found anywhere. He went back to the main camp where Dallen had his fire pit, tools, and stick-built shanty covered with a tarp to keep dry when a downpour of hard rain fell. Matt found Tiffany sitting on a log, watching the river with tears flowing down her cheek. Matt sat down beside her and put his arm around her comfortingly. He didn't need to say a thing; she leaned her head on his shoulder and began sobbing. He held her softly and let her weep. He noticed she was holding a flat river rock with two drops of dried blood on it.

She wiped her nose with the arm of the coat and wiped her eyes. "The last time I was here, my Pa and I sat right here talking. He asked me to try harder to get along with Danetta. That's when I first told him she beat me, threatened me, and showed him my bruises. He was so mad. He went home and threatened to kick her out if she ever did that again."

"And did she?"

She nodded. "She was nice for a few days. She threatened to pour boiling water on me yesterday. She was beating me with a belt buckle when I stabbed her with my pen. My Pa got me that pen for my writing and drawings for Christmas."

Matt took a deep breath. It angered him that anyone would treat a child like Danetta had. Any child that suffered at the hands of an adult was something Matt had a very hard time trying to understand. Spanking a child to correct them was one thing, but physically abusing a child was as dangerous and wrong as any other physical crime Matt had ever seen. Children were supposed to be loved, not hurt, tortured, and terrified by those who were supposed to love them.

"I'd like to get my pen and some other things of mine back before you go back to Branson," she asked more than stated. "Will you go there with me? I know you and William are leaving tomorrow."

Matt nodded. "Then let's go get your things."

"Danetta's going to be really mad at me."

Matt smiled comfortingly. "That doesn't matter. I'll be there, and she won't touch you. Are you up to it?"

She nodded. "What am I going to do when you're gone? Can you teach me how to punch her in the face?" she asked sincerely.

"Make a fist. Let's see what you got there."

She made a fist and held it out towards Matt. Her thumb was inside of her cliched fingers.

"No. You'll break your thumb like that. You make a fist like this. See? Now, your thumb is safe. You hit with these two knuckles. Like this." Matt touched the knuckles of her index and middle fingers. "She's probably taller than you are, so let me teach you a right cross to the jaw first. If you do it right, it might be all you need to lay her out or even break her jaw."

"You mean I can punch her?"

He looked at her sincerely as his eyes watered just a bit. "I will leave that completely up to you. You need to know how to hit so you don't hurt your hand and inflict as much pain as you can. And remember to put your weight into it by shifting your weight on your feet."

"I only weigh a hundred and twenty pounds. She's like two hundred and fifty or more!"

Matt smiled. He reached down and picked a fist-sized rock. "This rock weighs about five pounds. Can I drop it on your toe?"

"No!"

"Why not? It's only five-pounds, and you're a hundred and twenty pounds. Let me drop it on your toe."

"No! It'll break my toe."

Matt smiled. "Exactly. And your fist with a hundred and twenty pounds behind it can do the same thing to her or me, or anyone else no matter how big they are if you hit the right way and put your weight behind it. Let's practice a bit."

She smiled slightly. "I think your children are lucky to have a father like you. Do you have children, Matt?" she asked as she stood up.

Matt paused and frowned. "I have a son."

"How old is he?"

"He's Sixteen now."

"Wow, he's my age. Does he look like you?"

Matt nodded slowly. "He does a bit."

"What's his name?"

"Gabriel."

"Did you teach him how to fight too? I bet you did, huh?"

Matt smiled, sadly. "No. I'm afraid I haven't taught him much at all. He a…" he paused.

"He what?" she asked sincerely.

Matt sat back down on the log. "He doesn't know I'm his father. It's a long story, but I didn't know I had a son until I came back here a year ago. He has no idea I'm his father."

Tiffany sat down beside him. "Are you going to tell him?"

Matt shook his head. "No. His mother and I agreed to leave things as they are. He was raised by a good man who loves him like his own. I don't want to interfere with their home."

"So, the only son you have doesn't know you're his Pa? How sad. Have you met him?"

Matt nodded. "He's a great young man."

"Do you love him?"

He smiled slightly. "Very much." He looked at her. "You'll never know how much you can love someone until you have a child. I love him very much, and I didn't even know he existed. And I have no part of his life. Maybe someday that'll change, but for now, it is what it is. Anyway, let's teach you how to hit and some quick basics and then go get your stuff."

24

They rode to the edge of town and paused their horses in front of the narrow weathered clapboard home that looked to be in disrepair. Matt stepped out of the saddle and watched Tiffany sit nervously on Ace. She had a few moments of arguing with Ace earlier in the afternoon, but she was quick to whip the split reigns across Ace's rump and jerk the bridle to let Ace know she was in control. Ace wasn't giving up quite yet though, she tried to brush Tiffany off against a tree and bucked a few times when that failed. Tiffany, to her credit, stayed on with the help of the saddle horn. She had braved riding Ace and done well, but now she appeared too scared to step out of the saddle as she looked at the house and the smoke rising from the stove pipe.

"Are you all right?" Matt asked.

She nodded nervously.

"Then let's go. It's going to get dark pretty soon."

"Okay." She stepped out of the saddle and tied the reigns to a questionable hitching post at best.

"I'm scared," she said with her anxiety showing in her eyes.

"What's the worst she could do, yell? I'll be with you, Tiffany. Let's go get your things and get out of here," Matt said and stepped towards the door. He stopped and put out his hand out quickly to stop her. "Wait right here," he said. On the ground, there were thick droplets of dried blood. The trail led around the house towards the back. He followed the blood trail to the barn door. He could see where a body had been dragged out of the barn, and someone tried to kick dirt over the thick trail the blood left behind. Matt entered the barn with his gun's hammer un-thonged. He found a large pool of blood behind a room used to store the saddle and other tools. On the wall of the room was a bullet hole surrounded by the spattering of blood.

Matt exhaled. He had found where Ivan was executed. He bet if he were to ride out to Dewayne's house, he would find a similar scene. It was murder upon murder upon murder to cover one's own sins. The evidence was lining up, and soon he would face the head of the snake.

His thoughts were interrupted by the sound of Tiffany screaming and the sound of a heavy bump against the wall inside of the house. Matt ran out of the barn to the front of the house. Tiffany had gone inside without him. She was being attacked by the sound of her screaming for help, and the loud, deep voice of an enraged woman could be heard outside. Matt opened the door and stepped in to see a large red-headed woman holding Tiffany down on the floor while hitting her.

"I'll kill you!" the woman seethed between her teeth as she hit Tiffany. Beyond the woman, two young girls, both with red hair watched helplessly with tears streaming down their young faces in horror.

Matt grabbed Danetta by her shoulders and yanked her off Tiffany. . Danetta rolled to an abrupt stop and looked up in a fury at Matt. He pointed at her with his inflamed eyes and shouted, "Stay there!" He looked at Tiffany, who was crying from the beating she had taken. Her face was bleeding from her lip and a small cut above her eye. Matt helped her up. "Go get your things ."

She wiped the blood off her fattened lip and hugged Matt as she wept. He looked back harshly at Danetta as she began to laugh.

Danetta shook her head in disgust with a laugh. "So, you finally found another sucker to fall for your tears, huh?" Danetta stood up. "Fine, get your things and get out of here. Go!" She yelled at Tiffany and then looked at Matt with a slight smirk, "Well, Mister, where did you find her anyway in the gutter where she belongs, or was she begging like a two-bit whore? Never mind. My brother's will take care of you soon enough for throwing me around. Do you have a name I can give them, or are you just brave enough to push women around?"

Matt broke from Tiffany's hug and stepped towards Danetta. "I'm Matt Bannister and your'e coming with me," he said as he grabbed her upper arm tightly.

"Let me go! You're hurting me!" she said with a sudden panic to her voice. Her eyes revealed the fear that his name brought to her.

"Shut up!" Matt said irritably. "Tiffany, keep those girls in here!" He demanded and took Danetta out the door forcefully while her children began to cry in fear for their mother. Tiffany held them in her arms, trying to reassure them that everything would be okay.

"Where are you taking me?" Danetta asked nervously. "My brother's the Sheriff, and he'll kill you if you hurt me!"

"I said shut up!" he repeated as he led her towards the barn door. He took her inside and forced her to look at the wall where the bullet hole and blood spatter was. "Who shot Ivan?" he asked with a no nonsense look in his eyes.

"I...I don't know what you're talking about!"

"No?"

"No! I don't know what you're talking about! Now let me go, Please," she pleaded.

"Ma'am, I'll ask nicely one more time. Is this Ivan's blood?"

Her breathing grew heavy. . "No. Please let me go," she sounded like she was about to start to cry.

"Then whose is it?"

"I don't know! Dallen might've butchered a pig in here; I don't know!" she sounded afraid. He asked forcefully, "Who shot Ivan? You better tell me now!"

"Marshal Bannister, you better let me go before I tell my brothers your manhandling me."

"Ma'am," Matt said growing frustrated. "You can tell your brothers whatever you want, they don't frighten me. But I will tell you this, you better start talking before I get angry." He had dealt with many men over the years and wasn't afraid of getting physical to get the information he needed, but he had never had to be harsh with a woman before. He couldn't say he liked Danetta, but he refused to harm her in any way. He spoke sincerely, "Look at me, Ma'am, I have been very nice to you so far. Please, don't make me go any further. I'm giving you to the count of three to answer my question. Who shot Ivan? One! Two!"

"Okay!" she cried out in fear. She didn't know Matt Bannister, but she knew his reputation and it scared her. Very few men could intimidate her, but he had controlled her from the beginning. His presence exuded authority and the power in his eyes let her know he was not a man to trifle with.

"Who killed him? You better give me a name right now," he said staring into her eyes.

"Devin," she whispered. "Okay? It was Devin!" She said with a bitterness in her voice as she glared at Matt. "Now you got a name, you son of a ..." "

"Don't call me foul names, Miss! It's un-lady-like," he scolded. Now, why did Devin shoot him?"

She shook her head, anxiously. "I don't know."

"Yeah, you do. Tell me now, because I'm not playing with you!" His eyes were growing hard. It sent a chill down Danetta's spine.

207

She began to cry. "Please, don't hurt my brother. It was an accident. He didn't mean to shoot him. It was an accident..."

"And I'm sure killing Dallen was too, right? And those three other men? And the old man killed today to cover up for Devin! They're all accidents, right? Attacking Tiffany and threatening to kill her was an accident, too, huh? Ma'am, I don't believe a word you say! Let's go to the house; Tiffany has something she wants to say to you." He grabbed her upper arm and escorted her into the house. She was sobbing every step of the way. "Tiffany, we're back," he said as they entered the house.

Tiffany was hugging one of the younger girls. "See, I told you he wouldn't hurt your Mother."

"Are you ready to go? Do you have everything you wanted to get? Your journal?"

Tiffany nodded. She grabbed a pile of books and smaller things. The younger girls ran to their mother.

Danetta fell to her knees and hugged her daughters and began to sob.

Matt said, "Tiffany, do what you came over here to do. It's your turn."

"Now?" Tiffany asked in wonder as she watched Danetta sob like a whipped and broken child.

"If you want to."

Tiffany looked at the girls who were hugging their mother. She was shocked to see Danetta bawling like a child. It was strangely satisfying. Tiffany shook her head. An unexpected feeling of compassion had come over her. Whatever Matt had done to her had shaken her up so much that for the first time, Danetta's tears and sobbing were legitimate tears. "No. I just want to leave."

Matt knelt beside Danetta and looked at her. "Ma'am, I was always taught to be respectful of women. I was a bit irritated when I saw you hitting Tiffany so I apologize if I was a little rough. I hope I didn't bruise your arm."

Her face turned into a sharp grimace as her eyes turned cold as ice. She spat in his face. "Go to hell!" she shouted followed by a selection of bitter curses.

Matt wiped the spittle off his cheek with a slight chuckle. His eyes hardened as he said, "I'll let Devin know you said, hello." He finished wth a quick wink, and then stood up and turned to Tiffany. "Let's go."

They walked out the door as Danetta began wailing loudly.

25

Dane Dielschneider stood in the alley across from the hotel glaring at the dark window of room number two, wondering where Tiffany was. In his mind, thoughts ran rampant of Matt, holding her in the dark and thoughts of them getting married. Dane had fallen in love with Tiffany the very first time he saw her two years before. She was only twelve at the time, but she was the prettiest twelve-year-old he had ever seen. He knew right then and there that when she came of marrying age, they would be married. His siblings had teased him about it, but Tiffany was the only girl for him. He wouldn't let anyone steal her away from him, not anyone at all. He stepped back in the shadows as two horses rode by going towards the livery stable. He recognized Matt in his buffalo hide coat and felt a surge of anger rising within him when he heard Tiffany laughing as they rode by. She had never laughed like that for him

***

Dane followed them at a distance to the stable. He slipped through the door quietly and took a position kneeling behind a buggy kept inside out of the weather. He watched them talk to Jeffery McDonald, a stable employee who lived in a backroom behind the office to watch over the horses at night. They let Jeffery put the horses away in a stall, and Dane followed them back towards the hotel. Before they entered the front door of the hotel for the night, Dane could stand it no longer and run out in the street behind them. "Hello, Tiffany."

Matt and Tiffany turned around to see Dane staring at her with his eerily grin and penetrating eyes.

Dane continued before either could speak, "I want to apologize for earlier. I shouldn't have acted like that. Not to the girl I love. I still want to marry you if you want to get married tomorrow."

Tiffany shook her head in amazement. "No! Go away, Dane."

His smile faded. "But you said you would. You're not going back on your word, are you? A person should keep their promises," He said while raising his eyebrows pointedly. His voice though soft, revealed a threatening tone that seeped out.

"I'm not marrying you! You're disgusting. And it's crazy to think that I would. Get away from me and stay away from me!" She drew closer to Matt's side, unconsciously.

Dane's lips twisted, and his bottom lip quivered in rage. "That's a mistake," he said calmly. "Maybe you need to think about it. I know, let's get away from him and go for a walk. Come on, let's go." He reached forward and grabbed the sleeve of the bearskin coat. She jerked her arm away, and Matt put his hand out to create some distance between them.

"Go home, Dane. She doesn't want to talk to you," he said.

Dane glared at Matt with a murderous glare. "No one asked you! You better leave us alone. I won't let you have her!" He pulled out his knife with the three-inch blade and flicked his wrist to open it. "You should go on inside now and leave us alone!"

Matt's right fist struck hard and fast squarely on Dane's nose. He fell to his back, dropping the knife and holding his bleeding nose as he fell. Matt stepped towards him. "If you ever pull a knife on me again, I will shoot you! You're lucky I don't as it is. Get the hell out of here, and I don't want to see you again!"

Dane breathed heavily through his mouth as his eyes connected with Matt. "You're going to pay for that. She's mine, and she'll never be yours or anyone else's."

"No, she's not. And the sooner you realize that the less pain you're going to feel. Goodnight."

Dane watched Matt escort Tiffany into the hotel with a fire of hatred burned within him. The hotel door closed, and Dane stood up. "I'll show you!" he yelled. He stood in place and watched their hotel room window light up from the lantern being lit. He was breathing hard with fury, picked his knife up off the ground, and walked back towards the livery stable. "He stole my girl, let's see how he likes this!"

Dane didn't want to alert Jeffery McDonald to his arrival, so he couldn't go through the main entry doors because of the cowbell that rang when it opened. He entered the livery stable quietly by using his knife to unlock a wood-framed swinging door used as a window that was locked with a hook. He easily unlocked it and crawled through the window towards the back of the stable. He went from stall to stall, looking for Matt's horse. He knew Jeffery McDonald, was in his quarters behind the office. Dane stayed low and went towards the strawberry roan in a stall. Betty snorted and seemed uneasy as he drew near. To make sure Betty stayed quiet, he went to the grain barrel and got a scoop of grain and poured it in Betty's feed bin. When Betty went to the grain and began eating, Dane maneuvered to the side of the stall and pulled out his knife. He giggled with a wide grin on his face. "Now, we're going to be even."

26

Danetta Foster did her best to run but mostly walked as fast as she could to the Sheriff's Office, hoping to find her brothers there. She burst through the door just as Chuck and his men were getting ready to leave for the night. "Chuck! Oh, thank heavens, your still here!" She bent over hyperventilating as she began to sob.

"What?" Chuck asked with alarm jumping up from his chair. Danetta never was one to cry, and it was alarming to see her sobbing "What's wrong?" He grabbed her by the shoulders quickly to help her sit down. She was sobbing heavily and holding her side where she was stabbed the night before.

Troy Dielschneider looked at his brother Devin with concern as they both walked over to her. "For crying out loud, what is it?" he asked sharply, feeling some anxiousness.

She looked up at Devin and began sobbing again. "I'm…sorry, Devin."

Devin frowned. "Why? Did something happen

to Dane?" he asked worriedly.

She shook her head.

Chuck looked back at his deputy, Rocky Culp. "Get her some water." He addressed her, "What is going on?" he asked firmly.

She pointed at Devin. "Hide him."

"Why?" Chuck asked. He grew impatient. "Tell me what's going on? What are you crying about?" he asked sharply.

Troy kneeled beside her. "Danetta, talk to us."

She took a deep breath and wiped her eyes. She looked at Devin. "I told…" she began crying again. "I'm so sorry."

Chuck yelled, "Sorry for what? Stop crying and talk!"

"Here," Rocky said, handing her a cup of water.

She drank the water and took a few deep breaths. "I told Matt Bannister that Devin killed the Pinkerton, Ivan."

"You what?" Chuck yelled sharply. "Why would you do that?" He cursed a few times and stepped away to rub his thinning red hair. "What the hell were you thinking, Danetta? Do you think he's just going to ride back home? How stupid could you be?"

Devin sighed. "Great," he said lightly, shaking his head.

Troy stared at Danetta as he rubbed his braided goatee. "Why would you do that?" he asked in a calm voice but through narrowed eyes.

"I was scared! He hurt me! "

Troy looked at her with a growing angry expression. "He manhandled you?"

Danetta nodded. "He nearly broke my arm!" she lied. "I didn't mean to, but I was scared, and I just said Devin did it. It just came out! I'm so sorry! Chuck, you have to hide him. He'll be coming after Devin and all of you. He knows you killed all those men. Tiffany was with him. He knows Dallen, and the others were innocent." She began to cry. "I'm so sorry. I didn't want to tell him anything. I tried not to, but I was scared!"

"You better go see the doctor and and get your arm checked out. Did he say he was coming for Devin?" Chuck asked.

Danetta looked at him. " He just laughed and said he'd tell Devin hello for me. You have to kill him!"

Chuck took a deep breath. "We're running out of bodies to blame these killings on!" he cursed. "We don't have a choice. I'm not going to let him kill Devin." He walked across the room to think for a minute.

Troy stood up. "Well, we know where they'll be sleeping tonight. There's just two of them now that Matt's cousin's dead. Three or four of us should be able to do the job and be done with it."

Charles Hammond added, "A hooded adventure and no one will know it was us."

Troy shrugged. "And even if they do, they won't say anything."

Chuck turned around and looked at his brothers. "Okay. Charles, you, Rocky, Fred, and John wear your hoods and ambush them tonight. Dane, wherever he is, can get you inside quietly and find the room numbers, so you don't bust into the wrong rooms."

"Me?" John asked from the jail.

Chuck pointed at him and shouted, "Yes, you! This is all your damn fault to begin with! You and your personal vendetta! Well, now you get to finish it! I want you to kill Matt for making you look like a fool out there today. And he did!"

"What about you? Aren't you and your brothers going to fight too?" John asked bitterly.

Chuck shook his head. "No. I'm not risking my brothers. This is your mess, John! Clean it up."

Troy spoke to Chuck, "Let John out of jail, and I will be going too. If you think I'm going to miss an opportunity like this, you're crazy. If there was ever a time to put our family first and fight for our lives, it's now. I don't see how we can send our friends to fight our battle, Chuck. Matt manhandled our sister and Dane as well. Those are the two Ma always told us to look after. You, Devin, and I can all take care of ourselves. They can't. Matt's only a man. So am I. I'm going to kill him tonight and be done with this."

Devin spoke strongly, "Yeah, I'm not going to hide like a woman. If they want to fight it out, I'm all for it. He's coming after me after all. I won't surrender without a fight."

Chuck looked at Devin and sighed. "Gentlemen, you do understand Matt's not inexperienced. He's a dangerous man. I think we'd be darn lucky if we all got out of this alive. That's how much respect

I have for him. I don't know about the Pinkerton, Pete, but I know Matt is a hellcat to deal with. I've been reading about him for years, and no one's killed him yet."

"There's always a first time, huh?" Devin said with a shrug.

"Devin, I want you on the roof of the saloon across from the hotel. That will give you a straight shot across the street and the advantage in case they run."

Troy chuckled. " We don't need Devin across the street. Those two aren't coming out of the hotel alive. John, Devin, and I will make sure of that."

"What about the girl?" Charles asked.

Danetta spoke bitterly, "Kill her too!"

Chuck nodded in agreement. He spoke softly. "Yeah, kill her too."

"I've never killed a woman or a kid before," John said skeptically from inside the jail.

Chuck looked at his deputy harshly. "Yeah, you have, you just don't know it! How many fathers have you killed that had children waiting for them at home? What do you think that did to those wives and kids, huh? Don't play innocent with me, you hypocrite. You've killed a hell of a lot more than just the men you've shot. We've all destroyed homes and lives. So, don't go weak now when we have a job to do. Tiffany's got a big mouth and will only cause trouble later on. We don't spare wolf pups because they're cute, nor will we spare her. You all got it? We're going to massacre them and anyone else who gets in the way. We're fighting for our lives and what we have here."

Troy smirked. "I'd hate to be the one who kills Tiffany because Dane's going to make your life hell until he finds some other girl to be fixated on."

Chuck shook his head. "We'll order him a bride from Boston or somewhere."

Charles chuckled to himself. "Just make sure she's blind."

Devin glared at him. "I don't think you're funny at all. Dane can't help the way he looks any more than you can!"

Fred Johnson was the oldest and the quietest deputy of them all. He said little and was one of the most dependable of them all. He was an old outlaw who had done his share of crime throughout the west. As he aged, he had settled down with an ex-prostitute who had followed the gold to Prairieville and married Fred three years before. Since getting married Fred quit drinking and lived a quieter life. He sat at the large table with his feet kicked up on it. "Not to interrupt or anything, but if the Marshal's cousin was killed, why wouldn't he be asking about that instead of the Pinkerton? Your brother Dane isn't the brightest lad in the new land. I suggest we take his word with a grain of salt and be prepared for William Fasana too. He's no Matt Bannister, but he's no one to take lightly either. If you've ever heard of the Battle of Coffee Creek during the Snake War, you'll know the men who survived are a tough breed, and he was right there in the middle of it."

Troy shook his head. "Who cares? That was then; this is now."

Chuck spoke seriously, "Fred's right. William

might be alive."

Fred addressed Troy, "It means he might have more grit than all of you boys put together. Don't take him lightly."

Troy curled his lips and shook his head. "I doubt it."

"Boss," Fred said, "If I survive this, I think I'm gonna call it quits and take my misses out of this town where I can find some honest work. I'm getting too old for this stuff."

Chuck looked at his friend. He nodded slowly. "Okay."

Troy frowned. "That's what marriage will do to ya. It'll kill every once of manliness within you."

Fred smiled at his friend. "No. I've done my time and don't want to push it any further than I have to. The fact is, I'd rather not go with you at all tonight."

"I need you tonight, Fred. I won't ask anything more from you, though," Chuck said with a touch of disappointment in his voice.

Fred nodded.

A gunshot sounded from the other end of town. They all froze and listened to an eerie silence that followed. Devin's eyes widened with a frightful thought. "Dane!" he said and turned towards the door.

"Devin!" Chuck yelled, stopping him at the door. "I need you to stay here. If the Marshal's out there somewhere, we don't need a fight right now."

Devin looked at Chuck with disgust. "I'm going to look for Dane. Don't even try to stop me."

27

William shook his head as Matt explained to him and Pete what had happened that evening. The three men were standing in the hallway outside of their rooms. Pete Logan bit his lower lip in anger as he learned about the murder and cover-up of his friend, Ivan Petoskey. Matt continued, "We've been lied to this whole time by the Sheriff and his men. Like I said earlier, John was the one who killed Louis. Now we know Devin killed Ivan, and all the dead bodies they brought in were innocent men. Even her father." He nodded towards his room where Tiffany was. "And I'm sure their sister told them by now that we know."

William looked at Pete. "I came on this journey because I expected you and Ivan to be the enemy. I apologize for that if I was wrong. I liked Ivan. I wasn't expecting to be thrown into a war as such. But...what the hell, I came for the excitement."

Pete frowned. "You were about half right, William." He looked at Matt. "Ivan and I came here thinking we'd get even with you for killing our friend, Carnell. Divinity Eckman wired us from your own town to send you to South America with a thousand dollars apiece. In other words that we understood, she was offering us both a thousand dollars extra if we killed you. Don't worry," he said, holding up his hands. "I have no intention of doing that. You're a good man. Ivan and I both decided to let you be because occasionally, you find a man you wouldn't mind working for. Carnell was our boss and a friend, but you couldn't trust him. He'd turn on you like a snake if you messed up or if he was ordered to. I want you to know, I trust you more than I ever trusted him. I don't even know why, but I do. You can trust me. You both can. I'll fight side by side with you both."

"Thank you, Pete. Why would she want me killed?" Matt asked.

Pete took a deep breath. "Carnell and her had been having an affair for a long time. And when Louis was finally gone, and it looked like they could run the world together, you killed him. That's why."

"Do you think she'll continue to ask her people to do that? What about Sebastian? Was he in on that too?"

He shook his head. "Violence was never Sabastian's specialty. He's great at investigating and blackmail if necessary, but not violence. Those things were left to Ivan and me and a few other of my colleagues. I don't know what she'll want to do,

222

but I can tell you what I can do. I'll write an affidavit out for you if you want to charge her."

"You'd lose your job, wouldn't you?" Matt asked.

Pete nodded sadly. "Yeah. It's an odd thing; I see things in a different light here. Maybe it's because we're so far away from the city and I have time and the quietness to think. I see the people here and can't help but notice how friendly and content they are just to be here. Most of the people in town seem happy for the most part, and then you have people like the sheriff and his deputies who do nothing except terrorizing these simple people." He paused. "I've been watching you, Matt. You treat everyone you meet with the same respect that you'd give the Eckman's. Where I'm from, only the rich get treated that way. The poor can starve to death or live with rats, and the people I worked for didn't care. They treated people like the folks in town here, like dirt. They looked at them like they were fleas on a dog. The Eckman's said they were Christians and went to church and all of that, but I never," he paused. "I never thought anything about it until I met you. You're very different, and I would like to know why you are. I think if I lose my job, then maybe I can live with myself a little bit better then I am. All I do is hurt people. I've made a career out of being a paid strong man, collecter, thug, and assassin. Whatever Carnell wanted me to do, I did it. The same kinds of people you treat so well, I treated like street rats. I don't know what's going on with me, but coming here even for this short time has made me wonder if the money's worth it. I make a lot of money from beating people up and threatening folks. Then I met you, Matt. I've never experienced anything like this before, but you have a sense of peace about you that's so strong, I can feel it. I would like to know what that feels like because I have no idea. I have a hard time sleeping sometimes, and I know my Ma and Pa would be so ashamed of how I make my money. So, no, I don't care about losing my job. If you want me to write that affidavit, I will. It would guarantee she'd forget about you. She's a cold woman, but she's a coward when her reputation might be in trouble."

"Then it wouldn't hurt to have it, and we'll send it to the California Marshal's Office." Matt paused and looked at Pete thoughtfully. "That peace your talking about doesn't come from me. It comes from my relationship with Jesus. It's his peace that he gives to me, and he could give it to you too if you asked him to. We can do that right now if you'd like?"

Pete chuckled. "I don't know if I'm ready for that, Marshal."

"Well, when you are. Obviously, the Lord's knocking on the door of your heart. You have to choose to accept him or not."

"I'm afraid the Eckman's put a bad taste in my mouth for the whole Christian thing. It seems most of the so-called Christians I met acted like high and mighty saints until church was over, and then their drinks, women, deceiving, manipulating, and murdering nature came out. I'm not a religious man, but even I know they're hypocrites, each and every one."

Matt frowned slightly. "I don't think it's wise to judge a town by the first family you meet. The Eckman's or whoever else you may have known may have put on a show, but rest assured their day will come to give an account of their lives. And they might end up short. What they do should have no bearing on what you decide. In the end, it's just going to be you and God, one on one at the judgment seat. The Bible says, 'It's appointed for you once to die, and then the judgment.' You won't be able to blame anyone else for your decision to serve him or not."

There was a sudden ring of the bell as the hotel door opened and the sound of someone running up the stairs, "Matt!" a young man's voice yelled out. He reached the top of the stairs. It was the young man from the livery stable, Jeffery McDonald. He looked to be quite scared and in a panic. "You need to come to the stable. Someone hurt your horse. I went and got Bill, and we laid her down. But you need to go! I'm so sorry. I didn't hear anything, and I'm sorry."

Matt spoke loudly, "Tiffany, lock the door and don't open it for anyone." He hurried down the hall and past Jeffery. He ran out of the hotel and down the street to the livery stable. Inside he found the owner, Bill Bones, kneeling in front of Betty trying to comfort her. Bill stood up as Matt approached. "What's wrong with her?" he asked quickly.

"I'm sorry, Matt. Someone hamstrung your horse," he said with a strained voice. It was a combination of anger, disbelief, and shame all at once.

Betty neighed at his presence as Matt got down on his knees beside her and looked at her left hind leg. The hamstring tendon just above the knee had been sliced through with a knife. He felt his heart drop as did his head with a heavy sigh. He put his hand on her neck and closed his eyes. He bit his bottom lip.

"What's going on?" William asked as he reached the stall along with Pete. "Oh no! Matt, I'm sorry." He looked at Bill. "Any idea who did this?"

Bill shook his head. "No. Jeffery was here all evening. If he said he didn't hear anything, then he didn't." William turned to Jeffery. "What happened?"

Jeffery shook his head nervously. "I don't know. I heard his horse and went to check on her and seen her leg cut open. I didn't see or hear anyone, honest. I went and got Bill, and we laid her down so she'd stop trying to walk on her leg."

"Any other horses injured?" Pete asked Bill pointedly.

"Not that I'm aware of. Jeffery, go check the other animals."

Matt said sadly, "No other horses are hurt. This was personally directed towards me, I'm sure."

"By who? Little Red?" William asked.

Matt nodded as his breathing quickened a touch. The combination of heartbreak and fury began to fill him. "We'll find him. If you gentlemen don't mind leaving me alone for a little bit. I would appreciate it," he said without looking up.

"You bet," Pete said.

"Take your time," William said gently. If there was anything, William knew it was how lonely the road could be when you traveled mile after mile with no one but your horse. Matt had family and friends now, but for the years that he was a deputy marshal, Betty was his only constant companion and nearest to a friend that he had. "We'll be outside waiting."

Matt nodded while he petted Betty's neck. She tried to get up, but Matt held her head down. "It's okay, girl. You just lay here and relax." He bit his lip a bit harder as the moisture in his eyes grew. A hollowness moved from his throat on down to the pit of his stomach. He took a deep breath as he spoke through a soft voice, "It's been a long and tough road, Betty. You've been the best horse I've ever known. Through all those years and miles we shared, I never thought it would end like this. You deserve to retire at the Big Z and enjoy your final years in good pastures and teaching kids how to ride. Maybe even mine someday. That's what you deserve. I'm sorry I couldn't keep you safe, Betty. You deserve better."

A tear fell from his eyes as he dropped his head onto her neck. "You were never meant to be kept in a livery stable for long anyway. Maybe in Heaven, we can go for a long ride again," he said, sniffling as he stood up. He pulled his revolver out slowly and let it hang in his hand as he watched Betty try to stand. She fell back to the ground. A tear fell down his cheek. "I am so sorry, girl." He pointed the revolver at her head and pulled the trigger. He closed his eyes as another tear slipped down his cheek.

With her hamstring cut, there was nothing they could do for her. She would never be able to walk again. He had no choice but to put her down and leave her behind. Someone had intentionally crippled her. It was as intentional as any criminal intent had ever been. Someone was going to pay for it, and it didn't take long to figure out who it was either. Matt knew Dane Dielschneider was responsible for it. He holstered his gun. He looked around the livery stable and seen a back window with the solid wood cover open. He looked at Betty one last time and wiped his eyes dry before he left the livery stable and walked outside.

28

"Are you alright, Matt?" William asked as he came out of the livery stable. Matt's face was hardened.

"I will be," he answered and walked briskly past William and Pete towards the center of town.

William tapped Pete on the stomach lightly. "I've never seen Matt this pissed off before, so this ought to be fun."

"I would be too," Pete answered, as they followed behind Matt.

Matt walked into the Blazing Bull Saloon and yelled, "Dane Dielschnieder! Is he in here? And you better not lie to me! If you know where he is, you better tell me now!" His enraged eyes scanned the saloon and every man inside. They were all taken off guard, and many shook their heads. "Where does he live?"

A nervous man in his thirties spoke with a quivering voice, "It's kind of hard to explain, it's out of town a bit."

"Show me!" Matt demanded. "Get your coat and show me."

"Marshal...if I do and his brothers find out, um..."

"I don't care! Put your drink down and come on!" Matt yelled.

"Yes, sir..."

Pete Logan and William both remained quiet and scanned the room for anyone making a move towards a weapon.

The man grabbed his coat and put it on and went outside. They had barely left the saloon when they saw the Sheriff, Chuck Dielschnieder, with his two brothers, Troy and Devin. They were joined by deputies, Rocky Culp and Fred Johnson. They were all walking towards them and spread out as they neared, all accept Fred Johnson, who stayed slightly behind the others and just to Chuck's right side to be hidden from Matt if any shooting was to come out of the impromptu meeting.

Matt was the first to speak. "Where's your little brother? He hamstrung my horse, and I'm going to hamstrung his knee so he can stand as well as my horse could!" Matt's ferocity showed in his eyes.

Chuck was taken back by the initial greeting. He had his men spread out when he saw Matt in case there was any trouble. They would be smaller targets to hit than being grouped like Matt and his two men were. Now Chuck was second-guessing his decision to take an offensive stance. Matt's reputation was known far and wide, but he had seemed too easy-going to be as dangerous as his reputation made him out to be. Seeing Matt's hardened eyes, he was having second thoughts.

Devin spoke indignantly, "You have no proof, Dane did that, do you? Did anyone see him? You won't be touching my brother, believe me!"

Matt's eyes roamed through the men standing before him. He could see who was nervous, who was scared, and who was braver than their common sense could limit them to be. His eyes settled on Chuck, who stood in front of him about ten feet away. "Get your brother away from me before I shoot him for killing Ivan. Tonight, all I want is Dane."

Pete Logan had his pistol exposed, and his fingers twitching near it. He was resisting pulling his revolver and shooting Devin, but his eyes burned into him. William had both of his revolvers exposed and was standing near Matt, ready to reach for them at a moment's notice. His eyes watched everyone looking for the slightest sign of an aggressive movement.

Chuck held up his hands to calm Matt down. He spoke softly with a concerned voice, "I can't let you hurt Dane or shoot Devin, Marshal. Devin didn't shoot him anyway, my sister did. I'll arrest her in the morning; you can be sure of that. I'm just giving her another night with her children. I'll arrest Dane too, but I can't let you shoot them."

"Where is Dane?"

Chuck shook his head. "I don't know. I haven't seen him. How about we find him and put him in jail for you tonight? Okay? Obviously, your very upset and rightfully so. I understand that. We don't want any trouble. And for what it's worth, I am very sorry about your horse."

Matt shook his head slightly. "How about you tell me where to find him and when I'm done beating him senseless, you can have him back. No charges are necessary. I'll be perfectly happy with that!"

William Fasana chuckled. "He's going to beat him blonde."

Devin pointed at William and shouted, "And I'm going to bust your head open so wide they'll think your hairs red!" His blue eyes glared at William dangerously.

"Your brother already did! And if I were you, I'd hope Matt finds him before I do!" William replied sharply. "And I know my new buddy Pete's aching to put a bullet in the middle of your soul, so pick your target carefully, firey boy."

"You're already in my sights," Devin spat out coldly while jabbing his finger at William.

William answered quickly, "Should I turn around? That seems to be the only time you pull your weapon."

"I've never shot anyone in the back!" Devin replied indignantly. "If you think I'm coward enough to do that, then you have no clue what you're dealing with!"

William chuckled. "I'm a gambler by nature. Deal away." His face turned to stone.

Chuck turned to Devin and demanded, "Stop right there! This isn't getting us anywhere. Matt quiet your cousin down and let's be reasonable. We don't need to escalate this to a fight between our men. Okay?" he shouted to the others as he looked around. A crowd was growing outside of the saloon and on the main street.

Troy Dielschnieder looked at Matt and said, "You're outnumbered and bundled together. We could shred you three to bits if we had a mind to."

"What did I just say?" Chuck snapped at his brother.

Matt raised his eyebrows questionably towards Troy. "Maybe. But I wasn't looking for a fight tonight. Since that seems to be what your driving for, I'll let you know right now that if we did, you and your brothers would be dead before we fell. If you want to try it, as William said, we're game. It's going to happen eventually, right? Some of you, if not all, are dirty, and I'm going to bring you in one way or another."

Chuck grimaced. "Now wait a minute, we're not dirty, and I take offense of that. Are you threatening my men and me? We are no threat to you, and I thought you weren't a threat to us. Okay? But now I'm wondering what you mean by that? We've done nothing but help you. Now Dane crossed the line, and I'll find him and arrest him. You can come with me to find him if you like. But we've done nothing but try to help you," he said sincerely.

Matt took a step closer to Chuck and spoke pointedly, "There are five dead bodies, and not one had anything to do with that robbery. That's what I'm talking about!"

"Now that's not true! And unless you're calling

me a liar and have proof that I am, then I'd shut up and go get some sleep. Maybe tomorrow you'll be more reasonable to talk to. I don't like the way this conversation is going, Matt. We're both lawmen, so let's act like it, okay? I know you're mad and all, but you're crossing lines you shouldn't cross."

Matt looked at him with his hardened eyes. "Let me make this very clear. You are a liar and a murderer. You and your brothers and your deputies probably too. You'll all be doing yourselves a favor if you drop your weapons and surrender now before someone gets hurt," Matt said bluntly.

Devin spoke quickly, "What? The only ones getting hurt here are you three. If I were you, Marshal, I'd take your two sheep and lead them out of town."

Pete Logan answered coldly, "These sheep have a deadly bite. And I'm tired of the talking."

Chuck stared at Pete and then looked back at Matt. "No one wants any trouble. But before any of your boys get trigger happy, you should consider you only have four shots left in your gun. You're outgunned and outmanned. I don't think you want to go there with us any more than I want to cross shots with you. And I hope I'm right about that. We'll walk away and go home peacefully right now before you and your men say more than my boys can stand. Boys, let's go." He began to turn around.

"I don't keep an empty chamber in my revolver. I have five shots left, and that's plenty. I won't need more than four. Two for you and two for him." He nodded at deputy, Rocky Culp. "William has your brother Troy, and Pete's got Devin. That man," he nodded at Fred. "Won't even pull his gun. But if he does, I'll have one leftover for him too." Matt had noticed Fred slowly backing up as the tension built.

"No. We're not doing this tonight," Chuck said, waving his arms abruptly. "If you want to arrest us for some wild-haired idea you have, you'll have to shoot us in the back to do it! I already told you I'd be making some arrests in the morning. I don't know what more I can do for you. We'll see you tomorrow, Matt. Maybe you'll be more reasonable. Boys, turn around and let's go," Chuck said and turned around to his back towards Matt to walk away.

"Tomorrow then. I want Devin or your sister in jail and charged with murder by the time I get there in the morning. I also want to see Dane along with John in your jail tomorrow when I come by, Sheriff. Because if I have to do it, you'll be sorry you didn't."

Chuck turned around with a heavy sigh and walked the distance back over to Matt. He spoke softly, "Why don't you just go home? The robbery's solved. Ivan's murder is solved. There's no reason to push this any further. Because if you do, I'm afraid it will end badly for you and your friends. Save yourself trouble; you don't want. Trust me on that. From one lawman to another, accept what we've done for you and go home."

Matt shook his head slightly. "I have never turned my head to look the other way when innocent people are harmed, abused, or killed, and I won't start now."

"You're making a big mistake, Matt," Chuck said, raising his eyebrows threateningly.

"Doing what's right is never a mistake, Sheriff. It's just too bad you don't know that."

Chuck nodded with a sigh. "So be it. Get some sleep, Marshal. You're going to need it tomorrow. Because you're not taking us in without a fight," Chuck said bitterly.

"I figured so."

Chuck shook his head. "Why don't you just leave?"

"So you can rob the next stage and continue to murder whoever you like to cover your crimes? No. You could try to kill us and murder other men to blame it on, or you can surrender and take your chances on a jury. But whether it's now or tomorrow, your world is about to change, because I'm not leaving without you and your men."

Chuck's jaw clenched as he said, "Unless you have proof of anything you're saying, you're wasting your time. Don't push too hard, though, because you won't arrest any of my men without a fight. Sleep well, Marshal." He turned his back to Matt and began walking away.

"Okay. You too," Matt said sarcastically.

Pete looked at Matt bitterly. "We should've killed them here and now. Tomorrow they'll be better organized and have sniper positions, probably. We'll be walking into a trap like mice with their eyes gouged out! And you know it."

Matt watched the Sheriff walking away with his men. "If your enemy encourages you to get some sleep, and emphasizes it... I suggest you don't. I think they might be back tonight when we're supposed to be sleeping. Sleeping men are easy targets, and I'll bet these fella's don't want us rested up and feeling energetic tomorrow."

"So no drinks with the townfolks tonight, huh?" William asked.

Matt shook his head. "I could be wrong. If so, we'll be dragging our butt's tomorrow, but it's not the first time we've gone without sleep, right? If I were them, I'd attack tonight. It's the only way they can guarantee their survival. Well, let's go inside and get off the street." Matt led the way into the hotel and noticed Claudia and her husband standing behind the counter watching them.

Claudia stepped around the counter, stopping them. "We couldn't hear everything that was being said out there. But would you mind if we prayed with you, gentlemen? Come on, Harry, let's pray for the Lord to put his protection on these men. Tomorrow might be a very scary day with as much tension that was in the air."

Matt frowned with a heavy heart, "You may indeed. Afterward, I'm going to need you to move Tiffany to a safer room. I'm expecting them to attack us tonight right here in your hotel."

Harry suddenly looked worried. "Marshal, we can't afford to fix that kind of damage to the place."

Claudia looked worried as well but waved Harry away. "Then, let's pray for the Lord's protection on all of us and our place," Claudia said to her husband. She began to pray, "Jesus, I ask you to put your divine shield of protection around everyone in this hotel tonight. Our property and our very lives as well. You know the Sheriff and his deputies are a wicked bunch, and you know I hate violence, but I pray you'll allow justice to be administered as you will it to be done. And you know how I feel about Tiffany Foster, Lord. I pray you will be with her for the remainder of her life. She is such a sweet child. If we could take her in, Lord, you know we would. I want to thank you for these fine men and Jesus; please protect them from harm if it comes for them. These are good men, Jesus, and we put their lives in your hands. You are good, and we will trust you. In Jesus' name, Amen."

"Thank you," Matt said to Claudia and Harry. "I need a key to a room far away from ours and preferably on the backside of the building."

Claudia went to her apartment and came back with a key for the key drawer. She went to open it and discovered it was already unlocked. "The drawers been opened," she said awkwardly. She looked and said, "One of room Eight's keys are missing! Someone stole one of the keys. It must've been that rotten to the core, Dane Dielschnieder!"

"Give me the other key," Matt said quickly and went upstairs. He found the door to room eight locked. He unlocked it and opened the door all the way before he went inside. The room was dark and looked to be untouched. He peeked under the bed and opened the closet door to verify the room was empty. Satisfied that no one was in there, he closed the door and locked it behind him.

***

Dane Dielschnieder exhaled with great relief. He had been waiting outside of the hotel hoping Matt would get the news about his horse sooner than later. He grinned with excitement when he saw Jeffery McDonald run into the hotel to notify Matt. A moment later, Dane was a bit perplexed to see Matt leave the hotel with his cousin William Fasana. Dane could've sworn he had killed him. With them out of the hotel, it gave him the opportunity to sneak in through the front door and quietly make his way to room Eight. He had paused outside of Matt's room to listen for Tiffany, but he didn't hear anything. He knew he couldn't fool her again with a single knock, so he went to the empty room to wait. He didn't know for what he was waiting for exactly, he just wanted to be close to Tiffany in case he had the chance to talk to her or maybe sneak into her room in the middle of the night and persuade her to leave with him back to his room. In the morning, it was highly suspected that Matt and his cousin would leave town, and he would still be near her to protect her from his brothers and sister and win her affections.

He had laughed when he heard the single gun shot knowing it was Matt's horse being put down. A sense of satisfaction filled him to the core and the joy he expressed through his laughter was intoxicating. He watched the impromptu meeting outside on the street between his brothers and the Marshal from the window. He was elated to hear a gunshot a few moments earlier, but it pleased him greatly to see Matt so upset on the street. When his brothers and the deputies walked away, Dane put his ear to the door of room eight to listen for anything he could hear. He didn't hear Matt walking down the hallway until Matt checked to see if the door was locked. Dane pressed himself flat against the wall behind the door as unnoticeably as he could at the outside edge of the door and tapped the wall lightly with his knife hnadle to make it sound like the doorknob hit the wall. He held the doorknob so the door wouldn't swing back towards Matt. Dane didn't breath or move as he listened to Matt walk around the room and open the closet door. He could feel his heart pounding and knew if he was caught he might get hit again for what he had done. His eyes widened in alarm when Matt grabbed the door handle and pulled the door away from him. Matt had left the room and closed the door behind him. He never looked behind the door.

Once Matt locked the door, Dane put his ear against it to hear anything he could. About a half an hour later, he could hear Matt talking to Tiffany as he moved her directly across the hall into room Seven. Matt was saying, "You try to relax and get some sleep. And remember the new code is..." He knocked on the door with three knocks separated by about two seconds, followed by two quick knocks. "Do not answer the door for anyone else."

"Can't you come in and talk for a while?" she asked with a nervousness in her voice.

"Sorry, but not tonight."

Dane whispered, "Yes, I can." He grinned with a light giggle.

29

Devin stepped into the Sheriff's office as the others followed him in. He turned around angrily, with his eyes burning into Chuck. "I didn't want to say anything on the street, but what the hell are you doing?" he asked, raising his voice. "Why in the hell did you tell him Danetta shot that Pinkerton? We're supposed to protect her, not feed her to the wolves! She could hang for that, you stupid son of a..."

"Because the other Pinkerton was going to kill you!" Chuck shouted over his little brother. "You were so busy focusing on Matt and his cousin that you neglected to see Pete was this close to shooting you!" He held up his index finger and thumb with a fraction of space between them. "I was saving your life, Devin."

"And what about Danetta now, huh? You didn't think about that, did you? Are you going to arrest her like you said or what are you going to say tomorrow when she isn't in jail?"

Chuck sat down at the table in the middle of the

room. "Sit down, Devin. Even if I arrested her to-morrow, and she went to trial. We could persuade the jurors to acquit her, could we not? The Crowe Brothers are quite useful for that. Even John over there has nothing to worry about. We will be fine."

"So, you're going to arrest her?" Devin asked in disgust as he sat down at the table with the others.

Chuck shook his head. "No," he answered Devin. He turned to Troy. "Troy let John out of that cell. Come and join us, John."

"Then what? Matt's just going to cause more trouble tomorrow if you don't."

Chuck nodded. "As we talked about earlier, we're going to massacre them tonight in the hotel. I'm not taking any chances. Everything he said is true. We can't have him out there, suspecting us every time something happens. We need to take him out. I tried to work with him, and it's only dug us deeper in a hole. Sometimes when someone doesn't quit dig-ging, you might as well kill them and throw them in their own hole and bury it. Matt isn't giving us any other choice, so that's what we're going to do."

"Just John, Rocky, and Fred, like you said earlier or all of us?" Devin asked.

"All of us. If they failed, we'd be in a world of trouble tomorrow, so we'll take no chances tonight and make sure they're dead before we leave. It's going to cause a pretty big investigation by report-ers, more Pinkerton Detectives and U.S. Marshals and…everyone else who comes to town wanting to know what happened and who did it. Matt being killed will be a pretty big deal, so we need to be prepared for that too."

"Any ideas," Charles Hammond asked.

Chuck shook his head. "We'll have to come up with something and make it good. I wish we could knock them out without shooting them and burn the place down, but we won't be able to get that close."

"Smoke kills more people than the fire. If they're sleeping, we could catch the downstairs on fire," Fred offered.

Chuck nodded. "That's an idea, and if they wake up and start fighting it, we could shoot them like rats in a barrel."

Troy frowned. "Why not just burst into their rooms and blow them to pieces with two rounds with a scattergun? It's done, and we can disappear before anyone sees us. You're not going to be able to start a fire because the town's going to be there fighting it. Am I the only one thinking? The quicker it's done, the better."

"He's right," Deputy Rocky Culp agreed.

"I guess that's settled then," Chuck said, approving of the plan. "Rocky, do you want to make sure we have three shotguns loaded and ready to go. I know John wants some payback on Matt, right?"

John nodded with a slight grimace. The pressure from all the swelling of his nose and nasal passages hurt when he lowered his head.

"Good. Then I think we have a plan. Now, how to cover ourselves?" Chuck asked.

"Hoods, like always," Rocky answered simply.

"I meant as an alibi. We also need to track some-

243

one down for the crime, any ideas?"

Charles Hammond suggested, "Anyone who has a criminal record or might be wanted would have a reason to kill Matt and the others. And we know some of those people. How many times have the Wilken boys been arrested? That might be an idea."

Chuck nodded. "We'll think it over. But we'll have to hang them quick and blame it on vigilantes."

Troy shook his head. "You make things too complicated." He looked at his friend John, "How's it feel to be out of jail, John?"

John's face was black and blue under both eyes and had a swollen broken, crooked nose that nearly had swollen his eyes closed. "I look forward to sleeping in my own bed, thanks."

"Well, are you ready to get a little payback? You know, the percussion of the shotgun might hurt your face a bit, but just think you'll be the one who finally got the best of Matt Bannister. I think that's quite an honor even though he whipped you like a child today!" Troy laughed.

"Leave him alone," Rocky Culp said with a grin. "Matt got lucky is all."

"Sure, he did," Troy said sarcastically. "You got spanked by him!"

Fred Johnson sat at the table quietly, cleaning his revolver. "Troy, you're not facing three unarmed miners in a creek bed, you know? These men know how to shoot, and undoubtedly they're no strangers to killing. You might want to take a more serious view of what we're about to do. Because it may not go quite as planned."

Troy laughed lightly. "I know how dangerous the Marshal is, and according to you, how tough his cousin is. Didn't Dane tell us he was supposed to be dead? I swear when I see Dane, I am going to whack him upside his head. The boy is deaf to common sense and apparently blind to a man still breathing! The boy's just dumb."

"He's your brother none the less," Devin said quietly, resting his head on his arms tiredly at the table. "You have to protect him." He lifted his head to look at Troy. "Remember the marshal and his cousin want to hurt him. If we don't have any other reason to kill them, that's enough."

"We don't need a reason beyond saving our live-lihood!" Troy said pointedly.

"I wish I knew where that boy was. I don't know a better lock picker than he is. Some people have a knack for certain things, and when it comes to breaking in without anyone knowing, Dane is the best," Chuck said.. "Well, I think it's best that we all go home, get something to eat, and meet back here around midnight. We want to make sure those fellas are asleep. And remember to bring your hoods. I'll see you men around midnight."

30

Matt laid in the darkness of his room, reading the book of Psalms chapter 59 with a small bit of candlelight.

'Deliver me from my enemies, O'God; protect me from those who rise up against me.

Deliver me from evildoers and save me from bloodthirsty men. See how they lie in wait for me! Fierce men conspire against me for no offense or sin of mine, O Lord. I have done no wrong, yet they are ready to attack me. Arise and help me.'

He laid the Bible upon his chest and closed his eyes. "I couldn't read any truer words tonight, Jesus. I don't know if they're coming or not, but I pray you're in the midst of whatever happens in this town. There's not one of the Sheriff's men that I can trust, and I don't like the way this whole thing is going. I don't know how we're going to get out of this without a fight. I pray you'll put a shield of protection around Tiffany and keep her safe. And if I'm killed, I pray you'll give her a home where she is loved and treated like a young lady. I ask that you'll bless her in this life. I pray for the safety of William and Pete, as well. I want to thank you for Claudia and Harry and their hospitality towards Tiffany and us." He yawned. "I pray you will bless our intentions to bring justice to this community and do what's right. I pray we can make some arrests without any bloodshed, but if a fight breaks out, I ask you to help keep my hand steady and my aim true. And if you would, keep my friends and I safe. You are truly my shield of protection, and I put my trust in you. In your name, I pray, Lord Jesus."

He set his Bible on the bedstand and blew the candle out. He laid his head on the pillow and closed his eyes. There was no guarantee the Sheriff and his men would attack them during the night, and he didn't want to stay up all night worrying about it either. His gunbelt was on the bedstand, and his shotgun and rifle were lying on his bed beside him. He had the metal chamber pot in front of the door with a drinking glass sitting on an upside-down cup in the middle of it. The door was locked, but if by chance someone unlocked it and came in quietly, the door would cause the glass to fall, and that might be all the warning he needed to grab the shotgun and fire towards the door. He had already warned William it would be a bad night to play any jokes on him. William laughed and warned Matt of the same thing. And for Pete, he knew entering either of the men's room uninvited was a good way to get shot.

Matt was almost asleep when he heard a sound

coming from outside by the front door, which was under his room. He heard a pane of glass break lightly and the hushing of men's voices as they entered into the hotel. He sat up and stepped down onto the mattress on the floor that Tiffany had slept on the night before. He stood up and wrapped his gun belt around his waist. He stepped across the mattress that stopped the floor from creaking, he realized and silently thanked God for that as he pressed himself up against the wall nearest to the door. He raised his arm horizontally, pointing his revolver at the door, waiting for it to open. He could barely hear the men as they searched for the keys, Matt figured. He wished he could warn William and Pete in case they had fallen asleep, but he remained perfectly still waiting. He could feel his heart pounding, and his breathing was becoming heavier with the dread of anticipating what was coming ahead.

He heard the slight creaking of the stairs as the men came up them. There was no whispering or noise, except for the light touch of boots touching the hardwood floor of the hallway. The silence was excruciating as he knew momentarily hell was going to break loose and terrorize Tiffany and their hosts as well. He did not doubt that all three rooms would be attacked in unison. They might be planning an ambush, but people were a species of habit and patterns. Matt had expected that it was a possibility and did some preplanning of his own. He knew if he had hidden the registry book that the Sheriff would get their room numbers from the Richmonds and risk their lives in the process. He had verified the registry was left on top of the counter, and the key drawer was left unlocked just in case they came tonight.

Matt closed his eyes in a quick prayer when he heard the key slowly slide into the lock. The hammer of his revolver was already cocked and waiting for someone to enter the darkroom. The lock clicked open, and just as it did, the door was kicked open and slammed against the wall with a loud bang. A man stepped into the room, wearing a gray hood over his head. He had a shotgun aimed at the bed and fired both barrels at the empty bed before he noticed it was empty. Shotguns fired two shots in the other rooms at the same time.

Matt aimed at the man's head and pulled the trigger, and watched the blood splatter against the door along with a bullet hole as the man collapsed down to the floor.

"John's down! John's down!" the voice of the Sheriff yelled. He began shooting at the wall Matt was hiding behind. The bullets were penetrating the thin wall in front of him and moving his way about chest high.

Matt dove down to the floor.

"Coming! The Pinkerton's dead," a voice belonging to Troy Dielschnieder, yelled over the gunfire. He and his partner were running down the hallway. "Where's the Marshal?" he asked, full of adrenaline.

"Along the wall!"

A shotgun blast tore a few inches of wood out of the wall, and a stream of light bore through the darkness to the darkest corner of the room where the light from the opened door didn't shine. Another shotgun blast tore through the room, hitting the back wall.

Matt fired twice from the floor to the right of the door and heard the sheriff curse with a light injury. Matt fired twice lower and missed the sheriff with both shots.

"He's on the floor! Charles get over here with that scattergun. You and Troy fill this room full of lead! Shoot low!" Chuck yelled.

Matt fired his last two shots towards the door to buy a second or two. He grabbed his buffalo skin coat off a wall hanger wrapped it around him and ran and jumped out the window just as the two men stepped in the doorway and fired four rounds from their shotguns simultaneously. Matt fell with the broken glass onto the sloped porch roof and rolled over the edge and fell eight feet to the hard ground on the edge of the street below. The wind was knocked out of him when he hit the ground. He let go of his coat and slowly pushed himself up to his hands and knees.

"There he is!" Troy yelled, pointing out the window. He slammed the barrel of his shotgun closed and pulled back the double hammers and pointed it down towards Matt and pulled the trigger as Matt scrambled for his life. Troy's shot hit the street. "Damn! He's on the porch, let's go!"

The Sheriff yelled, "Devin, you and Troy come with me! Charles, help Fred kill that man!"

William had turned his bed on its side and turned it horizontal to the door and piled up every piece of furniture in the room on top of each other to create a wall to hide behind. He had set his bearskin coat's hood over a lantern that he set on the bedstand that was sitting on top of a dresser he had set up behind the bed. The weight of the coat was in an opened drawer, and the hood rested over the lantern. He knew whoever burst into his room; if they did, would be confused by the wall of furniture and their attention drawn to the bear's face staring at them. William had sat on the floor bored to death, playing solitaire with his cards in candlelight when he heard them coming. He moved to the closet, which was to one side of the room four feet from the door. He pulled the door closed just enough to peek out and waited. He held one of his revolvers in his right hand, and his left hand was itching to fan the hammer. Like Matt, he heard the key slip into the lock, and the lock click over. A half-second after hearing Matt's door being kicked in, his door was kicked open as well.

A man stepped inside wearing a white hood over his head and fired two shots with his shotgun hitting the stacked up furniture. He paused and said, "He's got a wall!"

"What? Did you hit him?" Devin asked as he stepped into the doorway to see for himself. He was wearing a hood as well.

"I don't know," the shooter said as he unhinged the barrels of his shotgun and quickly went to reload.

William exploded out of the closet fanning his revolver's hammer with his left hand while holding the trigger down with his right hand as fast as he could. He ran across the room in front of his make-shift wall. Devin spun around with an anguished curse out of the door reaching for his shoulder. He disappeared out of sight. The other man who was inside the room fell backward to the floor with four bullets in his chest and abdomen. William hit the wall and then dove down to the floor behind his wall and quickly began to reload his revolver while he watched the door.

He heard Devin say painfully, "Rocky's dead. And I'm hit!"

William smiled slightly when he heard Chuck yell out that John was dead. William shouted with a slight chuckle, "You better go home, Red, before you're next!"

Devin pointed his revolver into the room and fired twice at the wall missing William. Troy had shouted out that Pete was dead and stopped to see how Devin was.

"Go, help Chuck, me and Fred will finish this!" Charles Hammond said urgently. He had been teamed up with Troy to kill Pete Logan. Troy went to help Chuck in Matt's room. Charles Hammond turned into William's doorway and fired his shotgun twice, knocking part of the wall down. The metal chamber pot fell from the top of the mattress and hit William on the head. He grimaced and leaned out from the corner of the mattress and fired three quick shots hitting Charles in the leg, crotch, and stomach. Charles backed up against the wall across the hallway and sat down, crying out in pain.

"Charles!" Fred Johnson exclaimed. "Charles…" he said helplessly and not knowing what to do for his friend.

Charles grimaced as he tried to stop the blood from flowing out of him. "Kill him so I can get to the doctor."

"I don't think the doctor can help you, Charles," Fred said frantically from somewhere in the hall-way.

Devin spoke harshly, "Let me in there!" He turned around the corner and aimed his revolver at the pile of furnishings as he looked for William.

The sound of a window shattering followed by four shotgun blasts sounded loudly from across the hall. Devin was soon called away by Chuck, and he cursed and walked quickly away. It became silent except for the whimpering and yelling of Tiffany at the end of the hall. William slowly stood up as he heard the other three men run down the stairs and more gunshots being fired.

William began to whistle as he made eye contact with Charles, who sat against the wall staring at him. William smiled. "It's not quite working out like you planned, huh?" he asked while reloading his revolver.

Charles's eyes went up to William's left side of the door and then back towards William like he was motioning for someone to shoot him. William dropped his revolver and quickly pulled his other one out with his left hand and began fanning six shots into the wall beside the door.

Fred Johnson fell forward into the opposite wall and bounced off it and landed sideways in the doorway facing Charles. He had been hit in the back of his head.

William raised his eyebrows with surprise. He reloaded his revolver quickly and stepped towards the door. "That was lucky! Huh? Not for you, of course. Raise your gun, and I'll put you out of your misery or toss it down the hall and take your chances of getting to a doctor. But choose now because I have to go help Matt."

Charles tossed his gun down the hall a little ways. "Get a doctor, please," he said desperately.

Room seven's door opened, and Tiffany ran out of the room and down the hallway, screaming desperately. She jumped over the two men bleeding on the floor as she ran by William. William soon figured out why when Dane Dielschnieder came running after her. William grabbed Dane as he tried to run past him and slammed Dane against the wall harshly to stop him. William drove his right elbow across Dane's face and brought his arm back viciously to slam the bottom of the revolver's grip into Dane's head. Dane fell to the floor on top of Charles and Fred's dead body. Dane's head began bleeding as he laid there, nearly unconscious. Charles cried out in agony from being landed on and used his waning energy to push Dane off him and into a growing pool of mixed blood around Fred.

William watched Tiffany run down the stairs as he yelled out, "Tiffany!" He jogged to Matt's room and scooped up Matt's rifle off the bed and went out the broken window oblivious of the broken glass, cutting him on the arm and leg as he stepped quickly onto the porch roof.

***

Matt crawled onto the porch to take cover from Troy's shotgun. He couldn't catch his breath, and his left arm hurt from the impact with the ground. He frantically used his left hand to hold his revolver as he pulled bullets out of his gunbelt cartridge sleeves and shoved them into the chambers of the cylinder. He closed the cylinder and forced himself to stand up just as Chuck came down the stairs of the hotel, followed by Troy, and a bit behind them was Devin, who had been shot in the left shoulder. Matt could still hear shots being fired and knew William was alive still fighting.

Chuck fired his revolver through the window missing Matt by a fraction. Matt fired back, taking the top part of Chuck's left ear off as the bullet grazed the side of his head. Chuck cried out and spun down to the floor out of Matt's sight.

Troy raised his shotgun, and Matt dropped to the wood planks of the porch. He rolled to his side and pointed his revolver up and towards the window. Troy came bursting out of the door, and Matt rolled off the porch dropping down a foot to the street just as Troy fired his shotgun. It tore into the wood planks well past where Matt had been. He adjusted the shotgun toward Matt, but was met quickly by three continues shots from Matt's revolver. Troy fell back already dead from two bullets entering his chest and the third hitting under his chin and coming out the back of his head. His shotgun landed on the porch planks with a solid hit as his body fell too.

"Troy!" Devin yelled. "Troy!"

Chuck stood up and yelled out the door. "I'm going to kill you, Marshal!"

Matt remained quiet and crawled forward along the edge of the porch as fast as he could to get beyond the door and make his way to a water pump and trough near the hitching posts of the hotel. He got to his feet and ran the last ten yards and dove behind trough for what little cover it offered. He only had three bullets left in his gun and paused to eject the spent cartridges and replace them before the two injured men inside came out to finish him off. He got one in the cylinder when Devin fired at him twice from the window. Matt laid on the ground watching the door as he loaded the other two chambers.

Inside, Devin finished firing at Matt and looked at his brother Chuck. "He's behind the water trough!"

They heard Tiffany screaming and saw her running down the stairs, frantically. She tried to avoid the two brothers by darting for the door as fast as she could, but she was grabbed by Chuck and quickly under his control. His big hand covered her mouth to stop her from screaming, and his gun went to her head. "Shut up!" he snarled. "You've caused enough trouble, and when this is over, you and I are going to talk! And I doubt you'll like it!" He looked at Devin. "I have an idea. Go through the Richmond's place and out the back door and circle around. I'll keep Matt busy and draw him out into the street where you can shoot him. Hurry up and go!"

Devin kicked the Richmond's door, and it remained locked. He kicked it again, and the doorjamb cracked. He kicked it a third time, and the lock splintered through the doorjamb and flew open. He ran down the corridor into their place, finding Claudia and Harry were both huddled in a corner praying. He looked at them momentarily, and without saying a word, went to unlock the back door. He opened it and ran out into the darkness. He misjudged a step and fell off the back porch, which was three steps down and not one step like out front. He hit his shoulder on the ground and dropped his gun upon impact. He tried to control his voice as he groaned in pain. He held his shoulder with his right hand and rocked back and forth on the ground in agony. With a job to do he forced himself up to his feet and it took a moment to locate his gun. When he did he began walking quickly towards the corner of the house, still holding onto his shoulder.

Matt had heard Tiffany scream and stood up when he saw Chuck walk out of the hotel with Tiffany in his grasp. He had his revolver to her head.

"Let her go, Chuck," Matt said firmly as he

stepped out into the middle of the street, holding his gun at his side. Chuck stepped out into the street with Tiffany held in front of him. "Shooting her won't do you any good. I'll kill you as soon as you do!"

The left side of Chuck's face had blood running down it from part of his ear being shot off. He shook his head. "You should've left town when I told you too! Now my brother's dead and so are your friends! And before this is done, I'm going to kill you!"

"By holding a gun to a child's head? I would say that's a cowards play, isn't it? If you want to kill me, then do it. But let the girl go. Tiffany has nothing to do with this." She was terrified, and her tears streamed down her face. His hand covered her mouth to keep her pulled tight against him and to keep her quiet. His right hand held his revolver against her head.

"If she had kept her mouth shut, you would've taken her father and those other men and went home! I say she has everything to do with it!" he shouted without noticing William crawling out on the porch roof.

Matt wanted to keep Chuck's attention on him. He chuckled slightly. "You're wrong, Sheriff. She had nothing to do with this. I knew you were dirty as soon as I saw my old friend John. I knew he was the one who killed Louis Eckman as soon as I saw him. If you had hidden John from me, then you might've gotten away with it. But you didn't, and instead wanted to see a sideshow. That didn't go your way either. So what makes you think this will?" He waved to Tiffany.

"Because I'm in control! I'm taking Tiffany, and we're going to ride away. Unless you think you can shoot me quicker than I can shoot her."

Matt shook his head. "No, that's impossible. But if I were behind you, I'd aim to hit under your right shoulder blade when I could. You'd drop the gun out of pure reflex." He looked to Chuck's right and nodded.

"What?" Chuck asked and turned to his right to look behind him. By turning to his right, it exposed the right shoulder blade to William, who was upon the hotel's porch roof to the Sheriff's left. William smirked and fired. The bullet penetrated downward just under the shoulder blade, separating the scapula bone from his shoulder and tearing its way through the muscle and tendons that allowed the arm to move. Chuck's hand opened immediately, and he lost the grip on the revolver as he arched his back involuntarily and cried out in pain. He was stiff and stood with an arched back with his right arm dangling freely and screaming in pain.

Tiffany, now free, ran to Matt and wrapped her arms around him in a tight fearful hug. She was sobbing in terror. Matt holstered his revolver and put his arms around her to hold her tight. "You're okay," he said comfortingly. "It's over, sweetheart."

William stood on the roof, watching Matt hug Tiffany and the Sheriff stepping stiffly, trying to find some way to stop the pain of his agony. From underneath him, William watched Dane

Dielschnieder walk briskly out onto the street, carrying his little three-inch blade knife in his hand as he walked towards Matt. There was no question of his intention to stab or slice Matt as he had done to Matt's horse. William aimed the rifle carefully and fired just as Dane was nearing Matt's side.

The bullet penetrated the top of Dane's hand, where he held the knife handle. Dane dropped the knife and screamed in pain, and he dropped to his knees, holding his right wrist with his left hand and stared in horror at the blood pouring out of the hole through his hand.

William shouted from the porch roof, "I don't think you'll be holding a knife with that hand again, Little Red!"

Matt looked at Dane, surprised to see he had gotten so close unnoticed. He could feel the rage from having to shoot his horse earlier that evening, resurrecting within him. He realized that he would have been stabbed, sliced open, maimed, or quite possibly killed if it hadn't been for William. Matt pulled his revolver out of his holster while turning away from Tiffany and twisted his body to slam the side of his revolver's barrel across Dane's head. Dane fell to the street, unconscious.

A gunshot sounded, and the bullet zipped past Matt so close he heard it cut through the air. He looked up and seen Devin Dielschnieder walking around the back of the hotel with his pistol drawn and firing it at Matt with an enraged snarl on his face.

Matt raised his revolver and fired three shots as fast as he could. The first two hit Devin in the chest, and the third hit him squarely in the fore-head. Devin dropped back to the street with his legs crossed. Matt turned around to face a crowd of shocked townspeople who were gathering on the main street to see what was going on.

He took a deep breath and looked at the saloon keeper. "Find me the Reverend. The mayor and whoever else runs this town and have them meet me in the hotel right away. And you might as well fetch the doctor for those who are still alive."

"Yes, sir!" he said and jogged away.

William came out of the hotel and joined Matt on the street, still carrying the rifle. He looked at Matt and shook his head slowly. "I believe we are done here, Matt."

Matt sighed. "Almost. Tomorrow we'll go home. Hell, of a shot, by the way. I didn't know if you were good enough to make that shot with a rifle."

William scoffed. "You don't come out of Uncle James Ziegler's 7th Cavalry Company E Radical Badgers without being proficient in long arms, small arms, and your own arms. Unless your Adam. I don't know why he can't use a pistol worth beans. Like I always say, though, he might hit his thumb with a hammer, but that doesn't mean he can't build a solid shed. What do you say we go get a drink and call it a night, huh?"

Matt shook his head. "I have too much to do." He stopped William as he was walking away, "Hey William, I'm glad you're here. I wouldn't have sur-vived without you. If you want a deputy Marshal's job with me, you can have it," Matt said sincerely.

William nodded with a slight smile. "Let me think about that."

31

Matt had spent the night talking with the town leaders about appointing a new sheriff and deputies until a special election could be arranged. He talked about the damages to the hotel and funeral costs and the shipping costs of sending Ivan and Pete's bodies back to Sacramento, California. Most all costs would come from the bank accounts of the Sheriff and his deputies. It only seemed fair since most of their money was gained from robberies anyway. They discussed the future of where Tiffany would live, and three families agreed she could live with them. It had been a long night, and Matt was exhausted. After meeting with the town leaders, he went to the livery stable with Bill Bones and bought a new horse to get back home on. When he and William were packed, had eaten breakfast, and ready to leave, Matt went to say goodbye to Tiffany. She had stayed in the Richmond's home for the night. Matt knocked on their door, and Claudia answered it, looking as though she had not slept a wink all night.

"Is Tiffany awake?" he asked. It was still early.

"No. The poor girl was up most of the night. She's sleeping in our spare room. Should I wake her?"

"I will if you don't mind."

Matt sat down on the edge of the bed and woke her gently. She opened her eyes and looked at Matt. She noticed he was dressed and wore his buffalo coat and had his brown hat in his hands. "Are you leaving?" she asked with concern while waking up. Her exhaustion was clear to see on her face. She sat up in bed, full of emotion.

Matt nodded.

"I don't want you to leave," she said with a longing for him to stay in her troubled voice. Her bottom lip began to tremble.

"I know," he said softly. "I spoke with several townspeople last night about a lot of things. One thing I wanted to make sure of is that you'll be taken care of. Three good families agreed to take you in as one of their own. The Gremit family said they'd love to have you stay with them. And the Aggler and Harris family said the same. So you can choose where you want to live."

She nodded sadly, trying not to cry.

"Or, if you want, you can come back to Branson with me. You can't live with me, but I know my family would love you, and one of them would love to take you in and become part of our family. I could keep a better watch over you that way and make sure you're not getting in trouble, you know," he said with a wink. "Does that sound like something you'd like to do?"

She looked at him. "Why can't I stay with you? I wouldn't be any trouble."

"I know. And you'd probably keep the house cleaner than Truet, and I do. But I don't have room, and a young lady needs some privacy and a more womanish influence than Truet, and I can be. If you'll trust me, I know you'll be treated like family and never feel alone, scared, or like you don't matter again. And no one will mistreat you. I can promise you that. Come home with me, Tiffany. I don't want to leave you here."

"You want me to go with you?" she asked with tears filling her eyes.

Matt smiled warmly. "I do. Come here, kid, let me give you a hug." He hugged her while she sniffled in her tears.

"I'm not prepared to go yet. I don't have any of my clothes or anything except for what we got yesterday."

"Is there anything else you need from your house?"

She nodded. "My mother's wedding ring and things that belonged to my parents and my sisters. I want to take those if I could."

"Of course, you can. Well, how about you get up, eat some breakfast and then we'll go to your place where you can get the things you want to take, put on some warm clothes, take your Pa's horse and then we can get out of town." He stood up and looked down at her. "You'll be fine, Tiffany. You have nothing to be afraid of anymore."

***

They rode to the edge of town in front of Dallen Foster's house, and William said, "You call this living? I've seen run down chicken coops in better condition than this." William looked at Tiffany. "No wonder you're coming home with us. No princess has ever come from a chicken coop."

"I'm not a princess," she said with a smile despite the anxiety she was feeling about facing Danetta again.

William tossed a piece of hard candy to her from his pocket. "What?" he asked playfully. "You're going to be stealing hearts and living happily ever after before you know it. I think that qualifies as Princess language if I ever heard a fairy tale correctly."

"William, will you go around to the barn and fetch the Princess's horse and saddle. We'll meet you out here when she's ready," Matt asked as he stepped out of the saddle. William rode around to the back of the house while Matt and Tiffany went to the door. Matt knocked loudly.

Danetta's nine-year-old daughter, Thelma, opened the door. "Yes?" she asked, looking at Matt. Her eyes widened with a momentarily smile when she saw Tiffany. "Tiffany! Oh, Mama's going to be mad," she said uneasily as her excitement was replaced with fear.

"Where's your mother?" Matt asked with a friendly tone.

"Sleeping. Mama's mad. Uncle Dane lost his hand. And Uncle Chuck might lose his arm. And…"

"Get away from that door!" Danetta yelled as she came out of the bedroom into the small family room. She glared at Tiffany and Matt. "How dare you bring that man to my house! How dare you even come back here after you betrayed our family! We gave you a home, and this is how you treat us? You go to him! Get off my property, both of you! And I never want to see either of you again, or I swear I'll kill you both myself!" She yelled, pointing her finger at them. "Go!" She screamed.

Matt smiled slightly as he stepped inside. "Sorry, Ma'am," he said as politely as he could. He saw Dane sitting in a padded chair covered with a blanket with his hand amputated at the wrist. His lower arm was heavily bandaged with spots of blood showing through it. He looked to be in great pain. Matt looked back at Danetta, who glared him with deep wild-eyed hatred in her blue eyes. "We'll be leaving in a few moments. Tiffany wants to collect her things," Matt finished.

"What things? She's not taking anything. Everything here is mine! Now get out of my house!"

Matt said to Tiffany, "Go ahead and get your things."

Tiffany nervously stepped forward with her eyes downward as she walked across the family room. Danetta enraged, raised her right hand to strike the back of Tiffany's head, but Matt grabbed her wrist firmly. "I wouldn't do that!" he warned severely. "Go sit down by your brother and shut up!"

"What do you want?" she screamed in his face. "You murdered most of my family, and those you didn't will never be the same again! Dane's lost his hand because of you! Chuck's fighting for his life and may lose his arm at best! You've already taken Troy and Devin away from me! What more could you possibly take from me? How am I going to live without my husband and my brothers, Marshal? Huh? I have two daughters to raise on what, now?"

Matt raised his eyebrows. "Self defense is not murder, Ma'am. The murderers are either dead or maimed, and I won't apologize for either one. They chose to attack us. We didn't attack them. And quite frankly, I don't care how you survive. Other families will take your girls in and give them a better chance at living a good life than you ever will."

"How dare you! I'm their mother and a damn good one!"

"No, you're not."

"Who are you to tell me anything at all? You don't know me! You don't know anything about me!"

"All I have to do is look at the marks on Tiffany to know all I need to know about you. As I said, I recommend you sit down and wait before I force you to sit down right where you're standing."

"What is Tiffany doing in my room?" she asked bitterly. She turned towards the bedroom to see when Tiffany came out of the bedroom. She was carrying an armload of clothes, papers, books, and a framed photograph taken of her family shortly before her mother and sisters passed away.

"Where do you think you're going with my

things? That photograph I'm using for target practice later today! Put it all back!" Danetta yelled and knocked everything out of Tiffany's hands. The glass in the framed photograph of Tiffany's family shattered as it hit the floor.

"You broke my picture!" Tiffany yelled angrily. She pushed Danetta forcefully away from her. She wanted to pick up the photograph before the shards of glass damaged it.

Danetta grimaced and slapped Tiffany with a stinging blow to her cheek. "Don't push me, you wretched tramp! Now go put it all back! I won't…"

Tiffany tightened her fist and shifted her body weight from one leg to the other, followed by a hard right fist that landed on Danetta's jaw. Danetta spun around and fell to the floor face first. "It's my family's things! And I'm taking it all!" Tiffany yelled, furiously standing over Danetta with her fist still clenched.

Matt grinned.

Danetta got up to her hands and knees and moaned painfully, as blood flowed out of her mouth. She spat out two teeth. "You knocked my teeth out. She knocked my teeth out," she repeated to herself in disbelief.

Matt frowned slightly as he noticed the large diamond ring on Danetta's finger with small red rubies encircling the center diamond on a gold band. It looked to be worth a small fortune. "Tiffany, that ring she is wearing, have you ever seen it before?"

Danetta looked at Matt with a frightened expression and sat up to her knees, trying to hide the large diamond ring with her other hand.

Tiffany shook her head. "No. It doesn't belong to my mother, and my Pa never bought her a ring. He couldn't afford one."

"Did you happen to find a pearl necklace back there somewhere? One you've never seen before?" Matt asked.

"There's one hanging on the bedpost."

"Will you grab that for me." He looked at Danetta. " I'm going to confiscate your jewelry on suspicion that it's stolen property. You have a choice, surrender it to me, or I'll forcefully take it off your finger. And I might end up breaking your finger in the process, so choose carefully, but choose now."

She began to sob as she pulled the ring off her finger and tossed it at him. "There! Anything else you want to take from me?"

He nodded. "Yeah. Tiffany will be taking her father's horse and saddle too."

Tiffany gathered her things off the floor and set it on the floor by Matt. She went back to her room and put on her warmest clothes and some riding pants over her long johns. She hugged the two girls goodbye and grabbed her quilt made by her mother. She walked to Matt and said, "I'm ready to go."

"Okay. Let's get going; we have a long ride ahead."

"She's going with you?" Danetta spat out as blood ran down her chin.

"She is," he answered. He asked Tiffany, "Do you want to say anything to Danetta? You'll never see her again, so now's your chance."

Tiffany held her armload of things and looked at

Danetta as she sat on the floor crying. "No. Knocking her teeth out said all I have to say to her. It was a good hit, wasn't it, Matt?" she asked with a proud smile.

He chuckled. "Very good," he said as they turned towards the door.

Dane Dielschnieder looked at them with tears in his eyes. "See you later," he said awkwardly.

Matt paused at the door as Tiffany went on outside to meet William with her Pa's horse. Matt spoke evenly, "This is done here and now. If either of you show up in my city or my county and want to continue this, I promise you'll be shown no mercy. That means I don't want to see either of you again. That's the only warning I'm giving. Good day."

Matt stepped up into his saddle and looked at Tiffany with a slight smile. "Well, look around, Tiffany. This chapter of your life is over. And a new one is beginning. Are you ready to turn the page, so to say, and start a whole new chapter in your life?"

She took a deep breath as she looked around the outside of her father's home. The past would always be within her memories, but she could choose to let the bad ones go. And fill her heart with the times she had with her father, mother, and little sisters. She nodded as a touch of a cold wind tousled her blonde hair.

"Yes, I am. And I am not even going to flip the pages back to relive it."

Matt nodded approvingly. "Then you're going to be fine."

William yawned. "Well, let's turn to a new chapter and get to riding, huh?"

Matt kicked his new horse. "Yeah, let's go home."

Epilogue

Matt rode next to Tiffany as they reached the crest of the hill overlooking the Big Z Ranch homestead. They could look down over the two houses with smoke coming out of the chimneys, and it brought a comforting smile to his lips. At the barn nearest to the house, a corral held a couple of young colts who were playfully prancing around. "What do you think?" Matt asked, pausing his new Appaloosa mare to look over the ranch. The weather had warmed up a bit, but there were some very dark clouds on the horizon, threatening to bring some heavy rain.

"Pretty. Are you sure your sister is going to like me? She's not like Danetta, is she?"

Matt laughed lightly. "No, Tiffany. I think you'll be happier living here than you have been in a very long time. I know your Pa was a good man and a good father, but he wasn't able to provide the lifestyle you'll have here. I think you'll love my sister and my aunt and uncle as well. I bet in a few months when I ask you that same question; you'll laugh at the idea of it too."

A sad expression came over her face. "I wish I could have gone to my Pa's funeral. They shouldn't have buried him without me being there."

Matt nodded. He didn't know it until the morning they left Prairieville that Danetta and the Sheriff had Dallen's body buried early the morning after he was shot and killed. Matt and William took Tiffany to the cemetery so she would know where he was buried and say goodbye to her father. Matt ordered a tombstone for his grave at the Sheriff's expense and ordered smaller tombstones for the other four men the Sheriff had killed too. She was able to say some words at Dallen's grave but missing the funeral was a blow that had hit her hard.

"Thank you again for getting him a tombstone. I don't plan on going back for many years, but it will be nice to find his grave when I do someday."

"You're welcome. Well, shall we ride down and introduce you to the family?"

"You never answered my question about if you think they'll like me or not," she said nervously.

"They'll love you."

"Are you sure?"

"Let's ride on down and see. If I'm wrong, you can stay with me. Deal?"

"Deal," she said with a satisfied grin.

They rode down the hill and past his sister Annie's house to stop in front of his aunt and uncle's house. It had a new coat of white paint with blue painted on the trim around the windows and door. Matt tied their horses to the hitching rail and led Tiffany to the front door. He knocked as he opened the door. "Aunt Mary, Uncle Charlie, are you home?" he asked while entering the house. "I brought a new guest."

Charlie Ziegler looked up from a book he was reading and stood up. Mary Ziegler came out of the kitchen, wiping her hands on her apron. Her graying long dark hair was up in a bun. Her smile widened when she saw Matt.

"Matthew!" she said and hugged him. "It's sure good to see you. So who is this beautiful young lady you brought us?" She turned her smile and attention to Tiffany.

"This is Tiffany. She's going to be living with Annie."

Mary hugged her warmly. "Welcome home, Tiffany. Call me Aunt Mary, and this ornery looking man is Uncle Charlie."

Charlie smiled kindly. "Little Miss," he said with a nod. "William tells me you're a Princess. We haven't got any of those here, so welcome to the Big Z Ranch."

"Thank you, Sir."

"No. Thank you, Uncle Charlie," he clarified for her. His eyes cast to Matt. "William told us everything that happened to you down there in Prairieville and to you." He looked back at Tiffany. "Let me assure you right now, Little Miss, you have nothing to be afraid of here. And if you'll let us, we'll love you just like one of our own. So call me Uncle Charlie, and here's your Aunt Mary. Okay?"

he asked with a friendly wink.

She nodded shyly.

Mary grabbed her hand. "Come into the kitchen with me, and let's get to know each other. What's your favorite thing to eat?"

Tiffany shrugged. "I don't know. All we had to eat was soured cabbage for cabbage stew."

Mary paused and stared at her with disgust. "Well, we don't have sour cabbage around here. I wouldn't feed that to our hogs. I sure hope that's not your favorite meal because the aroma alone turns my stomach."

"It's not."

"Good. Have you ever tried chicken pot pie?"

She shook her head. "No."

"Well, that's what I'm making for dinner, but how about a piece of fresh apple pie? Come in here and let's get you fed. You're too skinny, girl." Mary walked Tiffany into the kitchen.

Matt looked at Charlie. "Uncle Charlie, how are you?"

"Good. It sounds like you and William got yourselves into a heap of trouble down there. I'm glad you both made it back alive. Do you ever think maybe it's time to retire and let someone else deal with that kind of garbage?" he asked as he sat back down.

Matt looked towards the kitchen and could hear Tiffany enjoying a piece of pie and his Aunt Mary talking to her about various kinds of foods. It occurred to him for the first time since Tiffany's mother passed away; she was being treated like a daughter by a woman who would be a positive influence on her. A touch of moisture came to his eyes as he looked at his uncle with a satisfied smile. He shook his head. "No. I'm…."

Mary called from the kitchen interrupting him, "Matt, are you coming for Thanksgiving?"

"Of course."

"And your friend? Christine? Is she coming?"

Tiffany spoke quickly, "She's so nice." She had spent a few days at Matt's and got to meet Christine and go clothes shopping with her while she was there. Christine bought Tiffany a whole new wardrobe of clothes for the approaching winter.

"No, Aunt Mary, I don't believe she is," Matt answered. "They are having a pretty big banquet at the dance hall, and she was requested to sing several songs. So, she's going to do that instead of coming here. She loves to sing."

"Oh, that's too bad. I heard Christine was very beautiful and nice," Mary said, nodding toward Tiffany.

"She is!" Tiffany agreed. "I really like her!"

"Are you going to be courting her, Matthew?" Mary asked.

He smiled. "We're just friends, Aunt Mary. I'm taking the courting thing slow for now."

Charlie waved his thumb towards the wall. "Rory's still single."

Matt laughed. "I know." Charlie had been trying to encourage him to court Rory Jackson since he had come back home. She was the daughter of Darius, Charlie's best friend, and cowhand.

Mary nodded towards the window in the family room. "Well, we know Truet will be here."

Matt looked out the window and seen his deputy and friend Truet Davis walking with Matt's sister towards her house coming up from the barn. They were holding hands and close together. They stopped and kissed.

Charlie frowned. "Did you know they were courting?"

Matt smiled, mischievously. "Yeah, but they don't know, I know. Watch this. I'm going to borrow your piece of wood here." He grabbed a piece of split firewood from beside the woodstove and stepped outside in a hurry.

"What the hell's is going on here?" he yelled angrily and threw the block of wood towards them. It bounced off to the side of Truet. He and Annie separated. They were both shocked to see Matt walking angrily towards them.

Matt pulled his hat off his head and threw it at Truet. "What do you think you're doing, Truet? Are you going behind my back to court my sister? How dare you!" he yelled with fury in his eyes.

"Matt...it's..."

"No!" Matt yelled as he stopped in front of them. He pointed at Truet. "What kind of a friend are you, huh? And I'm supposed to trust you? I have an idea. If you want to court her, you have to go through me to do so! Let's fight a few rounds and see if you can beat me. If you do, I'll let you court her, but I doubt you will!"

Truet spoke softly. His sincerity was visibly

clear. "I'm not fighting you, Matt. You're my friend. I'm sorry, but I tried to tell you…"

"Oh! So next you're going to tell me you love her or something stupid like that, aren't you?"

Annie spoke heatedly, "Matt, I don't appreciate you threatening him! He doesn't have to fight you to court me. We're adults, not children."

Matt fought from laughing but kept a serious expression. "Hush!" he ordered Annie loudly, with a pointed finger in her face. "I asked you a question!" he spat out at Truet.

Truet looked very uncomfortable and hurt by Matt's reaction. He felt the guilt of having a relationship with Annie while keeping it a secret from Matt. It wasn't honest, and it had been heavy on Truet's heart to tell him.

"Well? Are you in love, or is this just some passing phase you're going through like William does?" Matt asked, bitterly loud enough for his aunt and uncle to hear.

Truet took a deep breath. "Matt, I want to say, I am sorry for keeping this from you. I should've come to you long ago…"

"Long ago? You just met her at Saul's wedding!" he yelled.

Truet shook his head like a scolded boy. "No. I met Annie before that; you just didn't know it. I've been courting her for a while. But to answer your question, and you can beat me up if you want to. I deserve it. You can fire me and kick me out of your house, too, but I am in love with Annie." He looked at Matt, sincerely. "I hope you can forgive me, us, for keeping it from you."

He looked at Annie, who appeared most uncomfortable. He asked with disgust, "Don't tell me you're in love with him?"

She nodded. "I am."

Matt shook his head and looked up into the sky as the rain began to fall. "Truet…you're a hell of a man!" he said and began laughing.

Truet frowned. "You're not mad?"

Annie grimaced, noticing Charlie and Mary stepping out onto the front porch laughing. A pretty blonde girl stepped out with them but she wasn't sure what was going on. "You knew?" Annie asked.

"Of course, I did," Matt said, laughing.

"Since when?" she asked.

"Since I saw you two together at the wedding. Truet, I couldn't ask for a better man to court my sister." He reached over and shook his hand.

Annie smiled slightly. "You're a jackass!"

Matt laughed. "Here, come meet Tiffany."

Truet hesitated. "So you're not mad? I kept it from you."

Matt looked at him, sincerely. "I could see you struggling with it. And it would be a lie if I said I didn't enjoy seeing you sweat. No, I'm not mad. I'm excited for you two."

"Tiffany, this my sister, Annie. And you already met Truet."

Annie walked over to Tiffany and put out a hand. "Hi Tiffany, I'm Annie. Welcome home, young lady.

I have one son and two daughters, who are now your new brother and sisters. I hope you don't mind them too much. How about let's leave my comic brother behind and go see your new home. I got your bedroom all set up, and I think you're going to like it here. We haven't got too many rules, and there's a really cute boy at your school named Gabrial that's going to fall for you like a rock!" She shrugged. "I suggest you stick with him over any of the other boys who are going to be falling for you like a landslide. You're a beautiful girl, so you better get used to that. Come on, let's get you situated and feeling at home."

Tiffany looked at Matt.

He smiled gently. "Do you think you'll blend?"

Her lips turned upwards slightly. "I think I might."

Matt nodded. "I think you will. Welcome home, Sweetheart. Everything is going to be alright."

She pinched her lips together as her green eyes filled with tears and wrapped her arms around Matt tightly. She sniffled and held him for a moment with her eyes squeezed shut tight. Her body convulsed as she fought from sobbing. After a moment she let him go and wiped her eyes dry. She looked up into his eyes. "Thank you, Matt."

He nodded and watched her walk away with Annie with a slight warm mist filling his eyes. He looked at his uncle Charlie and aunt Mary. "To answer your earlier question, Uncle Charlie, I can't make a difference in everyone's life, but for those I can, like her: it makes everything I do, worth it."

Charlie smiled slightly with an approving nod. "That's all I wanted to know. Keep up the good work, Matt."

Mary looked at Matt proudly. " One person at a time, can make a world of difference. Now, how about you come on in and grab a piece of apple pie, and stay awhile."

"Aunt Mary, I think I will." It was good to be home.

About the Author

Ken Pratt and his wife, Cathy, have been married for 22 years and are blessed with five children and six grandchildren. They live on the Oregon Coast where they are raising the youngest of their children. Ken Pratt grew up in the small farming community of Dayton, Oregon.

Ken worked to make a living, but his passion has always been writing. Having a busy family, the only "free" time he had to write was late at night getting no more than five hours of sleep a night. He has penned several novels that are being published along with several children stories as well.

READ MORE ABOUT KEN PRATT AT http://christiankindlenews.com

d States
FL
2022

Made in Uni
Orlando
18 Januar